dark
mind rising

by Julia Keller

THE DARK INTERCEPT TRILOGY FOR TEENS

The Dark Intercept

Dark Mind Rising

Dark Star Calling (forthcoming)

THE BELL ELKINS SERIES FOR ADULTS

A Killing in the Hills

Bitter River

Summer of the Dead

Last Ragged Breath

Sorrow Road

Fast Falls the Night

Bone on Bone

dark
mind rising

Julia
Keller

**TOR
TEEN**

A TOM DOHERTY ASSOCIATES BOOK

New York

DARK MIND RISING

Copyright © 2018 by Julia Keller

A Tor Teen Book
Published by Tom Doherty Associates
175 Fifth Avenue
New York, NY 10010

www.tor-forge.com

Tor® is a registered trademark of Macmillan Publishing Group, LLC.

The Library of Congress Cataloging-in-Publication Data is available upon request.

ISBN 978-0-7653-8765-3 (hardcover)
ISBN 978-0-7653-8766-0 (ebook)

Our books may be purchased in bulk for promotional, educational, or business use. Please contact your local bookseller or the Macmillan Corporate and Premium Sales Department at 1-800-221-7945, extension 5442, or by email at MacmillanSpecialMarkets@macmillan.com.

First Edition: November 2018

Printed in the United States of America

0 9 8 7 6 5 4 3 2 1

To Andrea Lynn Voight and the
beauty of the dreams she dreamed

But I do know a kind of madness that lies low in the mind, half-buried in consciousness, which lives in parallel to sanity, and given the right circumstances or even just half a chance, creeps like a lick of flame or a growing tumor up and around ordinary perception. . . .

—JENNY DISKI, *Stranger on a Train*

PART ONE

TIME: 2296

The Intercept is dead. Two years ago, Violet Crowley raced into Protocol Hall and set a detonator, triggering the explosion that brought the tower down.

The Intercept had collected the emotions of every citizen 24-7, storing them for strategic deployment. It kept both New Earth and Old Earth under tight control.

But the Intercept also made people fear their feelings. They knew those emotions would be used against them whenever the government wanted to.

And so Violet erased it in a clean sweep. All traces eliminated.

New Earth now must stand on its own, because the Intercept is dead.

Or is it?

1

A Twitch in Time

Twitch.

Something weird was happening.

Twitch.

There it was again. A little crease of feeling, right behind her eyes.

Twitch.

Nothing serious, just annoying.

Amelia Bainbridge shifted in her seat. She glanced around the tram car at the other passengers. Was anybody else reacting? Was it some kind of glitch in the propulsion system, making the car bump and shudder? Nope. They all looked perfectly normal.

Twitch.

In the entire sixteen years of her life, she had never experienced anything quite like this. It wasn't painful, but it was definitely distracting. Something . . . *moved.* Something shifted at the edge of her thoughts, right on the outer rim of her mind. She tried to ignore it, but she couldn't.

Twitch.

Twitch.

It was coming even more frequently now, that jittery, fluttery thing, filling more of her head.

And just like that, Amelia's perfectly ordinary ride—the same one she took to school every weekday, traveling high above the bright serenity of New Earth—took a nosedive toward the strange and dark.

Twitch.

Stronger that time, more insistent. Like somebody had spun a dial from five to six.

Twitch.

Now the dial jumped from six all the way up to eight. Or maybe ten or eleven.

Once again, just to be sure, Amelia looked around the nearly full car. She sneaked a glance at the skinny old guy across the aisle two rows up, and at the girl roughly her own age, with reddish curly hair, in the row behind her. And once again, nobody else seemed any different, nobody else was reacting. So nobody else was feeling it. They all appeared to be doing what *she'd* been doing until just a few seconds ago when the weird twitches came along: enjoying the ride on another gorgeous morning on New Earth.

The tram traveled at a phenomenally high rate of speed, but it did so with such scintillating grace and absolute balance that there was no lurching, no bobble, no rocking back and forth; there was barely a sense of motion at all. The car followed the long sweep of elevated track with a whisper of perfectly modulated acceleration.

Someday, Amelia wanted to create things just as sleek and sparkling as this tram system. In her case, it would be buildings. She wanted to be an architect so that she could design amazing structures that would make people look up and utter a soft "Wow." And even though she got a bit discouraged sometimes because all the cool stuff had already been created—or so it seemed, which she knew wasn't really true, but New Earth was filled with intimidating wonders—she loved gazing out the window and dreaming. Any window would do.

Twitch.

The buildings she'd create one day flew out of her head, replaced by increasing confusion. And fear. The twitches were at it again.

She shook her head, trying to clear it.

Twitch.

Twitch.

Twitch.

Her desperation increasing, Amelia fetched a series of shallow, rapid breaths. Was she getting sick or something? Were these flu symptoms, maybe? The flu made you dizzy, right? This twitching thing could be the first stage.

People didn't usually get sick on New Earth. The serious, most-dreaded diseases were quarantined on Old Earth. If you didn't go down there, you'd be fine. The few maladies that *did* creep their way up to the shiny new civilization floating above the broken planet were annoyances—colds, allergies, and the like. And even those would soon be eradicated. Amelia had read a story on her wrist console just last week about Shura Lu, a young physician on the verge of developing a cold vaccine.

Until then, people had to put up with being a little bit sick now and again. Maybe that explained this twitching business. After class, Amelia would head straight home. Take a nap, maybe. Eat some soup. Whatever. Her mom would know what to do for her.

She made yet another frantic assessment of the other

people riding the tram. It was just before nine A.M., so most of them were probably on their way to school or work.

Nothing unusual.

A few seconds went by without a twitch. Amelia took a deep, relieved breath. Maybe it was over. Maybe the twitches would never come back. She relaxed. She let her head fall back against the cushioned seat, and she looked out the window again. The car was zipping across an aquamarine sky. The Color Blenders had done a nifty job today.

Each horizontal section of track was connected to a vertical strand of wire thinner than a human hair. The wires were made of a stunningly robust alloy developed by Arianna Prokop, chief engineer of New Earth. Every few feet they rose stealthily from the surface of New Earth, so fine that they were virtually invisible against the silver hills of the horizon. When viewed from the ground, the track looked as if it were attached to nothing at all, as if the tram system had simply materialized by magic and now wound in and out of the clouds in an elegant aerial cloverleaf. Tram cars swooshed along day and night, ferrying the people of New Earth with crisp speed and frictionless efficiency.

The car glided to a stop. The double doors jumped apart with a hiss, letting in another three passengers: an old woman in a floppy gray hat and two young children, a boy and a girl. Floppy Hat kept a hand on top of each child's head, shepherding them toward the trio of seats across the aisle from Amelia. The old woman sat in the middle, a kid on either side.

The doors smacked to a close, resuming their tight seal. The car oozed forward toward its ultimate destination, Mendeleev Crossing.

Amelia watched the newcomers out of the corner of her eye, wondering if Floppy Hat was the kids' grandmother, or maybe a friendly neighbor who had agreed to take them out for the day. There were lots of museums in Mendeleev Crossing, art museums and history museums and science museums. Amelia could spend hours hopping from museum to museum. Her mother used to take her there all the time. Now she was old enough to go on her own, and so she'd call her friends and—

Twitch.

Amelia's happy thoughts vanished. Anxiety roared back in. She tried again to focus on something else.

They were entering Hawking, the capital city of New Earth, which lay between Amelia's home in Higgsville and her school at Mendeleev Crossing. She saw Floppy Hat pointing out at the tall, skinny spires outside the window, murmuring a history lesson to the kids about the construction of the buildings when New Earth was still young.

Twitch.

Amelia shuddered.

Twitch.

Twitch.

The twitch expanded into her shoulders—or so she felt. Amelia looked at her right shoulder and then at her left, and she saw that they were still. So it was all happening in her mind. An invisible quiver traveled up the right side of her face, starting at her jaw and forking toward her temple.

Her lower lip began to tremble, the way it sometimes did when she was starting to cry—but she wasn't starting to cry. She was too scared to cry. She reached up to feel her lip. It was perfectly still.

Everything was happening on the *inside*, not the outside.

Twitch.

Twitch.

Twitch.

Twitch.

Twitch.

Amelia let out a short, sharp little blurt of a sound. Not a yelp, exactly, and not a cry, but a sort of half burp.

That attracted the notice of one of the kids. He whispered something to the old lady. She put an arm around him and drew him closer to her, as if she—*she*, Amelia Bainbridge, who'd never hurt anybody in her *entire* life, who felt bad if she accidentally stepped on an ant or a spider, especially because they'd been so carefully bred up here on New Earth—was dangerous.

Twitch.

Twitch.

Twitch.

She was losing control of herself. Her knees banged against each other. Her arms and her legs jerked and stuttered—and yet, when she looked down, she saw that her body was *completely still.*

The only thing that had changed was the tiny bruise in the crook of her left elbow. She could swear she saw a small blue flash there. Once, twice.

And still the twitches continued.

Something had its hands on her brain and was squeezing tighter and tighter. The twitches had linked up to make a single long chain of unbearable hurt.

I want to die.

Never before had such a thought occurred to Amelia. Her life had not been totally painless—nobody's life was perfect, right?—but overall she had it pretty good, and she knew it. She had a tight circle of friends. She was doing fantastic in school. She was making excellent progress toward her dream of becoming an architect. She loved her mom. She even loved her annoying little brother, Jeff.

So life was great.

Life is terrible.

I want to die.

I WANT TO DIE.

The sentence exploded in her mind like a Thought Bomb. In its wake came another noise—a rising scream that ricocheted off the inside of her skull again and again. She couldn't stop herself from visualizing small, awful things like cold rain and soiled floors and moldy food and crushed bugs and smelly kitchen drains and dirty windows. And big, awful things like death. Her grief was cataclysmic. It was gigantic and devouring. It seemed to scoop up all the sorrow that had ever come to her—every minor disappointment, every small loss, every failure, every time she had ever felt lonely or confused or embarrassed or afraid—and shouted the details back to her, again and again, louder each time.

New Earth wasn't pleasant. It was disgusting. It was horrible. It was a dead, doomed place.

All of the good things in Amelia's life dropped over the edge of her brain, never to be seen again. They were replaced by the idea of oblivion—of erasing herself, of not being here at all. And self-destruction seemed like a tremendous relief. It seemed logical and rational and . . . *inevitable.*

The beautiful notion of nothingness filled every fissure and crevice of her heaving brain.

Fleetingly, Amelia wondered if the other passengers could hear the needle-sharp scream, the one that was jabbing holes in her brain. She didn't think so. Nobody else looked any different at all. So it was true: She was alone. Trapped inside her mind.

I want to die.

Die.

Die.

Die.

The word *die* scuttled like a poisonous lizard back and forth across her thoughts, its tail whipping and showering her with acid drops of despair.

I want to die.

I want to die.

I HAVE TO DIE.

I HAVE TO—

The door slid open. This was the stop for Hawking. A young woman in a long purple coat stepped into the car.

Amelia bolted past her, nearly knocking her down, running headlong toward the space created by the sprung-open doors.

"Hey," the woman called out. "Hey, what the—"

Amelia didn't pause on the platform. She didn't even slow down as she crossed it, shoving more people out of her way. There were angry shouts and grunts and a few startled shrieks. Still Amelia rushed forward.

When she reached the waist-high white metal barricade bordering the platform, the final threshold before a yawning three thousand–meter gap from the track to the surface of New Earth below, she gripped the top rail with her left hand and leaped over it with ease.

For a moment she was suspended in the air, her head twisted back toward the passengers on the platform, as if to give herself the gift of one last look at the living, a final reminder of what it had been like to be human—the pain and the joy, the questions and the contradictions, and the fierce, simple beauty that crowned it all.

The people on the tram that day—the people who watched, even though they didn't want to—would later say that Amelia Bainbridge had appeared to be smiling.

And then she dropped into the vastness below.

2

Crowley & Associates, At Your Service

Vi? Vi? Hey, Vi!"

Violet Crowley refused to respond to the very familiar—and very annoying—voice. It flew out of the room connected to hers, sailing through the open door and settling on her thoughts like . . . like . . .

Like a pesky fly.

Her thoughts drifted. Why did New Earth even *have* flies? No matter how many times Violet's father claimed there was a good reason for it—*We must continue to promulgate species diversity, my dear, and rigorously maintain standard biological archetypes* blah blah blah—Violet's thought was always the same: *So you had the chance to build a perfect new world* exactly *how you wanted it and you included* FLIES?

"Vi!"

Violet still hadn't answered. She hadn't and she wouldn't, because she had told Jonetta a thousand times—okay, more like a million—not to call her *Vi*.

Vi was not her name. Her name was Violet.

How hard was that?

"Hey, Vi! Viiiii!"

Violet shook her head and narrowed her eyes. She pushed a hand through her thick dark-blond hair. She was frustrated all the way from her fingertips down to the soles of her shoes. At present, those shoes were piled up on the rickety desk. Her left foot was stacked on top of her right foot, although a few seconds from now she would be switching things up and her right foot would be stacked on top of her left foot. And then back again.

Which means, Violet reassured herself, *it's not like I'm sitting here in my office doing nothing. I'm not totally motionless. You could even say I'm keeping busy.*

At the moment, the only thing higher on Violet's list of Things That Would Drive Any Sane Person Crazy than Jonetta's inability to remember her name was the Headache. The Headache was no ordinary inconvenience. No simple pain. It was much, much worse than that. She'd stayed out too late the night before—and the night before that and the night before *that*—dancing at Redshift, her favorite club on New Earth. Which naturally resulted in the exceedingly icky reality of the Headache.

Violet grimaced. She blinked a bunch of times. The sun rippling in through the window behind her kept the Headache revved up. It also spotlighted the very few—and distressingly dingy—objects in her tiny office. The smart play would've been to pull the curtain shut. But the window didn't have a curtain. Curtains cost money.

The *real* truth—and Violet knew this deep in her heart, even though she'd never say it out loud to anybody, except maybe her best friend, Shura, or her second-best friend, Kendall—was that the core source of her frustration wasn't a lame nickname.

Or sunshine. Or the price of curtains. Or dancing too much. Or the *knock-knock-knock* pain of the Headache.

Or even the crinkly document in her grip, the one she'd been reading when the first infuriating *Vi* had come buzzing her way from the outer room.

The problem wasn't any one of those things. Or even several things. It was *everything*.

It's my whole, entire, miserable life.

Violet restacked her feet again. And one more time after that, too. She was feeling more than a little lost these days. She was moody. She was restless. She was jumpy.

She glanced down at the small blue bruise in the crook of her left elbow. Frustration was a *massive* emotion, a thrashing, rattling, towering one. The Intercept was surely having a blast right now as it—

She caught herself.

Nope.

There was nothing to see in the crook of her elbow. No blue flash, no crackle of heat from the tiny chip embedded there. Not anymore.

Which, in a weird way, made her feel even worse.

Because nothing had turned out the way she'd thought it would two years ago, when the Intercept first lay in steaming shards and the world seemed new again, filled with wonder and promise.

Wonder.

Promise.

What a joke. These days, everything—*everything*—seemed to be part of the same general mess.

Exhibit A was the very document she held in her hands right now. It was a bill, a bill she couldn't pay, and it squirmed with numbers that were stunningly ugly. They attested to the grim reality that Crowley & Associates Detective Agency was deeply, dismally, and perhaps irretrievably sunk in debt. Most bills were zapped directly to consoles, but when you didn't pay on time, they came at you from another angle. And the paper parade started up.

"Hey, Vi!"

Jonetta Loring's infuriatingly sweet-as-pie voice and that ridiculous nickname.

Enough already, Violet thought. Time to lower the boom. Time to head out to Jonetta's desk and deliver the ultimatum: If she called her *Vi* ever again, that would be it.

So long.

Buh-bye.

Violet unpiled her feet and yanked them off the desk. She jumped up, side-arming the paper bill to her right. It fluttered to a landing in the corner, joining a pile of similar-looking documents with earlier date stamps that made the same general point as the one she'd been reading:

Girl, you're dead broke.

"Hey, Vi?"

There it was again. Violet barreled into the outer office. She'd set up a wobbly desk for Jonetta and plunked a secondhand computer on it. The computer, like the desk, was a mostly broken-down piece of junk that Violet had foraged from the Refuse Sector over in L'Engletown, with a keyboard that occasionally delivered a mild electric shock.

Right now, Violet didn't much care if Jonetta was electrocuted by the thing.

"I've told you over and over and over again," Violet said in the meanest voice she could muster, her eyes focused on

Jonetta's, "*not* to call me *Vi*. Vi is *not* my nickname. It's never *been* my nickname. It will never *be* my nickname. Never, never, never. And did I mention 'never'? Because—*never*."

A lot of people considered Jonetta, with her cascading corkscrews of black hair and twinkly smile and creamy brown skin, adorable. And sweet. For the record, Violet did *not* think of her sixteen-year-old secretary as adorable or sweet. She thought of her as flighty. And annoying. And a really bad listener.

"If you call me *Vi* one more time, I swear I'm going to—"

She stopped. Jonetta was pumping her eyebrows up and down, as if trying to convey an important concept without resorting to words.

"Uh," Jonetta said.

"Uh?"

"Uh." She gingerly lifted her right hand, using her index finger to point to the other side of the room, the part blocked from Violet's view by the open door to her own office.

Violet peeked around the edge of the door.

A woman had stationed herself stiffly on the small blue sofa by the entrance. Her back was straight, and her hands were clasped tightly on her lap. Her body was so rigid that for a moment Violet wondered if she was a recently uncrated statue instead of a flesh-and-blood person. Her straight brown hair was combed harshly back from her face. That face was blank. She was, Violet speculated, around forty years old.

"Oh," Violet said. "Um . . . hi. I mean, welcome to Crowley & Associates. Sorry to keep you waiting." She gave Jonetta a sideways glare of unmistakable reproach.

"Tried to tell you," Jonetta whispered defensively. "Called you a bunch of times."

Violet ignored her. To the woman, she said, "Would you like to come into my office?"

"Yes." The word was spoken with no inflection whatsoever. Some people might have described the visitor's voice as robotic, but Violet had worked with a few robots during her years at Protocol Hall and generally found them to be warmer than this stranger. Some robots even had a decent sense of humor.

The woman nodded. Just once.

Later, Violet would look back on this seemingly ordinary moment as a hinge point, a perilous pivot. Because even though she didn't know it at the time—and really, how *could* she have known?—she had just taken the very first step on a road that would lead her toward a startling revelation, plunging her and her friends headfirst into chaos and terrible danger, a danger that threatened the very existence of New Earth.

In just a few short days, Violet Crowley would get the shock of her life. The most important thing she knew about her world would be revealed to her as wrong.

And nothing would ever be the same again.

The Dare

Violet plopped down behind her desk, waving her visitor toward the chair that faced it at a slight angle. The woman still hadn't officially made eye contact.

"Okay," Violet said. "How can I help you?"

"My daughter."

Violet waited.

"My daughter," she repeated.

"Okay, but why are you—"

"My daughter," the woman said yet again.

"Look, I'd like to help you, but I'll need a little more informa—"

"She's dead. I want to know why. I *have* to know why."

The word *dead* made Violet sit up straighter in her chair.

"What happened?"

"They say she killed herself. She . . . she jumped from the tram track."

Now Violet got it. She had checked the news update on her console that morning and saw the horrible story: Shortly after nine A.M., a sixteen-year-old girl had rushed out of a tram car and plummeted to her death.

The victim must have been this woman's child.

"I'm sorry," Violet said. "But the police already ruled it a suicide. So I don't see what I can do."

The woman's response was quick and sure. "My daughter didn't kill herself."

"But the police say—"

"The police are wrong." She looked at Violet—*really* looked at her now, seeking out Violet's eyes and locking on, not just staring at the world in a glassy, abstract way. There was passion in her voice. It was almost as if someone had seen an unattached cord trailing from the heel of her shoe and suddenly plugged it into a power source. "I'm *telling* you. Amelia didn't kill herself. She wouldn't."

But everybody believes that, probably, when somebody they love commits suicide, right? That's what Violet was thinking, but she might as well have said it out loud, because the woman had an answer ready.

"Of course that's what a mother is expected to say. But you can check with anybody who knew her. Amelia was happy. She loved her classes. She loved her friends. She loved her life. She was very close to her little brother, Jeff. You should've seen her eyes when she learned something new in school—they *gleamed*. They actually *gleamed*. There's just *no way* she would've done what they say she did." The woman leaned forward, stretching her hand across Violet's desk so that she could thump the surface with her palm, in time with her next four words. "*It can't be true.*" With each word, she thumped harder. "And I want you to prove it. I want you to find out what really happened to my girl."

The words *my girl* caught in the woman's throat. Stricken,

she swallowed hard. Her eyes instantly grew misty. She fell back against her chair, and as she did so her hand slid off the desk and came to rest in her lap. She bowed her head. It was as if the cord had been yanked out of the socket again.

"I can see you're in a lot of pain," Violet said.

Totally lame, but she had to say *something*. She'd never been very good at the whole sympathy thing. Even when Shura's mother was hovering near death in the hospital two years ago, Violet had forced herself to hug her best friend and murmur supportive clichés. Feelings—other people's feelings and her own, too—embarrassed her.

Back in the days of the Intercept, Violet had learned to keep a tight rein on her emotions, holding them in check, forcing herself to stay on an even keel so the Intercept wouldn't have much to work with. It was a hard habit to break.

"Amelia," the woman said, "was my life." Her chin quivered.

Violet resisted the urge to sneak a glance at the crook of her visitor's left elbow. All she'd see there, of course, was a small scar. The same scar that everyone else had. No blue flash. No brief sizzle as the Intercept's Wi-Fi signal scooped up the emotion and sent it off to Protocol Hall to be added to her file.

The only thing visible there would be a bruise. A slight discoloration that never glowed, never hummed.

"I'm really sorry," Violet said. "But I'm still not sure how I can help."

"I told you. Find out the truth."

Violet decided to deploy what she thought of as her Warm Supportive Voice. It didn't come naturally to her, but she'd been working on it. "I know you think you're doing the right thing by not accepting the police report, but—"

"I don't think it. I *know* it." Abruptly, her visitor stood up. "Never mind. I can see you're not the right person for the job.

You're too much like your father. I met him a few times, and everything they'd said about him was true. And now I can see it in you, too. You trust authority too much."

"Hey," Violet said. Now she stood up, too, energized by her umbrage. "I'm a good detective," she insisted. "In fact, I'm a *very* good detective. If there's anything suspicious about your daughter's death, anything at all, I'm the one who can find it."

"So you'll take the job?"

The words popped out before Violet could stop them.

"*Of course* I'll take the job."

Her pledge had come from wounded pride, but maybe not *only* from wounded pride. Because a lot of things were happening all at once. Just as Violet was making her declaration, her eyes happened to slide over to the piles of unpaid bills in the corner. Even if the inquiry into the girl's death was a pointless waste of time, she could charge the woman by the hour. Which sounded cold and calculating, but then again, there was nothing dishonorable about wanting to stay in business. Violet was more than a few months behind on the office rent. And there was also the teensy matter of the rent on her apartment. She was a couple of months late on *that*, too.

Not to mention tomorrow's court hearing for breaking New Earth Statute No. 293874-A-392876, Subsection 39887-HYV, Article 983746. Even if she beat the rap, she'd have to pay her attorney.

For heaven's sake, Shura had asked her last week, *why don't you just get a loan from your dad?*

Shura should've known better. *That*, Violet had informed her friend with heat in her voice, *will never, ever,* EVER *happen*. Violet didn't want anybody to think she depended on her family connections. Sure, her company name linked her to New Earth's founder, but she still stood on her own. Essentially.

So Violet didn't withdraw her offer. In fact, she doubled down on it. "I'll find out what happened to your daughter," she stated. "Guaranteed."

A single curt nod was all she got in return, but Violet could sense the hot wash of relief and gratitude surging through Amelia's mom. "I'll send an initial payment to your console," the woman said. "You have to start right way. There's not a moment to waste."

"I'll need a list of her friends and classmates. And remote access to her console. And—"

"Already done. It's in your console. Plus, I added your name to the list of approved contacts. The police department is authorized to speak with you about my family."

Violet blinked. "When did you do all that?"

"Right before I came here."

"You were sure I'd take the job?"

For the first time, the woman smiled. "I've met your father, yes, but I *also* knew your mother. Lucretia Crowley never backed away from a fight—if, that is, the fight really mattered, if it was about doing the right thing. I figured that if you were even half as decent and determined and wise as your mother, you'd try with all your might to help me find out who did this to my girl—and *why*. And bring them to justice."

By the time Violet had escorted the woman out of the office and returned to her desk, Jonetta had the goods.

"Check your console," Jonetta said. She was blowing on her fingertips after enduring a brief but vicious electrical charge from short in the keyboard.

Violet tapped her wrist console. Five iridescent dots—green, blue, black, red, yellow—rose an inch above it like a synchronized dance of fireflies. Each dot contained a cache of messages, sorted by sender and subject matter, viewable only from the console-wearer's perspective.

She touched the red dot. The other four sank and faded. She read Jonetta's report. It was impressively thorough, and it reminded Violet why she kept Jonetta around, even though she couldn't really afford her, and even though Jonetta never seemed to get her name straight. She actually did a very good job.

Violet skimmed the report a second time, making sure she had all the facts straight. Amelia's mother was named Charlotte Bainbridge. She was forty-three years old. She lived in Higgsville. Her husband, Frank Bainbridge, had been a member of the original team of engineers who created New Earth to Ogden Crowley's specifications. Frank had been in charge of the transport system connecting New Earth to Old Earth, a collection of pods and docking stations at both ends. He was killed a year ago in an accident when a decommissioned pod exploded on one of the abandoned tracks.

First her husband dies, Violet thought. *And now her daughter. No wonder she's a little strange. She's got to be out of her mind with grief.*

"Get me the police report on Amelia's death," Violet called out to Jonetta.

Then she shot a quick text to Kendall. Having your second-best friend be a top officer with New Earth Security Service was a definite advantage when you were a professional detective.

She wouldn't hear back from Kendall right away. He was on duty. That meant she had some time to think, and so she sat back down, turned around in her chair, and gazed out the window.

New Earth was laid out in a rigorously symmetrical grid that gleamed smartly in the morning sunshine. Broad white boulevards replicated themselves until they merged with the honey-colored blur of the horizon. Beyond the downtown area and its soaring silver towers, neighborhoods bloomed into view; from Violet's window they showed up as pale pink smudges.

It was a warm, luscious day. But then again, it was almost always warm and luscious on New Earth. The only time it wasn't that way was when the weather algorithm dialed up a brief spike of rain or a quilt of fog, just for contrast. Too many warm, luscious days in a row could be as oppressive as gray, chilly ones, or so the psychologists hired by her father in the early days of New Earth had advised him. People needed variety. They craved it. And so even an atmosphere maintained by the computers that ran the mammoth magnets over in Farraday occasionally included some less-than-ideal conditions.

The analogy occurred to Violet in a sad flash. What if Amelia Bainbridge's mood had been like the weather on New Earth? Most of the time, it was sunny; most of the time, it was sweet and mild. That's what Amelia's mother saw. But occasionally something else might have crept in: gloom, anxiety, doubt. Maybe Charlotte Bainbridge never saw that part. And maybe it grew inside the girl. And maybe today, Amelia hadn't been able to fight it off anymore. Maybe it just got the better of her. So even though she was generally happy and positive, the truth was that a different kind of mood, coming at the wrong moment, might have been enough to . . .

"Hey, Vi! Vi?"

Jonetta again. And again with the *Vi* business.

"Look," Violet snapped. "How many times do I have to tell you not to call me by that stupid—"

"Line two. It's Rez."

All at once Violet forgot all about what Jonetta did or didn't call her. She forgot about Amelia Bainbridge. She forgot about how much she owed which creditor. She forgot about the Headache and the court date she faced tomorrow and the fact that none of her office furniture matched and that the case she'd just let herself be bamboozled into accepting was, in all likelihood, a lost cause.

She was happy. Because whenever Violet got the chance talk to Steve Reznik these days, she got something else, too. She was gifted with a glimpse of another world—a world that was the opposite of New Earth and its studious beauty, a world that was frayed and dangerous and bleak and broken down, a world that was toxic and tattered and teetering on the brink of ruin but that still enthralled her, captivated her.

It had been her mother's birthplace. Her father's, too. And so it was a place that perpetually featured in Violet's dreams.

Old Earth.

4

Home Is Calling

"Try again, Rez," Violet said.

"What?"

"TRY AGAIN!" She was shouting, hunched over her console, trying to force her voice through the dense atmospheric interference that could make communication between the two worlds a challenge.

The fuzzy gray blob on her screen was Rez. Now the blob seemed to be trying to say something. She assumed he was asking, "How about now?" but it came out sounding like *bow-wow-wow*.

"Huh?" she said.

"I can *see* you, but I can't *hear* you!" Rez yelled. "Can you hear me?"

"I can *hear* you, but I can't *see* you."

"Let me try another channel," he said. At least that was Violet's speculation, because all she could make out was a series of beeps, squeaks, and squawks that indicated a console-channel change.

Finally, a clear channel emerged, wicking up through the writhing vapors in Old Earth's atmosphere, punching through the thick, sticky goop of pollution into the clear, pure air that swaddled New Earth.

"Gotcha," Violet said at last, nodding emphatically because now she could see Rez's face and hear his "Roger that!" loud and clear.

She adjusted the image on the feed by touching the shimmering purple dot that hovered above her console. His face emerged with an even crisper clarity.

"Can I see where you are, Rez?" Violet said. She was trying not to sound too eager. "Please? Just for a second?"

He grunted. He wouldn't refuse her. Regardless of all that had happened between them two years ago, he was still deeply attached to her. Or at least she assumed he was, because she couldn't know for sure. Without the Intercept, she couldn't be certain if he was feeling anything at all—unless, that is, he chose to reveal his emotions to her the old-fashioned way, by saying them out loud, which, Rez being Rez, he would never do. His emotions were invisible now, just as they'd been before the Intercept came along. Just as everyone's were.

Rez held his console facing away from his body. He turned in a circle, giving Violet a tantalizing visual taste of a world she loved but didn't really know.

She gazed at the tattered remnants of a city, its buildings mostly toppled and lying in great heaps of jagged ruins. There were enormous holes in the street, rendering it impassable by anything but foot traffic, and even that required a lot of leaping and dodging so as not to stumble headfirst into pools of inky black goop. Abandoned vehicles, their windshields smashed and their tires and doors long ago wrenched off by desperate scavengers, lined the streets. A fierce wind seemed to be blowing; Violet could tell by the trash that scuttled in front of Rez's console. She could make out, in the roiling mix, rags and sticks and cans and crates. There could have been precious things in there, too; there could have been diamonds and sapphires, but no one would know, because on Old Earth everything was swept along by the scouring winds in a great democracy of debris.

Then Rez turned and her perspective changed; she found herself peering down a long gray road that led away from the city, twisting its way toward a somber horizon above which the kidney-colored sky seemed to throb in mute agony.

He turned again. Now she was back in the city. Two women hurried along the warped and mangled sidewalk with bent heads, drawing up the collars of their threadbare coats to keep out that relentless wind. A skeletal-looking dog skulked by, going in the opposite direction; its brown fur was greasy and matted, and it paused to drink from a culvert that sloshed with a filthy liquid that may or may not have been water. Anybody's guess. A huge black bird swooped into view and then ascended again out of the frame, delivering as it departed an eerily raucous cry that echoed through the hollowed-out streets like a wordless warning, a savage sound that foretold of even worse to come.

"Wow," Violet murmured, transfixed. "This is great."

It was an odd thing to say, perhaps, given the bleakness of the scene—or it *would* have been odd, if the speaker were anybody but Violet. But she had always been obsessed by the shattered place that her parents had left behind when they opted for the new civilization built atop the bones of the old.

She was born on New Earth, after the Great Migration had severed the worlds. Yet because of her parents and their heritage, Old Earth was the home she felt in her soul, even if it wasn't the one listed on her birth certificate. She couldn't go down there often—the trip aboard a pod was jarring, and visiting more frequently than twice a year affected all kinds of body systems. And so whenever she talked to Rez on her console, she asked him to let her see Old Earth. Just a few quick scenes.

"Thank you," Violet added quietly.

He shifted the direction of his console feed. Once again, it showed his face—a frowning face, of course, because Rez was always frowning.

"Sure," he said.

"How are you doing?"

"Okay."

"By the way, I'll be seeing your little sister tomorrow," Violet said. "She's helping me out with a court thing."

"She told me."

"Really." Inwardly, Violet winced. She didn't want Rez—or any of her friends—to know about the stupid thing she'd done to get herself in trouble again, minor as it was. Rez's sister, Rachel, was her lawyer. She was one of the top lawyers on New Earth. *And isn't there*, Violet asked herself, *some kind of ethics thing? Lawyers aren't supposed to tell people about their cases, right?*

It didn't really matter, though. Rez wouldn't judge her. Not about that, anyway.

"Yeah," he said. His voice was distracted.

"Are you keeping busy down there?"

Now he perked up. *People* were hard for Rez, but work wasn't. Violet knew that very well. She and Rez had shared a cubicle in Protocol Hall, the nerve center of the Intercept, until both the building and the technology that rumbled and churned beneath it were demolished. However he'd decided to spend his time, it would have something to do with computers, and he would be totally absorbed by it.

Rez loved computers more than he loved human beings—almost any human beings, Violet thought, except for his family members, although she wasn't really sure about that. And he understood computers better than anyone Violet had ever known—except for Kendall, of course, who had invented the Intercept.

"Yeah," he said. "I've hit a couple of snags. But it's nothing I can't deal with."

She took a quick second to study his face. It had changed since the days they had shared a cubicle. It was still pale. But during his exile on Old Earth, his face had gotten hard. It had edges now. It had new angles and shadows. And there were other changes in him, too, beyond the physical. Not-so-good ones. He was more subdued. Violet missed the zeal that used to be a part of Steve Reznik, the constant fizzing excitement over a new line of code or a counterintuitive app. There wasn't quite as much brightness in him these days. Part of that, she assumed, was the fact that his mother had died six months into his prison sentence, with only Rachel there to attend to her. Rez never had a chance to say goodbye.

"What kind of snags?" she asked.

"You wouldn't understand."

He was right. She wouldn't. The extent of Rez's brilliance still astonished her. After all the months Violet had spent sitting beside him in Protocol Hall, she had decided that Rez's brain was maybe as much of a burden to him as it was a help, as much curse as gift.

"I can try," she said.

She said it because no matter what had happened two years ago, she and Rez were friends. They would always be friends.

True, he had betrayed her profoundly when he illegally accessed Intercept files, sending one of her father's emotions back into his brain and causing him terrible pain, but Rez was paying dearly for his actions. He had a felony record now. And Violet knew he was sorry for what he had done. That was enough for her. She'd been the beneficiary of forgiveness herself. Everybody had.

He licked his lips. She guessed that he was reconsidering the reason for his call, wondering all over again about the wisdom of confiding in her the way he used to.

"Okay," he said. "Thing is, I'm having a few problems with access codes down here. According to the terms of my probation . . ." His sentence trailed off. He didn't like to talk about his conviction, a conviction that meant every time he touched a computer he had to secure permission from Captain Kendall Mayhew of NESS, the New Earth Security Service.

Rez coughed. The console feed wavered then cleared again.

"According to the terms of my probation," he said, trying again, "I can't do any quantum computing at all. But I need to."

"Can't you ask Kendall to make an exception?"

"Guess so. But there's no guarantee he'll say yes." Rez shrugged and looked away. The console feed wobbled again, the picture interrupted by jumping lines of static.

"Maybe," Violet said, "I could ask Kendall about it myself. Tell him what you're working on. As much as you want me to reveal, that is." *As much as you're willing to tell me,* she added silently.

She hadn't planned to make that offer. It just came out—the same way, now that she thought about it, she'd agreed to take the Amelia Bainbridge case. She really needed to work on her impulse control.

But the sight of Rez's troubled face, plus the discouragement in his voice, had moved her. Concerned her. If Kendall didn't agree, she could always go to his boss. And the truth was, any intervention from Violet Crowley would probably be effective.

She had clout. She knew it, and she knew that Rez knew it, too. She didn't like to *use* it, but she had it all the same. She might be a struggling detective with a load of bills, but she was also the only child of Ogden Crowley, founder and former president of New Earth. And that mattered. It mattered a lot.

"Okay," Rez finally said. "If you want to—okay, fine. But if you change your mind, I get it."

"I'll talk to him."

He shrugged again. Shrugging was Rez's go-to gesture. "Like I said, it's totally up to you."

"So just to be clear, what do you need the clearance for? What are you working on?"

Rez's face softened. His eyes seemed to shine with their old familiar light.

"When they first sent me down here," he said, "I had to come up with a way to pass the time. I mean, I couldn't just sit around and brood. So I got an idea. It started the same place all ideas start—with a question. What can we do with Old Earth? How can it be more than just a prison? More than just a haven for disease? Then it came to me—maybe we can *repurpose* it. Take what we find here and make it new again."

Violet was skeptical. How could anybody revive Old Earth? And why would they *want* to? Sure, she had a deep bond with it, but for most people, Old Earth was dreadful wreck, a dismal has-been of a planet.

"So then I had a brainstorm," Rez declared, breaking into her thoughts with what almost sounded to her—could it be?—like *enthusiasm.*

He took a deep breath and then plunged on. "We could make Old Earth into an amusement park. Olde Earth World or something. I've already started. I've been using whatever I find on the ground—wood, scrap metal—to build it, so nobody can complain about the cost. There's tons and tons of salvage down here. Amazing stuff that was left behind." Another deep breath. "All the rides," he said, "relate to the fate of Old Earth, to what happened here and why. So it's fun, sure, but it's also a place where people can *learn.* The roller coaster with the watertight cars and the track that loops under the ocean and back out again, spiraling through those ginormous blobs of plastic bottles that go for miles—that's already designed. And the hovercraft that zips along the edge of the melting ice caps at both poles—that's going to be great, too. I've decided to call that one the Ice Cap Zapper. And then—"

"Hey, hold on, hold on," Violet said, interrupting him but doing it in a gentle, good-natured way. "I get the picture. I don't want to overwhelm Kendall. We just want him to approve your access to quantum computing. Not book season tickets."

A sheepish smile. Rez's smiles were so rare that Violet had started to count them.

"Excellent point," he said.

This is a good place to leave things, she thought. *With Rez in a newly awakened good mood.* "Okay," Violet said. "Well, I'd better get back to work right now. I'm running a business, you know." *More like running a business into the ground.* "I've got a new case."

"Hope you solve it." His tone had reverted back to its normal flatness. He didn't care about her case—at least that was Violet's interpretation.

"Thanks."

"So is it worth it?"

Whoa. Was Rez actually asking her about her detective agency? This might be a first.

"What do you mean?"

"Having to deal with people all the time," he said. "And only when something has gone wrong in their lives."

Violet's surprise intensified. Not only was he asking her about her business—he even seemed to have given it a bit of thought.

"The dealing with people part is okay," she replied. She had to actively resist adding, *Only YOU would think other people are automatically a negative, Rez.* "But the other part—meeting them when they've lost something precious or when they're in some kind of trouble—well, it's not so okay. But that's the job."

He appeared to be ruminating about her answer.

"Hey," he said.

"What?"

"You're not doing anything dangerous, right? You're being careful?"

She was instantly miffed. "I've already got a dad," Violet snapped. "I don't need two."

"Never mind," Rez snapped right back at her.

"Okay," she said.

"Okay."

She started to sign off when she saw that he had more to say.

"Hold on," he said. "Something I need to tell you about."

"Yeah?"

"It's no big deal. Probably not important, but I thought you should know."

She waited. She was still mad at him. She didn't feel like being nice.

"So I was running a few calculations the other day, just for fun," Rez said. "And I used some of the declassified Intercept code. It's like scrap paper now. And guess what?"

"What?" It came out testier than she'd meant.

"Wow." Rez reared back his head, blinking a few extra times. "Take it down a notch, Violet, okay?"

"Sorry. Go on." Why was she so emotional around him these days? It was confusing. This was just Rez, after all.

"Well, it's kind of weird—I mean, maybe it's not even worth talking about. But some coordinates just sort of ghosted across my console this morning. And I could swear that somebody else was accessing the Intercept protocol."

Violet's breath caught in her throat.

"How is that *possible*?" she said. "The Intercept doesn't *exist* anymore. It's gone. It's dead. It's actually deader than dead. How could somebody be using it?"

"Well, like I said, it's probably nothing. Sheer coincidence. A couple of random algorithms probably overlapped. And it happened to echo a part of the Intercept foundation code. I'm sure it's nothing."

"Right."

But Violet wasn't reassured. She pretended to be, but she wasn't. Because she knew things about the Intercept's destruction that Rez didn't know. Things that nobody else knew.

Except for Kendall. And he would never betray her.

TAP

iolet made a mistake. In fact, she didn't make just one mistake; she made the same mistake three times over.

It wasn't anything she did.

It was something she *didn't* do.

And it was all set into motion when she arrived at the Tram Assembly Point—TAP—shortly after winding up her talk with Rez. She'd gotten here before Kendall, but not by much. In fact, she'd just spotted him striding toward her with his purposeful, straight-line, outta-my-way walk, dressed in his regulation blue tunic and black trousers. Kendall had a long face with gray eyes, a thin mouth, and a straight nose. He wore his hair in a severe buzz cut. His build was slender but sturdy. You wouldn't exactly call him handsome, Violet thought as she watched his approach, but he was the kind of guy who snared your attention.

When he was seconds away from her, Violet made a quick, fateful decision:

I'll tell him later.

That was the first time she made the mistake. It was a bad one, and it was to have terrible consequences down the road. People would end up dying because of it—even if, at the time, Violet had her reasons. Good ones. Or so she'd thought.

"Hey," Kendall said.

"Hey." Violet looked around. "Wow, this place is really noisy. Makes me want to rip my ears off. And that *smell*. What is it?"

"All kinds of chemical solvents mashed together," Kendall answered. He was standing close enough to her so that he didn't have to yell. "You've never been here before?"

"Once. When I was a kid. My dad brought me. He was check-ing on the recycled tram cars."

"And you don't remember the smell?"

"What can I say? I guess I blocked it out." The truth was, she hadn't even noticed it back then. She was so thrilled to be hanging out with her father that everything else just fell right out of her head. Usually, he was too busy to spend time with a little girl—even his *own* little girl.

"Well, if you can pull that off today, let me know how you do it." Kendall grinned. The grin faded as he turned and spot-ted the tram car isolated in the far corner. "There it is. Come on."

Violet had asked Kendall if she could join him here at TAP in L'Engletown. The official police report listed Amelia's death as a suicide, but there would still be an investigation. And it would start here, in the vast, frenetic facility with the concrete floor and the enormous glass bubble of a roof, held aloft by an elaborate grid of thin steel girders that let in gobs of sunlight.

"So this is the car she was riding in," Violet said. "Before she . . ."

"Yeah." Kendall detached one end of the taut crisscross of

yellow police tape that protected the entrance to the sleek silver lozenge.

He stepped inside. Violet followed him. Kendall went right to work, taking measurements and making notes on his console, which meant Violet had a chance to look around the car.

The shadowy interior gave her a mild case of the creeps. It was cool and self-contained, a world away from the controlled chaos that existed just outside its door—the thick acoustical stew of drilling and hammering and nonhuman shrieking. The shrieking resulted from the fact that immensely large hunks of metal were constantly being pulled apart by the extended clamps of opposing teams of robots. To Violet, they looked like kids playing tug-of-war.

"It's so quiet in here," she said. "You don't expect that. Not with what's out there."

"Yeah," Kendall said. He ran a thumb along one of the car's welded seams. Then he got down on his hands and knees, exploring the bolts that linked the seats to the floor.

Tram cars were retooled every ten days, Violet knew, and brought to TAP to be spruced up and rejuvenated and then returned to the elevated tracks. Thus there was a perpetual round of cars going from track to TAP and back again. Everything on New Earth had to be recycled, with the position and density of every speck and spark and dab and stray ounce accounted for, second by second. This ceaseless calibration was what enabled New Earth to remain poised over Old Earth. The tremendous cumulative weight of its streets and its buildings and its machines and its people had to be meticulously balanced by the power-generating magnets and wind turbines.

Violet stood in the center of the aisle. She was trying to put herself in Amelia's mind, in hopes of understanding what might have happened. *I'm sixteen years old, it's early in the morning, I'm on my way to school, and I'm feeling...*

"Identification. Identification. Identification."

The tinny, annoying voice crashed into Violet's reverie. She looked down. It was a ConRob, a shorthand term for construction robot. The bullet-shaped ConRobs were built for strength and efficiency, not friendliness or companionship, and this one had an especially nasty streak. Even though he only came up to her waist, she was a little alarmed by his telescoping pincer; he tried to grab her wrist as he repeated his stupid little mantra: "Identification. Identification. Identification."

"She's okay," Kendall said. He had trotted over from the other end of the car.

"Authorized personnel only," the ConRob snapped.

"She's authorized," Kendall said. "By me." He pulled out his police ID. The ConRob scanned it with a blue light, line by line, and then backed off.

"*Jerk,*" Violet muttered at him as he wheeled away.

She was sure he was a guy, even though ConRobs didn't have assigned genders. She also knew they didn't have personalities, and yet she would have sworn he'd sneered at her—and had been a little snarky to boot.

Kendall laughed. "You know what, Violet? I don't think you can hurt a robot's feelings by calling him names."

"Worth a try."

So this was the second time she made the mistake. Because even if she hadn't told him when he arrived, this was her next-best opportunity. The mood was temporarily lightened by her attempt to bad-mouth a robot. Kendall was taking a break from his careful analysis of the car.

It was the perfect spot.

But she didn't do it. She didn't fill him in about Rez's suspicions.

Why bother him with something that might turn out to be nothing? I'll tell him later.

If she had told him then, everything might have turned out differently.

Twenty minutes later, Kendall was still crawling around the floor of the car. Violet was getting antsy. His forensics team had already examined the place. So what was the holdup?

"Is the autopsy ready yet?" Violet asked.

"I told my assistants to move it to the front of the line." He stood up, dusting off his hands. "The moment it's done, you'll have it—along with whatever my team found on their initial sweep in here."

Violet nodded. "Appreciate it. To tell you the truth, though, I'm not really sure how much an autopsy's going to help. Obviously, the fall is what killed her. It's the *why*—not the *how*—that I need to figure out."

They stood side by side in the wide aisle of the tram car. Instead of channeling Amelia, Violet realized that now she was sort of channeling the car itself. The car was totally out of its element here, marooned and useless. No longer doing its job. No longer part of a smooth line of identical cars, busy and important, racing along a track with cool speed.

Violet could almost sense the car's loneliness at being isolated here in a distant corner of TAP, cut off from its destiny.

Ribbed steel ran the length of the floor. Three seats were grouped on each side of the aisle. The seat in which Amelia had been riding before she fled from the car was covered in a plastic wrap. On the wrap was a label: DO NOT REMOVE BY ORDER OF THE NEW EARTH SECURITY SERVICE.

"You never know," Kendall said. "I've seen cases turn on the smallest things. You just have to be patient and methodical."

Two words that happened to define him perfectly, Violet thought. Running the police forensics lab was the ideal job for him. He was a crusader-scientist with a brilliant mind as well as a deep hunger for justice. That hunger had been honed and sharpened by the years he'd spent as a street cop—and before that, as a kid on the wild, lawless streets of Old Earth. He knew how important justice was because he'd seen what could happen to the world without it.

He didn't usually handle cases in the field anymore. But he was doing this for her, Violet knew.

"How about the toxicology report?" she asked. "Any hair and fiber evidence found in the—"

"Under way. I'll keep you posted."

"Right. Okay." Her shoulders rose and fell with a long, slow breath. "This is my first job in forever, so I'm eager to get started."

"Right," Kendall said. "But before we talk any more about the case, tell me how you're doing. You didn't answer my console call yesterday. Or the day before."

Because I knew you were going to ask me how I'm doing. And I don't want to talk about anything . . . personal.

"Well," Violet answered, "the thing is, I've been busy. With work."

"I thought you said this was your first job in a long time."
Oops.

"Well, yeah. Yeah, it is. I've been busy with . . . other stuff." She tried to recover her footing in the conversation. "How about you?"

"I'm fine."

"You look good. I mean it. Your uniform . . . it almost looks *ironed.*" Violet leaned back, as if the concept was so totally amazing that she needed a little distance to fully appreciate it.

"Yeah," he said. He grinned. "My clothes are getting a little more attention these days. But not by me."

"So the Ironing Fairy stopped by your place? Any chance she'd make a detour over to mine one of these days?"

He shook his head. "I hired somebody to help out. Frees me up to spend more time at work."

"Just what you need," Violet murmured, her sarcasm friendly but pointed. "More time at work." Kendall was a notorious workaholic.

He ignored the dig. "I think you know her—Sara Verity. Used to work at the Old Earth transport site until she lost her job. She's great."

Violet nodded. She liked Sara, too, and she'd heard about her misfortune. Layoffs in the Old Earth transport division had escalated sharply over the past several years, ever since Ogden Crowley had opened the borders of New Earth. Now that anybody from Old Earth who wanted to come had already been allowed in, there was no need for a large staff at the checkpoints. No need for people to review the credentials of legions of travelers or operate the pods or keep the tracks in good repair.

Violet felt a surge of sympathy for Sara. She knew how much her friend had loved her work in transport logistics. Ironing tunics and sweeping floors didn't sound like much of a substitute. But then again, it was surely temporary. Sara would find something better soon. And everybody had to deal with change.

Especially me and Kendall.

Violet realized he was looking at her . . . in *that* way.

For a long time, she'd wanted so much more than a friendship with him—but that was back when Kendall was passing as his brother, Danny.

She had forgiven him. She knew that he and Danny had had a good reason for switching their identities when they emigrated to New Earth from Old Earth: Danny—the real Danny—wanted to protect his brother. Kendall was a dazzlingly bright scientist who had invented the Intercept.

Over the next three years, after they'd destroyed the Intercept together, Violet and Kendall had hung out. She needed to see if she was still in love with him. She'd recently decided that the answer was probably . . . *no.*

He was the same person she had been in love with before, when she knew him by another name—but somehow he *wasn't* the same person, too.

Sometimes, she thought, everything she was doing these days—running around like crazy as she tried to make a go of her detective agency, dancing all night until she was so tired the next day that she could barely stand up—was just a way to distract herself so she wouldn't think about what had gone wrong with her and Danny.

With her and *Kendall*, that is. Kendall, not Danny. Because Danny—the *real* Danny—was long dead. And she couldn't even mourn him, because she'd never really known him.

"Do you want to grab a coffee when we're done here?" Kendall said.

"Wish I could. But I've got a ton of work to do."

"Okay." His face revealed nothing. "Got it."

A long, fraught moment went by.

"So," Kendall said. He was ready to return to the case. "I'll send the toxicology report to your console, but the bottom line is— Amelia Bainbridge was clean. No drugs, legal or otherwise. No medications. No antidepressants. And no evidence of any sort of neurological condition. No brain tumor, no seizure disorder, no concussion, no infection. She was sound in mind and body when she took her own life."

"Obviously not."

"Why's that?"

"Because she took her own life," Violet said, repeating his words back to him. "Nobody kills herself for no reason."

Kendall snapped on a pair of gloves. He stepped toward the row of seats that included Amelia's.

"Okay," he said, crouching down in the aisle on one knee, facing the seats. "So you've added psychiatry to your many fields of expertise."

The sarcasm stung. "Just my opinion," she clarified. "I'm only saying that it's unusual. Amelia had everything to live for. Jumping off that track doesn't make any sense."

Kendall unwrapped the plastic from the seat. He went over the surface with a sweeping hand. The seats were covered with black fabric and bolted securely to the floor. "So the eyewitness accounts are all in agreement. Amelia's sitting right here." He tapped the back of the seat. Then he stood up and pointed toward the open door of the car. "The car stops at Hawking, and the doors open up and off she goes—running as fast as she can, almost knocking down a woman who's boarding the tram. Amelia can't *wait* to get to the edge. She's frantic. But why?"

"Did she get a call on her console? Some kind of bad news, maybe?"

"No call. That's what the witnesses said and her console record confirms it." Kendall walked slowly up and down the aisle, checking each row of seats. "It all looks normal. Nothing out of the ordinary."

"Except for the fact that a girl with her whole life ahead of her suddenly rushes out the door and jumps to her death."

Violet shook her head in exasperation. "And nobody saw or heard anything that was unusual."

"One person did."

"Who?"

"The woman Amelia bumped as she ran out. I interviewed her on my way over here."

"What did she tell you?"

"She said Amelia was murmuring something about New Earth being awful. And about hearing a scream."

"A scream? None of the other passengers said anything about hearing a scream."

"No. They didn't. But the woman wasn't certain about Amelia's exact words. She was too shaken up by what happened just after that, she said, to be sure of anything."

Violet thought about the word *scream*. It was such a brutal word. There was nothing soft about a scream. Had Amelia meant that she *wanted* to scream? Or that she had *heard* a scream? Or—

"Hey."

A third voice.

Violet looked up.

Somebody else had entered the car.

Rez's Request

The entryway was thickly webbed with shadows, and thus Violet couldn't make out the visitor's identity right away. All she knew for certain was that it wasn't the pesky ConRob, back to torment her once again. The new arrival was too tall.

"Oh—hi, Sara!" Violet said, the moment she realized who it was.

Kendall's greeting was less friendly. "Sara, what are you—"

"I came by to apply for a job at TAP and saw you guys in here," Sara said. She looked quickly around the car, up and down, back and forth. The motion made her copious reddish curls bounce in a nervous cluster, like a bunch of grapes somebody was trying to shake dry. Violet had not seen her in several months—honestly, she couldn't remember how long it had been—but Sara looked basically the same. She had a round, pretty face, with a paintbrush-swipe of freckles across her nose and cheeks. "I'm not going to be a housekeeper forever, right?

And this is my area of expertise—transport. I just finished the application paperwork."

"That's great, Sara," Kendall said, "but this is a restricted area. I'm conducting an official police investigation."

"Investigation?" Sara said. "Into what?"

Kendall and Violet exchanged glances.

"Come on, you guys," Sara said. "You can trust me."

In a quiet voice, Kendall said, "The girl who committed suicide this morning. Amelia Bainbridge."

Sara closed her eyes and shook her head. "Oh, *right*. That was awful. Just awful. I saw it on my console feed." She opened her eyes. "But if it's a suicide, what's to investigate?"

"Just wrapping up loose ends," Violet said.

Sara gave Violet a sharp look. "You're not a cop."

"I was hired by the victim's mother to investigate her death."

Sara smacked her forehead with the heel of her hand. "Oh, geez. Of course. Sorry if I sounded rude. I just didn't expect to see you here. And I'm pretty nosy."

"Me too," Violet said with a smile. "But in my case, I get paid for it. Being nosy is sort of a detective's job, right?"

The smile wasn't forced or fake. Two years ago, Sara had risked her job in transport systems—the one she now missed so much—on Violet's behalf. That was a gesture Violet would never forget.

"I hope you get a position here," Violet added. She wished she could hire Sara herself. But at this point, she still had no idea how she was going to pay Jonetta's salary, much less add somebody else to the payroll.

"Thanks," Sara said. "But it's a long shot. I don't really have the right experience. I've never supervised robots. I worked on transport to Old Earth, not transport here on New Earth." She shrugged again. She seemed to be cheering herself up. "But no matter what, I'll keep looking."

Violet gave her a thumbs-up. "Let's hang out sometime. Okay?"

"Great. I can tell you funny stories about *this* guy and how many of his socks straight up go missing every week." She pointed at Kendall, who threw up his hands as if he'd been caught doing something naughty.

Sara moved toward the exit. She paused. Her face was somber again.

"Found any clues yet?" she asked. "Anything to tell you why Amelia Bainbridge would want to end her life? She seemed like a nice girl."

"Nothing yet," Violet replied. "Did you know her?"

"No. Only what I read in the news stories. But I think I sort of get her. Life can be hard sometimes, you know? For everybody. Even on New Earth—which is supposed to be almost perfect." Sara waved and ducked out through the doorway.

"It's exactly what the investigating officers said in their preliminary assessment," Kendall declared. He had finally finished his examination of the car and now stood in the middle of the aisle. He gave a last appraising glance fore and aft. "Amelia Bainbridge died of injuries sustained when she plunged from a tram track at 9:02 A.M. today. No foul play involved."

"But why did she want to die?"

He paused. "Not all questions have answers, Violet. Anybody who works in science will tell you that."

She shook her head. "No way. There's always an answer. But sometimes it's not the answer you want to hear." She sighed.

"It's going to be really tough to go back and tell Amelia's mother that her daughter died because she didn't want to live anymore. If that's what I find out, I mean. After my own investigation."

"You owe her the truth."

"I know." Violet could tell that he was trying to wrap things up so he could get back to the station. "Listen, Kendall. I need a favor."

"Aren't we already in the *middle* of me doing you a favor?"

Violet ignored that. "Rez called me today." She watched Kendall's face to see if she could spot any reaction. The tension between Kendall and Rez was subtle, but it was there.

"How's he doing?" Kendall's expression didn't change.

"As well as can be expected. I mean, it's Old Earth, you know? He's enduring it."

"His probation must be up soon."

"Year and a half."

"Wow," Kendall said, his voice somber. "Sounds pretty far away."

"Exactly. The thing is, he needs clearance to do any quantum computing."

"Given the nature of his crime, I guess I'm not surprised."

"Yeah," Violet said, "but he's paid a high price for that. And now he has some good ideas for Old Earth. He's already started on them. That's why he wants to do quantum computing."

"Ideas?"

She paused. "An amusement park."

"A *what*?" Kendall made a sound that was halfway to being a snicker.

"An amusement park. Remember the Culture Portal in history class? Does the word *Disneyland* ring a bell? Or *Six Flags*?"

"Yeah. Yeah, they do. You forget, I was raised on Old Earth.

I've seen the remnants of a bunch of Disneylands—a lot of dangling wires and empty lagoons and crushed pop cans and twisted coaster tracks that break off and go nowhere. And by the way, even if I *had* gone to school on New Earth, I would've automatically skipped anything called a *Culture Portal*." He scrunched up his face. "I would've subbed it out for molecular biology."

"It was a requirement."

"Then I would've quit school. On the spot."

Violet laughed. "Yeah, you're such a dropout. Anyway, that's what Rez wants to create down there. Some really cool rides. Things like coasters and Ferris wheels and haunted houses. Real retro stuff."

"Why?"

"He thinks that maybe it could turn a dead place into a living one. So people will want to go back down there again and again. They'll have a stake in keeping Old Earth fixed up and halfway decent. It'll become a vacation spot."

"A vacation spot." Once again, Kendall made the half-snicker sound.

"Okay, whatever." Violet knew she was coming across as defensive. She didn't care. She was tired of having Kendall repeat Rez's words back to her, vaguely mocking. "You don't have to believe in what Rez is doing. Just help him get the tools he needs to do it." If she'd had the nerve, she would have added a few extra sentences: *You're not the only one who gets to have cool ideas, Kendall Mayhew. Other people like to invent things, too.*

"Okay," he said.

"Really?"

"Sure. Why not? I'll send a note to Chief Singleton's console. Tell her it's fine by me if she wants to sign off on it." Two years ago, Laura Singleton had replaced Michelle Callahan as chief of police. "And I'll double-check with President Shomo's office, too. Keep everybody in the loop."

Violet waited for more explanation. When it didn't come, she had to ask.

"So why are you suddenly so cooperative? I thought I'd have to argue with you for at least ten minutes to get you to vouch for him."

"Maybe I'm mellowing." He shrugged.

"Yeah. Like *that's* gonna happen." Kendall was the most intense person she had ever known. When he was pretending to be Danny he had ratcheted down that intensity, presenting himself as more easygoing and low-key; now that he was Kendall again, he could be his real self—which meant passionate and focused and driven.

"The truth is," Kendall continued after a thoughtful pause, "Rez is brilliant. New Earth needs him. As soon as his parole is up, I'd like to hire him to work in my lab. Until that day comes, I want him to be as happy as possible, given his situation. I want him to be fulfilled, you know? Not bored. And not frustrated."

"Makes sense."

Now was her chance. They were ending the conversation. The moment was here.

This was yet *another* perfect opportunity to tell him about Rez and the Intercept. And he was the only person she *could* tell, because Violet and Kendall shared a secret: They had not destroyed it. On the day of the Intercept's death two years ago, they had made a swift, mutual, momentous decision. They rescued the loose pages of Kendall's notes from his original blueprint. With those notes, the Intercept could be remade.

Once again, she said nothing.

Countdown

Two more days.

That was it. Only two.

The girls had been counting down for a month now. Twenty-nine. Twenty-eight. Twenty-seven . . .

Finally, they'd crossed the threshold into single digits. Ten, nine, eight, seven.

This morning, it was two.

Two! Yes!

Thinking about it, letting the beautiful number bounce around in her head, Rita Wilton pumped her fist. She was lying on the bottom bunk, and so the pump sent her fist crashing into the underside of the top bunk. Hard enough, in fact, to make her twin sister, Rosalinda—who was sleeping on that top bunk, or trying to—yelp.

"Hey," Rosalinda said, following up on the yelp. "Cut it out." Her tone was cranky.

"Two days!" Rita said.

"Got it." Rosalinda groaned. "Let me sleep. It's not even light outside yet."

The window in the twins' bedroom was still a black rectangle. Technically, they didn't have to start getting ready for school for another half an hour. But Rita didn't care. In a mere two days, she'd be thirteen years old—which meant, of course, that Rosalinda would also turn thirteen—and being thirteen meant that they could load a bunch of new jewels onto their consoles.

Console regulations were very clear. Up through age twelve, you were only allowed a single jewel; a single jewel limited you to simple data searches or brief text exchanges with your parents. But the moment you turned thirteen—*jackpot*. You could add two more jewels. With three jewels—*jewels* being the shorthand designation for the shimmering holograms generated by wrist consoles, embedded in iridescent dots that drifted up from the console face like reverse snowflakes—you could start corresponding with friends. You could access music and social media. The whole world of New Earth would open up for you like a blossoming flower.

It was a totally cool milestone. Rita couldn't wait. And so she jumped hungrily into each new day, hoping that if she moved fast enough the days, too, would go faster and her thirteenth birthday would arrive that much more quickly.

"Come on," she declared. "Let's go!"

Rita popped out of bed. She ran to the window and gazed out. Despite the darkness, she was able to make out a shadowy shape moving quickly along the sidewalk in front of their house. *Probably a jogger*, she guessed.

Even before the sun rose, Rita could tell it was going to be a glorious day. She could just feel it.

Rosalinda didn't heed her sister's command to get up.

Instead she groaned again. This time, it was a longer, slower, *leave-me-alone* kind of groan.

Rita headed toward the closet. Time to get dressed for school. She almost tripped several times as her bare toes bumped into shoes and socks and T-shirts and tennis rackets and toy sailboats and other junk they discarded in a wild rush every night, when they raced in from whatever they were doing and flung themselves into bed—Rosalinda always in the top bunk, Rita in the bottom one—just ahead of the moment when their mom would come in to check on them.

She was always lecturing them about keeping their room picked up. And they tried. They really did. They loved this room; their dad had been a sailor on Old Earth, and he'd added wooden rafters across the ceiling to make it look like the galley of a schooner. If it were humanly possible, they would've kept the space tidy.

But there were *so* many more interesting things to do than clean up *their* room.

Rita promised herself that she'd do better. She wanted to help her mom. She knew that her parents struggled to pay the bills and to make sure she and Rosalinda had everything they needed; she had heard the murmurs from the living room late at night, when her mom and dad went over their expenses. Rita couldn't hear the details—and in fact she didn't *want* to hear the details—but she knew from the worried sound of her parents' voices that the conversation was about money. It was always about money. The lack of it, that is.

A burden. I'm a burden.

Rita had been reaching for a shirt in the closet when an odd thought showed up in her head.

If they didn't have me, they'd be okay. But all I do is cost them money.

She blinked several times. Was she dreaming? She felt a small flicker in the crook of her left elbow. But when she looked down at her arm, she didn't see anything.

I'm just a stupid nuisance.

The world would be a lot better off without me.

The room was lighter now. Sunrise was here. Rita turned around slowly. To her surprise, Rosalinda hadn't gone back to sleep. Her sister was sitting up in bed. Rosalinda's face wore a shocked look. Her eyes were wide. Her lip was quivering.

If we weren't around, Mom and Dad would have a lot more money. They wouldn't worry so much. They'd be happy. They'd be free.

The thoughts came like jittery little twitches.

"Rita," Rosalinda said. Her voice was hushed. She sounded scared. "Are you thinking—?"

"Yeah," Rita said. "I am. I'm thinking it, too."

"What is it? Why is this happening?"

Rita shook her head. "I . . . I don't know."

Our parents don't really love us. How could they? I'm a loser. Both of us are losers. We don't matter. If we were gone, nobody would miss us. Least of all Mom and Dad.

"It's got to stop," Rosalinda said. Her voice had dropped even lower and sounded even more strained. It sounded like a plea that came from the deepest part of her soul. "I can't stand it, Rita. I can't stand being a burden." She clutched the bedsheet in her balled-up fists. She felt her body starting to shake, as if overtaken by a sudden intense chill. But when she looked at her fists, she saw they were still. "Please, Rita."

Nobody cares about us. Nobody. Why should they?

Rita tried to move back toward the bed so that she could take her sister's hand. So that they could ward off the thoughts together. Fight them as a team. But she couldn't move. The thoughts blocked her. Those thoughts came in waves now, great dark waves of hatefulness.

Mom and Dad would be so much better off without us. I can see that now.

Rita started to shake. Her shoulders shuddered as if an invisible bully was roughing her up, pushing her around. She was losing control.

But when she looked at her feet, her hands, she saw that her body wasn't moving at all.

I'm stupid. Stupid and selfish. All I care about is my dumb little birthday.

"Rita?" her sister said. Her voice was little more than a gasp now. "Rita, I can't get it out of my head. It won't stop. Why is it screaming at me? Help me, Rita. Please."

I know what to do.

Rita opened her mouth. She wanted to say something reassuring to Rosalinda, to tell her not to listen to the screaming in her mind. But when she tried to speak, the screaming voice got louder, drowning her out.

I'm ugly. I don't matter. Nobody likes me. Mom and Dad wish that we would just die. Both of us. So why don't I do it? I know what to do. Don't I?

Rita's brain was made of snakes now. Black, twisting, writhing snakes, with tongues darting and striking, darting and striking. And she knew that Rosalinda's brain felt the same way, because they'd always pretty much known what the other twin was thinking.

I know what to do. And if I care about Mom and Dad, I'll do it. I'll put them out of their misery.

Both girls climbed onto the top bunk.

I know what to do.

"Rosalinda," Rita said. "It's time."

I know what to do.

Rosalinda nodded. "It's time," she repeated back to her sister.

Rita tied the bedsheet around her neck. She reached up toward the rafter that ran the length of the ceiling. She tied the other end of the sheet around the rafter. Her dad had taught them how to tie a good, sturdy knot; he knew all about knots.

While Rita was doing that, Rosalinda tied one end of her own bedsheet around her neck. She, too, tied the other end around a rafter.

They shivered. The screams, vivid and high-pitched, clawed at the insides of their skulls. Because they were both hearing them, and because each knew the other one was hearing them too, their agony was doubled.

I KNOW WHAT TO DO.

I KNOW WHAT TO DO.

They stood up, side by side. Sisters.

"Rita?" Rosalinda said. "Do we have to?"

"You know we do," Rita said.

"Yes," Rosalinda said.

Rita took her sister's hand. She hesitated for a second, but then the screaming came barreling at her again, slamming and banging against her brain, destroying everything in its path— all of their hopes, all of their dreams, all of their joy. There would be no thirteenth birthday. There would be no new jewels. There would only be a whirling and terrible voice, echoing forever, shrieking at them, unless they made it stop.

Mom and Dad hate us. They want us dead. We know what to do.

Yes.

Hand in hand, Rita and Rosalinda jumped off the edge of the bed, hurling themselves into the air. They went up, up, up—they jumped so high, in such perfectly synchronized rhythm, that when their bodies plummeted back down and the sheets stretched taut, anyone listening would have sworn that there'd been only one crisp snap, not two.

Ambush

Sometimes, in the privacy of her own mind, she missed the Intercept.

Violet couldn't admit that to anybody, not even Shura or Kendall. But sometimes she missed it.

She had awakened the morning after her visit to TAP with a deep, insistent feeling that she needed to run. So she pulled on sweats and a hoodie, laced her sneakers, turned off her console, and ran.

And as she ran, she was reminded, with every step, of what wasn't there anymore: the feeling of the Intercept beneath her feet, like a living, breathing, watchful presence, and she missed it.

She didn't miss what the Intercept *did*—spying on people's feelings, grabbing them, storing them, and redeploying them to control behavior—but she missed the vibration produced by its constant operation. And the way that subtle motion made her feel: *protected*, somehow. Surrounded and supported by something bigger and more powerful than herself.

From its underground lair at Protocol Hall, the network of computers had branched out beneath the straight silver streets, spreading for mile after mile after mile after mile. As the Intercept went about its frenzied work of collection and deployment, collection and deployment, it had created a small but perceptible ripple. The movement was tiny—it barely riffled the tea in a teacup—but if you paid attention, you always knew it was there.

Now the feeling was gone. The streets of New Earth didn't move anymore.

They were absolutely still.

And she was alone.

She'd been running more and more often lately, as her detective agency teetered on the brink and the bills kept piling up. She liked to flash past the coolly elegant spires and darkly gleaming towers. Running took her mind off her troubles even more effectively than a crazy night at Redshift did.

Last night was the first time in a long while that she'd stayed home from the club. She needed to review the files on the Bainbridge case that Kendall had sent to her console. And she'd studied some notes sent over by her lawyer. Because she had to show up in court to account for the stupid—no, the very, very, *very* stupid, not to mention thoughtless and reckless, even if indisputably minor—thing she had done. Even a small fine, given her present financial predicament, could be disastrous.

Dawn had brought a striking mix of shades to the New Earth sky. Looking up as she raced along, Violet picked out ballerina pink and buttercup yellow and the scuffed-up orange of an old basketball, along with skittery dots of gray that looked like the speckles on the underside of a dove's wing, all swirled together like cotton candy on an invisible stick. The Color Corps engineers over in Farraday who were responsible for creating the daily blend must be in a good mood today. Usually they just switched on the randomness algorithm and one or two colors popped up, but sometimes they got inspired—a little whimsical, even—and did it by hand. You could tell.

The streets were too ordinary to go along with a sky like this one, Violet thought. Too bland. Too firm. They didn't murmur with magical secrets, which was how she had thought of them as a kid, when the Intercept was in control.

The Intercept wasn't the only thing she missed, of course. She missed her mother, too, with a whole different universe of intensity. Lucretia Crowley had given her daughter this strong, vigorous body, these powerful legs. She had also passed along her fierce and abiding sense of justice.

Violet was ten years old when her mother died of a fever caught while she was treating patients on Old Earth. Violet remembered her well, and never more so than when she hit the streets of New Earth first thing in the morning, when the sky was coming to life and the air was crisp and the great promise of a new civilization was gloriously evident.

She pictured her mother's long, wavy hair, the snap and fire in her eyes, the tilt of her chin when she laughed, and the gentle, loving way she would—

What's that?

Something jerked at the corner of Violet's eye.

She didn't slow her pace, but she was on alert now. Her mother's face slipped out of her thoughts. Whatever she'd spotted had been somewhere off to her right side, just at the edge of her range of vision. It was a . . . well, a *flash*. A flash of . . . well, of *something*.

Violet's gaze whipped around as she rapidly took in her surroundings. Before, those surroundings had been a blur. Now she concentrated.

She was still in the business district of Hawking. The city was an intricate silver forest of immensely slender, terrifically tall, sumptuously sleek-sided structures. The offices were generally empty at this time of day. Most people hadn't gone to work yet.

Wait.

There it was again. A flash of reflective light between the buildings. Keeping pace with her. Speeding up, slowing down when she did. Turning when she turned.

Violet kept moving, because the worst thing she could do right now would be to tip off her shadow that she'd seen her or him. The best strategy was to fake nonchalance and head for the police station. Pretend to be oblivious. And vulnerable.

But who was it? Who in the world wished her harm? Why would anybody go to the trouble to—

The idea came to her all at once, in a twitch of sudden insight.

Maybe Charlotte Bainbridge is right. Maybe somebody did kill Amelia.

And maybe I'm next.

And maybe I deserve to have something bad happen to me. I'm a loser, right? I'm embarrassing my father. My friends probably don't really like me and—

Whoa. Where did that come from?

She shook off the negative thoughts and made a sharp right turn, darting across a small brick courtyard that linked the parking lots of two massive office buildings, then scooting through a narrow alley before emerging two streets over from where she'd been. Nobody knew these streets as well as she did.

That'll show 'em.

Didn't work.

Because she was still being followed.

If Violet had doubted that even for an instant, the doubt

vanished now. She could sense her pursuer moving as she moved, just to the right of her, hidden by the buildings except for the brief spaces between them. Zigging and zagging, darting in and out.

The street was just deserted enough to make her nervous, even though she was fully capable of taking care of herself. She was in good shape, and she knew how to throw a punch. Kendall had taught her how to defend herself, because she'd been attacked by a gang two years ago during her first trip down to Old Earth. In the aftermath, she had promised herself that she'd *never* be so silly and weak and ridiculously helpless ever again. That attack had left her bloody and breathless, but she considered it a gift. It showed her how tough she needed to be.

She sensed that whoever was tracking her had nosed ahead of her. So this was a pro. That was the secret of a good tail: You never stayed exclusively behind your prey. Kendall had taught her that, too. Sometimes you let yourself get a little bit ahead, before looping back around. You had to make it look natural. Natural helped you stay unnoticed.

In the near distance, Violet spotted a gap between two buildings, a crevice that looked like a great hiding place. Her purser had surely seen it, too. And now waited for her.

Ready to pounce.

Violet moved ever closer, keeping the rhythm of her pace. Acting as if she hadn't seen a thing. But she was on high alert. Her fists were tight. Just in case.

And then something glinted. Something . . . *metallic.*

A slab gun. Had to be a slab gun. Violet's heart gave a terrified twist. But now that she'd seen it, she knew she could handle it. She'd be able to kick it out of the shooter's hand before the firing mechanism engaged. She'd practiced that very maneuver with Kendall in the police gym, going over it again and again; whirl, kick, disarm.

Suddenly she swerved. She peeled off her straight course, diving toward the shadowy space in the chasm between the buildings. She aimed herself like an arrow. A figure crouched on the ground. Violet was a quarter of a second from what she envisioned as Full Attack Frenzy—punches, kicks, jabs, and then maybe a few curse words for good measure. This creep who'd been following her would be sore for a week, with plenty of time to regret having even *considered* messing with Violet Crowley.

She pulled back her fist, ready to deliver a solid roundhouse blow.

"Hey, wait! Wait! Don't hit me!"

Violet hesitated. The voice was young. Her eyes adjusted to the darkness, and she realized she was looking at . . . a *kid.* Just a kid. He was about ten years old. His mouth hung open, and he was panting in frantic desperation, having followed her for well over a mile on much shorter legs.

What had caused the glint? The answer winked at her: It was the kid's console, an old-fashioned clunky one. Its wide metallic face had caught the early-morning light and reflected it back.

"I'm not going to hit you," she said.

"Sure looks like you are." He nodded toward her cocked fist. Violet looked at her fist, too. Pretty impressive, if she did say so herself.

She dropped it.

The kid stood up—slowly, cautiously—and Violet grabbed his shoulder. She hauled him out onto the sidewalk. She wanted a better look. He tried to resist but didn't put much oomph behind his resistance.

He had large ears that stuck out on either side of his narrow head, big round eyes, and dark brown hair that jumped off his scalp in a fuzzy spray.

"So why were you following me?" she said.

"Because," he said. Or rather snarled, there being enough razor-edged pugnacity in his tone to scrape the paint off the hull of a transport pod. The moment Violet let go of him, he plunged his hands into his pockets.

"Because why?"

"Because you're not doing your job. And I wanted proof. You're not really trying to find out what happened to my sister."

"Who are you?"

"Jeff Bainbridge."

Amelia Bainbridge's little brother.

He was still glaring at her. His feet were spread and his chin was thrust out in what looked like a tough-guy pose he'd practiced for hours in front of a mirror.

"Why do you think I'm not doing my job?" she asked.

"My mom hired you to find out what happened to Amelia. She told me. So I came to Hawking to see if you were making any progress. I saw you leave your office yesterday. Followed you to some factory. They wouldn't let me in, but it didn't matter. I could tell you were just goofing off. And then you went home. It's pretty clear that you're a big fake." He sounded thoroughly disgusted.

"Did it ever occur to you that maybe that factory's related to your sister's death?"

"Is it?"

"As a matter of fact—yeah, it is."

The next thing that happened took Violet by surprise. Jeff Bainbridge—the tough kid who'd had the nerve to follow her, the punk with the chip on his shoulder as big as one of the mega-magnets on Farraday—began to cry. But it wasn't ordinary crying. He wept great gusty, swirling, sloppy bucketfuls of tears until he was barely able to catch his breath.

By now a couple of early risers had shown up on the street; one woman slowed down to make sure the sobbing kid wasn't seriously hurt. "He's okay," Violet said. "Just doesn't want to go to school today. You know how it is." She grinned heartily and slung an arm around Jeff's shoulder. "Really. He's okay." The woman moved on.

In the meantime, the boy had moved from sobbing to wailing. "Hey," Violet said, because she didn't know what else to say, and "Hey" was a sort of all-purpose, fits-anywhere word. "Hey. Hey. Hey." She tried to ruffle his hair, the way she'd seen some of their friends do with their younger siblings, but it was hopeless. Utterly hopeless. She simply wasn't very good at comforting people, not even a ten-year-old who had just lost his sister.

"Hey," she repeated, even more feebly.

He blinked at her. Tears clung to the ends of his eyelashes. Violet felt a quick zing of envy. People younger than she was— Jeff would have been seven at the time the Intercept was destroyed—barely remembered the technology and what it did. They might be embarrassed by their feelings, but they never had to worry, as she'd had to worry, that their heartbreaks would be raked up and then used against them. They were free.

She was free now, too, of course, but she was still cautious. Still nervous. Worrying about the Intercept was a hard habit to break.

Jeff was snuffling now. The wails and sobs had tailed off. With the back of his hand, he wiped the snot that dangled messily from his nose, leaving a smeary yellow trail that spread across his face all the way to his right earlobe.

"How do you *know* it'll be okay?" he asked, his voice thick with phlegm and sorrow. "How do you *know*?"

Bright kid. He'd put her on the spot again. *It's just something people say, Jeff. Got that? They're trying to be nice. They don't mean it. And I don't mean it, either.* Truth was, Violet was convinced—despite the lingering questions, questions she might not ever be able to answer—that Amelia Bainbridge had killed herself. The girl was upset and depressed and she had needed relief, and she had made a bad decision. A *spectacularly* bad decision.

That was all there was to it. Amelia's mother and brother could search for a reason as long as they liked—and hire all the detectives they wanted to hire and try to complicate it with tangles and nuances and complications—but the reality was pretty simple: It was suicide. And they might never find the specific trigger amid all the potential troubles that must have haunted Amelia Bainbridge. Without the Intercept, human emotion was a locked box again. A riddle. A mystery. A conundrum.

And suicide was a sudoku puzzle that no survivor ever solved.

Which didn't necessarily mean she had to give back Charlotte Bainbridge's deposit. Did it?

"I'm trying my best to find out what happened," Violet said.

"Starting when?"

His sentence came at her like a bayonet lunge. Despite his tears, he really *was* a tough kid. Violet's admiration for him was rising by the minute. She sensed that she would've liked his sister, too.

"Starting yesterday at TAP," she answered. "I went over the tram car she was riding in. And by the way, I *do* have other cases, you know. This isn't my only one."

The look of skepticism he aimed at her was bold. It unsettled her. Had he somehow sneaked a peek at her console appointment calendar? Or was it just a lucky guess? Because of course this *was* her only case at the moment. She'd get more. Absolutely, she would.

And in the meantime, it was high time she got to work on this one. The kid's courage had inspired her. Okay, so Amelia had killed herself; Violet would try her best to find out why. There would be no lurking uncertainties. No lingering questions. This boy and his mother would know that Crowley & Associates had done everything possible to get to the truth. That truth might be hard to swallow—but it would be the truth.

"I need to tell you something," Jeff said. He jammed his hands even deeper into the pockets of his jeans.

Violet waited. He studied the sidewalk, twisting the toe of his sneaker against the surface that glittered in the morning sunshine of New Earth.

"My sister really loved her life," Jeff finally said. "She studied all the great buildings in Old Earth history so that she could build them up here—only she'd do it *better*. She had dreams and plans. There won't ever be anybody like Amelia." He gulped hard. "My sister would've understood how hard it was for me and my mom to lose her. She would've *known* that. She was sensitive that way. Sometimes too sensitive. She worried that she'd never be able to do all the things she wanted to do. But she always tried. As hard as she could. Always. So there's *no way* she'd kill herself, okay? Never." He gulped again. "Which means somebody did this to her."

Violet let a few seconds pass. In a soft, gently probing voice— she wanted him to understand the illogic of his position all on his own—she said, "How, Jeff? How would they do it? And why?"

"I don't know." He raised his eyes. The tears were gone, and the sadness suddenly was replaced once again by fierceness. He'd turned back into the mean kid, the one who'd followed her that morning. "But that's *your* job, isn't it?" he pressed her, yanking one hand out of his pocket so that he could jab a stubby finger in her face. "*You're* the one my mom hired. *You* find out what happened. *You* catch whoever did this to her. And when you do, you let me at 'em. I'll beat 'em up. I'll rip 'em to shreds. I'll tear 'em apart until there's nothing left but a pile of stinking—"

"Whoa. Settle down, okay? Don't get all worked up again. And aren't you supposed to be in school right now?"

Reluctantly, he departed. Violet watched him go. She felt a mixture of irritation and sympathy for this pushy kid who'd followed her, challenged her—and who, given what he'd been through, had a perfect right to do both.

Her console chimed. When she touched the screen, a shimmering pink jewel rose. It hovered in the air for an instant and then opened. Jonetta's face appeared. Violet knew in a flash that something was wrong.

"Vi," Jonetta said in a trembling voice. For once Violet didn't jump in and correct her. She could see how upset she was.

"What happened?"

"Don't you know? It's all over the news. It just happened."

"I've been busy. Haven't checked my news feed. What's going on?"

"Two more suicides. It's . . . it's just awful, Vi. They were little girls. Twins. And they—" Jonetta couldn't go on.

Violet's stomach was doing its funny twisty thing again. One suicide? Okay, maybe. That could happen. But two more? In such a short space of time?

No.

Something was wrong. Something was very, very wrong. And if something struck you as very, very wrong—and if, by sheer coincidence, the person with the expertise to help you figure it out *also* just so happened to be your best friend—then you knew where you needed to go. Right away.

And that's where Violet went.

Shura Lu, M.D.

"Could you hand me that catchspark triple-wattage agitator?"

Shura's voice sounded hazy and preoccupied. Violet wasn't even sure she had fully realized yet that she had company. For all Shura knew, the body-sized bundle of heat emanating from an area near the door of her lab—a bundle otherwise known as Violet—was a random TechRob, and the energy was just runoff from a power cell. Shura had six Technical Assistance Robots working in her lab.

Well, five, actually, Violet reminded herself. One of the TechRobs had perished last week when the emergency shutoff on the sonic intensifier failed to engage. Shura had told her all about it. The mess on the floor was large and off-puttingly gooey.

But despite the possibility of being ignored for a long period of time, there was nowhere else Violet wanted to be just now. She was upset and confused, and she knew that, eventually, Shura would be a great help. In the meantime, having dropped in unannounced, Violet had to take what she could get.

And what she got, when she visited Dr. Shura Lu in her lab, was this: a highly focused physician-researcher who was probably working on a project that would change New Earth forever and save millions of lives—or working on a painting, Shura's other great passion. Violet's apartment was filled with Shura's paintings, including the most precious one of all: a portrait of Violet's mother.

But today was a science day, not an art day. Violet had figured that out the moment she walked in and saw Shura perched on a stool, her back to the front door, crouched over a microscope while two TechRobs, one on either side, switched out slides with the speed of an aide-de-camp supplying artillery in a firefight.

"The what?" Violet said, looking around at the crowded but superbly well-organized lab.

"The catchspark triple-wattage agitator," Shura said. She still hadn't lifted her gaze from the eyepiece. Instead she gestured with one hand, waving it vaguely toward the shelf across the room. "It's that red metal thingy with the iron hoops on the side and the crooked antenna. These guys always get it mixed up with the catchspark *double*-wattage agitator." By *guys*, she'd meant the TechRobs. "Rookie mistake." Shura sounded miffed. The good thing about robots, she'd once told Violet, was that you could insult them all you liked and they never got mad.

Violet rummaged for a bit.

"Um, Shura?"

"Yeah?" She still didn't look up from the microscope.

"I don't see . . . oh. Wait. Yeah, there it is." Violet scooted through the room, sidestepping bundles of thick black wire that rested on the floor like sleeping pets and nearly capsizing an entire row of test tubes sitting perkily atop a metal table. She reached to retrieve the catchspark triple-wattage agitator.

"STOP!"

Shura's mighty shout was accompanied by a large crash as she leaped up from the stool, knocking over a nearby box filled with springy purple wires and oil-encrusted engine parts. She lurched toward Violet, whose hand was just about to close around the handle grip of the catchspark triple-wattage agitator.

"DON'T TOUCH THAT!" Shura yelled again. She grabbed Violet's arm. She was breathing heavily. "I forgot. I rigged it to explode if it's touched by any entity that hasn't received a dose of synthetic lexco-megachloridactive-oblator compound. SLMO. Slo-Mo, I call it."

"And you rigged it that way because . . . ?" Violet was shaken by her brush with annihilation, but still curious.

"It's a new chemical I'm testing to counteract explosive components. So far, I've only injected the TechRobs. It's not safe yet for human trials. The only way to see if Slo-Mo works is to rig something to explode when the compound *isn't* detected in whoever touches it."

"Which would've been me."

"Yeah. Sorry." Shura gave her a rueful, please-forgive-me smile. "When it's just me and the TechRobs in the lab, I *never* slip up like that. I've got to pay better attention when humans come around." Shura tilted her head and looked at Violet. "Why *did* you come around? I mean, it's cool and all, but you hardly ever just drop in for no reason anymore."

"There's a reason. Can you take a break?"

"Um." Shura was very busy. Violet knew that. She hated to ask, but she needed her friend's help. She couldn't come back later, because she had to be in court that afternoon.

Their eyes matched up. Over the years they had endured so much together—good things, bad things, in-between things. They'd consoled each other through bad grades and bad break-ups. Shura had been there when Violet's mother died. And Violet had been there when Shura's mother was critically injured.

It was true that they'd been drifting apart lately. Shura didn't like the idea of Violet being a detective, and she also thought Violet hung out too often at Redshift. And Violet wished Shura would spend more time with her paintbrush and less with her microscope. There were other issues, too, but their shared history kept them tethered to each other, even through the rocky patches and occasional stretches of silence.

"Of course," Shura said. "Go grab some chairs. I'll clear out a spot on this table and make us some coffee." She started to pick up the catchspark triple-wattage agitator to relocate it elsewhere.

"NO!" Violet yelled, snatching back her friend's arm just in time.

"Oh. Right." Shura grinned. "I save your life and then you save mine. We take turns. Just like old times, right?"

"So you've heard about the suicides."

"The what?"

Violet looked at her friend in disbelief. "Don't you ever watch the news?"

"No. I don't. If I took time to do that, Violet, I'd never finish redesigning the HoverUp." Shura pointed to an especially crowded area along the wall of her lab, where a passel of short steel rods twisted like pretzels were stacked next to a smorgasbord of switches and dials, and next to the switches and dials, an endless assortment of red-and-gray wires were gathered into huge loops. "I had a real breakthrough the other day. I think I can eliminate the operational noise entirely." HoverUps were devices used by people with spinal cord injuries; they enabled limbs to move by sending powerful jets of air to manipulate them, triggered by a user's thoughts. Among the flaws was the soft but incessant *whish-whoosh* sound created by the HoverUp's propulsion system. "Kendall's given me a ton of great pointers. I'm still running the computer simulations. There's a lot left to do. But if I'm right, I actually might finish it before I'm an old lady." She smiled at Violet. "Because I don't watch the news."

Genius might have a little something to do with it, too, Violet thought. *Shura Lu and Kendall Mayhew are the two smartest people on New Earth, and they* both *happen to be my friends.*

Sometimes Violet had the distinct impression that she was a total slacker.

"Okay, fine," she said. "But I need to ask you about a case I'm working on."

"A case." Shura's words were superficially neutral. Violet knew better. They weren't neutral at all; they were negative.

"Yeah," Violet said. She didn't want to argue again about her choice of profession, so she ignored her friend's tone. "A suicide. Well, three of them. Everybody else on New Earth knows about it, apparently, except for you. The first victim was named Amelia Bainbridge. Her mother hired me to find out what really happened."

"She hired *you*?"

Violet started to send forth a snappy retort but stopped herself. She deserved that. She wasn't exactly a superstar in the detective world.

"Yeah," Violet said. "Me. And now there's been a second incident. Two little girls. They hung themselves in their bedroom.

So I was hoping you could tell me what to look for. Any similarities that might show up in the autopsies."

"Why?"

"Well, Amelia's mother doesn't think it was suicide. She says her daughter would never have killed herself. So maybe the other two weren't, either."

"What would you expect a mother to say?"

A beat. "So you don't think I should've taken the case?"

"I'm just saying that she's a mom. She might not have known everything that was going on in her daughter's life." Shura looked directly at Violet, so directly that it made Violet uncomfortable. "Sometimes," Shura added, "you think you know somebody really, *really* well—and then their behavior can surprise you."

Violet understood what Shura was trying to say to her, but she couldn't get into any of that now. They both had too much to do.

"So there's nothing I should look for in the autopsies? Nothing that might be suspicious?"

Shura hesitated. She was a very good doctor. Violet knew that. Her friend lived in the world of facts, and that was what Violet needed.

"Well, there are a couple of possibilities," Shura said.

"Like?"

"Like puncture marks in the skin. Those would indicate that they might have been injected with something. And maybe that something induced them to harm themselves."

"Right. Anything else?"

"I'd have the lab check the hair."

"The hair? Why would that matter? Would having a bad hair day cause somebody to end it all?"

"No," Shura replied patiently. "But if you're poisoned, traces of it can wind up in your hair follicles. Certain kinds of poison might make somebody behave irrationally."

"Wouldn't the police lab check for that, anyway?"

"Not if they think it's suicide. They're busy. Why bother?"

"Got it," Violet said. "Anything else?"

"I'd try to find some links between the victims. If you really don't think it was suicide and somebody killed them and then made it *look* like suicide, the question is, why pick these particular people? Was it random? Who stood to gain from their deaths?"

"Right."

"And maybe it all ends now. With three deaths."

"Maybe."

They were silent for a moment. The only sound in the lab was the slow idle of the TechRobs' power cells, and the occasional *pop!* when a bubble of liquid inside a beaker on the lab bench rose to the rim and disintegrated.

"I hope you solve your case," Shura said. "I hope you can help the girl's mom—and the other parents, too—find some peace."

"So you're wishing me luck? Even though you think it's a wild-goose chase?"

"I'm wishing you luck *because* I think it's a wild-goose chase." Shura smiled. For just a brief flicker of an instant, the old Shura was there again: funny, sincere, good-hearted Shura. The Shura whom Violet had known since they met on the very first day of their very first New Earth kindergarten class. The Shura whose paintings could make Violet cry—and make her think, too.

And then the distance between them returned. The warm moment winked away as quickly as that air bubble on the rim of the beaker.

They weren't the people they used to be. They were growing apart, and nothing could stop it.

"Take care of yourself," Shura said.

"I will." Those were the words Violet used, but it's not what she was thinking.

What she was thinking was this:

Change can be a real bitch sometimes.

She also realized something else. With all the excitement in her life since yesterday, she'd forgotten about Rez's suspicion that someone was trying to resurrect the Intercept.

No word back from him. So it was a false alarm. Right?

Wendell's End

T*witch.*

Wendell Prokop squinted. He coughed. His head felt funny inside. Actually, it felt like five different kinds of funny.

He thought that maybe an ant had crawled in his ear and was dancing. Or maybe the ant was just rooting around, looking for whatever it was that ants generally spent their time looking for. Other ants, probably. Sexy ones.

Twitch.

This was really messing with his lunch break. He sat at his office desk, with wrappers and an empty soda can littering the top in a ragged little half circle. He was all alone, but that was a good thing, because based on what he was going to do next, he figured he'd look kind of weird, and he would've been embarrassed if anybody had been there to witness it.

Wendell took the heel of his hand and smacked it twice against the side of his head. That, he hoped, would show the ant who was boss. Or at least scramble his brain cells enough to make the funny twitching feeling go away.

He didn't really believe the ant theory. It was pretty far-fetched to think that an ant could end up in his brain while he was finishing his shift at transport logistics.

He had three hours to go before he clocked out. Then maybe he could meet a few friends at Redshift tonight for a beer. That ought to make his head feel right. Wendell had just turned eighteen, the legal drinking age on New Earth, and he intended to make the most of his newfound freedom.

Twitch.

He used the heel of his other hand to pound on the opposite side of his head. He thought maybe he could balance things out.

Twitch.

Wendell put his head down on the desk; his forehead hit the metal with a dull *thwunk*. He closed his eyes. He rolled his forehead back and forth. Then he quickly jerked his head back up again. Dizziness swept over him. He felt like he might slide right out of his chair. Just ooze on down to the checkerboard tile floor.

Twitch.

Before this stupid twitching started, Wendell had been bored. There wasn't much to do around here anymore, so he'd ordered a pizza. The Delivery Robot had come and gone without a word a few minutes ago, which was fine with Wendell. Like he wanted to hear preprogrammed pleasantries from some DevRob.

Being bored was a new thing in this job. It marked a huge change from two years ago, when—for a brief time—the main launching station for the transport pods was just about the busiest place on New Earth.

Shortly after he'd ordered the demise of the Intercept, President Crowley had opened the borders. Great throngs of Old Earth people who had been denied entry for years were invited in. Immigrants arrived from Old Earth in a constant stream, and each newcomer had to be thoroughly vetted, processed, issued an ID, matched up with an occupation, and then assigned to one of the six cities of New Earth.

During that period, a thousand metal desks spread out across that checkerboard floor here in the processing division. Each new arrival would step up to one of those desks, take a seat, and begin the journey to becoming a citizen of New Earth. Thus it was a happy place, as well as a fantastically jam-packed and rackety one.

Not anymore.

Wendell's desk was the only desk left. And he hadn't processed a single immigrant from Old Earth in a month and a half. All of his colleagues had been assigned to other jobs or let go. Staffing levels had been slashed again and again, because by now, everyone on Old Earth who wanted to relocate to New Earth had done so. The only people left on Old Earth were prisoners serving out their paroles or scientists who were conducting experiments on the decaying planet. Or a few rogue souls who liked solitude and a rugged life. A life of deprivation and hardship.

But Wendell still had a job. Not because he was smart or hardworking. He wasn't either one of those things. What he was, though, was lucky. He kept his job because his mother, Arianna Prokop, was a big shot in the government. She used her influence to keep him employed, because she didn't want him hanging out in their apartment all day, doing nothing—which is what he'd be most likely doing, if he didn't have this job.

Here, at least he was getting *paid* for hanging out all day and doing nothing. The thought made him grin.

Twitch.

The grin faded. By this point, the funny-feeling twitch was more than just annoying. It was starting to hurt. He looked down at the inside of his left arm. Had he seen something there? Probably not. Probably it was just his imagination.

Anyway, he needed to focus on his *head*, not his arm.

Twitch.

Twitch.

It felt like it was coming from the *inside* of his head. Weird. He blinked rapidly.

Twitch.

Now the thing, whatever it was, had burrowed even deeper into his brain. He felt a hot, curved finger of intensity prying at the base of his skull, digging and twisting, like somebody trying to peel an orange.

He thought about calling his mother. Should he do that? If he *did* do that, what would he say? *Um, Mom? I've got this, um, funny twitch in my head, and I think I'm going nuts.* Naturally, she would assume he'd been drinking in the middle of the workday. He'd be in big trouble. Grounded for a month. He wouldn't be allowed to go to Redshift. He wouldn't be allowed to go *anywhere* except here, to his stupid job in the stupid transport sector. Boring as hell.

Eighteen years old and my mom still treats me like a little boy.

The thought had just jumped into his brain. He had no idea where it had come from. It didn't come from *him*, because even though it was true, he never let himself think that way. It was too depressing. And way too embarrassing.

Eighteen years old. And she'd probably tuck me in at night, too, if I asked her to. Like a little boy begging his mommy.

Where the hell did *that* come from?

People think you suck your thumb. They think you've got a special blanket that you sleep with.

This was ridiculous. Why was he thinking like this? These thoughts were humiliating. He was blushing. The heat rose in his cheeks. At the same time, he felt a quick jab in the crook of his left elbow. When he looked at the spot, he could swear he'd seen a small blue flash.

And then he forgot all about cheeks and elbows and flashes, because the voice in his head was screaming even louder now.

Baby boy. Baby boy. Look at the baby boy.

He couldn't breathe. His throat was tight, so tight. With two frantic fingers, he dug at the collar of his shirt, digging and pulling, wondering why the collar was—all at once—cutting off his breathing.

Eighteen years old, and I do what my mommy tells me to. Where's your widdle stuffed bear, Wendell? Widdle Wendell.

He had to tell somebody what it felt like. He had to leave a message, like a trail of bread crumbs . . . or even one bread crumb. Just one.

He grabbed a slip of paper and a fat yellow pencil, and he scrawled a word:

SCREAMING

It was the only word he could think of because his head was filling up with the screaming, like a pool filling up with water. There wasn't room for anything else in there. He tore himself away from his desk. He lurched and he staggered across the checkerboard floor. He dug so fiercely at his shirt collar with frantic scrabbling fingers that he scratched his neck, drawing blood. He tripped, falling face-first onto the tile. He picked himself up and hurled himself forward.

Widdle Wendell.

I'm Widdle Wendell. Baby boy.

The supply cabinets along the far wall had once overflowed importantly with massive stacks of equipment required to process thousands of immigrants as they entered New Earth. All of that hardware had been moved to other offices in other administrative portals. Now the "supplies" consisted of a few scruffy cubbyholes crammed with orphaned cords and useless lengths of wire and stubby pencils and rusty scissors—old-fashioned gear shed by newly arrived Old Earth citizens who didn't want to take it with them into their new lives.

Poor Widdle Wendell.

He had to make the screaming stop. He had to claw it out of his head, stab it, kill it, rip it apart. In a desperate frenzy, he grabbed at the biggest pair of rusty scissors. His hands were too slick with sweat, though, and he ended up knocking them onto the floor. Panting and sobbing, he leaped at the scissors, going down on all fours like a dog ravenous for a scrap of food, his knees skidding across the slick tile until he could lurch forward and—finally!—he had the scissors firmly in his grip.

Baby boy.

Die, baby boy. Widdle Wendell wants to die.

With the scissors in hand, he found himself overwhelmed by an immense feeling of relief. Pure, dazzling, anticipatory relief. Because now he had the means to end his torment. He held the answer. He could get rid of the screaming voice in his head. He could make it shut up. He didn't have to feel this way anymore—the shame, the certainty that he was a loser, a pathetic moron, a miserable and hopeless failure. People laughed at him. They had always laughed at him and they always *would* laugh at him. They would never *not* be laughing at him. He could hear it right now, that horrible laughter; his head echoed with the hoots, the jeers, the snickers, the cackles.

And the screaming.

But he could stop it. He had the power to stop it. He could make the screaming go away, and once the screaming went away, the laughter would go, too, the horrible laughter. He would be free of the shame and the grief and the guilt and the chaos roaring in his head.

Baby boy wants to die.

Die, Widdle Wendell.

Bye-bye, baby boy.

One vicious blow, driving the points deep into his heart, and he could end the torture and the screaming. Forever.

So that is exactly what he did.

11

Statute No. 293874-A-392876

I'm guilty.

She actually *was* guilty, but that's not why Violet's mind rang like a thumped tambourine with the mantra *I'm guilty I'm guilty I'm guilty* the moment she crossed the magnificent, ostentatiously ornate threshold of the NEJC—the New Earth Judicial Center.

The place would make anybody confess to anything, up to and including ritual torture and mass murder. It was *that* intimidating. And grand. And spectacular. Violet always had the same thought each time she glimpsed it after any interval, long or short: The NEJC seemed specifically designed to make human beings feel as puny and powerless and pitiable as possible.

She'd seen pictures of the courthouses on Old Earth, from centuries ago, and the planners of New Earth apparently wanted to channel all that stately spaciousness, all that lofty, chilly magnificence, the kind that could leave people humbled and afraid.

And that could, quite frankly, make you want to pee your pants.

The columns ranging across the front were massive and cream-colored, held in place by elegant square plinths at top and bottom. The double doors were a dull, cold steel; decorative buttons of a darker hue had been hammered in symmetrical rows across the wide surface, like medals spreading across the chest of a decorated general. Once you opened those doors, the lobby flooring—ginormous squares of gray, separated by thin ribbons of black grout—looked terrifyingly vast and also menacingly insubstantial, as if it might drop away beneath your feet at any second, plunging you toward a fiery doom.

Prison floors are cuddlier than this, Violet told herself with a shudder as she hurried to keep up with her lawyer, Rachel Reznik.

Her trial was scheduled for one P.M. and it was not yet noon. But Rachel believed in getting everywhere early, and she had made Violet promise to show up when she told her to. The lawyer—black suit, black boots, spiky black hair—had greeted Violet out front in the long shadows of those colossal columns and delivered a rapid-fire series of instructions, her voice the aural embodiment of bullet points.

"First, turn off your console," Rachel said. "This judge *hates* interruptions. If she hears so much as a whisper from a single rising jewel, she'll put you in jail. For the rest of your life."

Rachel was probably exaggerating—the trial, after all, was for a minor infraction—but who knew? Violet switched off her console.

"And once the trial starts," Rachel went on, "don't say a word unless I tell you to. Not a *word*."

With Rachel marching in the lead, they entered the maze of bright, high-ceilinged corridors. Violet struggled to keep up.

That was more than a little bit amusing, because her lawyer—in addition to being fiercely smart and ferociously well-educated—had an attribute that tended to eclipse the first two:

Rachel Reznik was eleven years old.

Like her brother, Steve, Rachel was a dazzling prodigy. She'd breezed through the first several years of New Earth schooling until her teachers finally realized that she knew a lot more than they did—a lot more, in fact, than they ever *would* know—and gave up, assigning her to tutors at New Earth University. She'd graduated at ten. Law school took her another six months. And now here she was, still too young to vote in New Earth elections or drive a car on New Earth streets but very capable of rescuing screwups like Violet from the clutches of the New Earth judicial system.

"Can you walk a little faster?" Rachel said.

"Trying," Violet replied, although she was breathing so hard that it came out as a sort of squawk.

All the doors along the corridors were closed. The knobs were polished globes of brass that looked far too grim and important to be the medium for a simple function such as opening a door. The lettering on each frosted, wood-trimmed slab was done in an imposing gold with black trim, as if the occupants intended to grind visitors' faces in the fact that crucial decisions were made therein and ordinary mortals should keep their distance.

"This way," Rachel barked.

They turned a corner and found themselves facing another long corridor, just as immense and austere as the first ones they had traveled through. They passed courtrooms labeled one through seven. Then they turned another corner and passed courtrooms eight through thirteen.

At number fourteen, Rachel came to a sudden stop. Violet,

who'd been admiring the fretwork on the coffered ceiling, almost smacked into her. Given the disparity in their heights, the results might have been dire.

I would've crushed her like a bug.

"Here," Rachel stated.

A long wooden bench extended along the wall on either side of the door. Witnesses and lawyers for other trials—that was Violet's guess—had arranged themselves uncomfortably on the benches, looking forlornly at shut-down consoles or staring at the same decorated ceiling that had snagged Violet's attention a few seconds ago.

All at once, Violet saw her.

She pushed past Rachel and barreled toward an older woman who sat on the left-side bench. The woman wore a red bandana around her curly gray hair as if to shush its corkscrewing exuberance. Spotting Violet, she jumped to her feet, opening her arms like a flower suddenly aware of a soft rain. Violet let herself be embraced, but it was an awkward moment because Violet was a terrible hugger, even when she was doing it willingly.

"Delia!" Violet said. She extricated herself from the hug and stepped back. "Why are you here? What—"

"Your lawyer called me." Delia Tolliver shrugged. One sleeve of her shabby gray tunic hung longer than the other, and she used the dangling fabric to rub her chin. "Said you needed a character witness so they won't throw you in jail. Frankly, I don't see how it's going to help—who cares what an Old Earth troublemaker like me has to say?—but she claims it might do the trick. Being as how I'm old and mature and all, unlike your other friends." Delia laughed. She scrunched up her face and looked around the corridor. "So where *is* that lawyer of yours, anyway? Rachel Somebody, right?"

"Here." Rachel stepped forward.

"No way." Delia snickered. "No *way*. You look like you should be at home eating a bowl of cereal and watching cartoons on your console."

Delia had a habit of speaking her mind. That's what Violet had liked about her when they met for the first time two years ago on Old Earth. With Ogden Crowley's help, Violet had arranged for Delia and her son, Tin Man, to relocate to New Earth. Now that Ogden had moved into a retirement center, Violet spent her holidays with Delia and Tin Man in their cozy little house.

"Not only that," Delia added, sensing with delight that she was getting under Rachel's skin, "but you oughta be wearing feety PJs instead of that fancy suit."

"I *assure* you," Rachel said, steely umbrage turning her voice haughty and stilted, "that I was admitted to the New Earth bar four months ago and am *fully authorized* to represent any and all—"

"Lighten up, sweet cheeks." Delia snickered again. Once she'd seen how sensitive Rachel was, she couldn't resist digging in. She had nothing against the girl, Violet knew; this was purely for sport. In fact, the more Delia liked you, the more she teased you. "And take that stick out of your butt while you're at it, Little Miss Lawyer," Delia added. "You're a kid, okay? You might have more brains than the rest of New Earth put together—and from what I've seen of the place, I wouldn't be surprised—but you're still a child. So act like one. Go run. Go play. Go build a fort."

Rachel's mouth opened and closed. She'd been ready to unleash a scathing retort, Violet speculated, but held back. She needed this strange, pugnacious woman who wore her Old Earth bluntness like a badge.

"I appreciate you coming here today," Rachel said carefully.

"I did it for Violet, honey, not for you," Delia shot back. She turned to Violet. "Okay, so what kind of crazy nonsense did you pull *this* time? What sort of hot water have you gotten yourself *into* already? And why can't Daddy get you off the hook? That's the whole point of being the daughter of the former prez, right? Beating the rap?"

Delia knew perfectly well why Violet didn't get her father involved. It was a point of pride—one of the few scraps of pride Violet had left, now that her detective agency was on the skids—to not allow herself to receive any special treatment. The only time she asked Ogden to pull strings was on behalf of others. Not herself.

There was an excellent chance, of course, that the judge would know who she was, anyway. But she didn't have to draw attention to the fact.

And yet pride had its price. Because if Violet couldn't squirm her way out of this current jam, she'd be facing a fine she couldn't pay. Unless, that is, she stopped spending money on frivolous trifles like food and rent.

She gritted her teeth. *Onward.*

The heavy doors opened with a slow, ponderous creak. A blank-faced bailiff in a stiff red tunic motioned to them. They stepped inside. The courtroom was a blur of brash lights and blond wood. The ceiling was immensely high and dramatically distant. So high and so distant, in fact, that as Violet stood there and let her gaze climb up, up, up, she realized that pigeons could be roosting on those rafters and you wouldn't know it until you felt something warm and goopy and gross plop on your shoulder.

Rachel poked her in the ribs, scattering all thoughts of pigeons from Violet's head. She shuffled nervously toward the front of the room.

For the next hour, she was subjected to the humiliating ordeal of responding to a complaint that an anonymous witness
had seen her in flagrant violation of New Earth Statute
No. 293874-A-392876, Subsection 39887-HYV, Article 983746.

Translation: littering.

It sounded trivial. It *was* trivial.

Except that on New Earth, nothing that involved material
objects could really *be* trivial. Not when the position of even a
thousandth of an ounce had to be accounted for at ten-second
intervals. New Earth was kept aloft by a precise calibration of
weights and measures that were then juxtaposed with the
wind pressure and gravitational parameters maintained in
Farraday—and a thousandth of an ounce mattered.

The relative location of one one-thousandth of an ounce
meant the difference between the ability of New Earth's engineers to maintain a mirroring of the earth's movement as it
orbited the sun and *not* being able to maintain that mirroring.
And *that*, according to the preponderance of computer mod-
els, would result in the swift disintegration of New Earth as it
was ripped to shreds, bringing instant death to all inhabitants.

All because Violet had tossed an empty coffee cup into the
wrong container.

On the day in question, she had had many things on her
mind—"many things" being her handy shorthand for "unpaid
bills"—and, as a consequence, had a temporary brain fade.

So she littered.

That was the sole extent of her transgression.

Next thing Violet knew, she'd been slapped with a ticket.
And because she understood the rudiments of the crucial phys-
ics of New Earth as well as anybody but, say, Kendall and Shura,
Violet *also* understood why it was a big deal. Which in turn

made it difficult for her to resent the ticket or the ordeal she was presently undergoing.

"And so," the judge intoned, "is it true? Did you fail to place a biodegradable cup into a recycling container in Mendeleev Crossing at approximately 8:47 P.M. last Thursday? And is it true that the aforesaid container was clearly and specifically marked 'Recyclables'? And is it furthermore true that, when confronted about said infraction, you said to the citizen who approached you"—the judge paused to adjust her gold-rimmed spectacles as she looked down at her notes—"and here I quote, 'Mind your own business, you idiot'?"

"Objection," Rachel said. "Prejudicial. My client was under stress at the time. The use of an epithet was atypical."

The judge peered at her over the top of the glasses. "Stress from breaking the law, or stress from having been *caught* breaking the law?"

Delia sprang up from her seat. "Who's the idiot now? *Of course* the stress came from getting caught! Geez."

Before the judge could react, Rachel asked permission to approach the bench. She and the judge conferred in harsh whispers. When Rachel retuned to the defense table, she glared at Delia. The glare had an unmistakable meaning: *Do you want your friend to be in even more trouble than she already is? No? Then shut up.*

Rachel was eloquent and forceful in Violet's defense. She said very nice things about Violet. And then Delia said very nice things about Violet. And then Violet said very nice things about Violet.

In the end, the judge shook her head and scowled and pointed a finger at Violet and declared, "Have you learned your lesson, young lady?"

Yes, she had. Yes, yes, yes. Definitely, she had. She really, really, *really* had learned her lesson.

"Then it would behoove you to try," the judge declared, "to act a little more responsibly."

It wasn't the first time in Violet's life that somebody had suggested that. It wasn't even the first time *today* that somebody had suggested that.

Outside the courthouse, Violet thanked Delia again and gave her another hug. This hug was—if such a thing were possible—even more cumbersome and awkward than the first one. Delia made Violet promise to get more sleep—*You look like you've been up for about three weeks straight, honey*—and to take better care of herself. And to come by and see her and Tin Man more often.

I don't need another mom. Those were the words Violet was tempted to sling right back at Delia. But she kept quiet.

Because sometimes she *did* need a mom.

Delia left to catch a tram home. Violet switched on her console.

It promptly went bonkers.

That's what it sounded like, anyway, as the console face leaped to life and the beeps overlapped and the chirps multiplied. Jewels of red and white and yellow and purple and green and orange spun and tumbled in a confusing aerial circus.

Violet touched the red jewel to activate the message marked URGENT.

"Oh, Vi—*Vi*—you won't believe it. It's *awful*. There's been another one." The holographic image of Jonetta's face was streaked with tears, and her voice faltered. Violet had rarely seen her secretary so distraught. It was even worse than the last time she'd had to deliver bad news. "Another suicide," Jonetta clarified. "His name was Wendell Prokop. It's just like Amelia Bainbridge. And the twins. It's just . . . just *horrible*. What can we *do*? There can't be any more suicides. This has to be the end, right?"

Violet was totally absorbed in the shimmering dot and Jonetta's grim message. Then she looked up. Rachel stood right next to her, reading the news on her own console, and when she looked up, too, their eyes met. Violet didn't need an Intercept feed to read Rachel's feelings, to know that her lawyer was just as shaken as she was.

Both of them were grappling with a terrible question.

What in the world was happening to New Earth?

12

At the Station

don't know, Violet. I just don't know."

As he spoke, Kendall rubbed his hand over the top of his head. He did that frequently when he was thinking hard. His hair was cut murderously close to his scalp. Maybe, Violet thought, he needed contact with those little nubs and bristles to jump-start his brain. Or maybe it was just a nervous habit.

"You agree with me, though, right?" Violet said. "It's getting weird."

She sat across from him in what was surely *the* most uncomfortable chair that existed anywhere on New Earth, a mild monstrosity of misaligned metal and wobbly bolts and sagging plastic—designed, Violet surmised, to discourage long visits from pesky citizens. All around them, the police station was churning with activity and bubbling with noise. Consoles chirped, suspects yelled, coffee machines offered clicks and whirrs and adenoidal gurgles as they dumped gelatinous black goo into an endless succession of biodegradable cups. Cop coffee was always bad. Violet had refused Kendall's initial offer to grab a cup for her. She always did.

"Huh?" he said. Worry distracted him.

"I said it's getting weird," she repeated. So weird that she had raced right over here from the courthouse.

"Unusual? Yes. Weird? I'm not sure." Kendall rubbed his head again. "Suicide's not unknown on New Earth. A certain percentage of any population is going to be afflicted with mental illness. Sometimes that's going to manifest itself in self-destructive behavior."

"Is that why you're not making the cases a priority?"

She'd touched a nerve. He dropped his hand and glared at her, sitting up straighter in his chair.

"Every death," he said curtly, "is investigated to the extent we believe is necessary. This might be nothing more than just an unfortunate coincidence."

"You've got four young people committing suicide in two days," Violet said. She could be curt, too. "Coincidence? Come on."

He looked around the station. She realized that he wanted her to do the same thing, and so she did. Her gaze hopped from chaos-spot to chaos-spot across the hot, crowded, humming space. It reminded her a bit of TAP, but with humans, not Con-Robs, in constant motion, packed in so tightly that you almost expected to see sparks when they bumped each other, which happened every few seconds.

"We're not exactly slacking off here, Violet," Kendall said. "Nobody even takes vacations anymore. We can't."

He didn't have to tell her why. She knew why. Until two years ago, the Intercept had kept tight control over New Earth, like a way-too-strict parent.

But things were different now. And the cops were falling behind. They had too many cases and too few officers.

It wasn't that New Earth was filled with especially bad people. It was filled with people, period. And some people did bad things. Cops had gotten rusty during the Intercept years; force levels were allowed to dwindle. Now they were playing catch-up.

"I get that," Violet said. "But what if these deaths *are* related? Why are so many people suddenly deciding that life's not worth living? Or what if they're *not* suicides? What if somebody's trying to make them *look* like suicides?"

"So they were murdered? Is that what you mean?"

"I know you've considered that, too."

"Sure."

"Well?"

"What's the motive? The victims were *kids*. If you're going to kill somebody, why go to all the trouble to make it look like a suicide? And anyway—what do these people have in common?"

"I've been trying to figure that out."

"And?"

"I've gone through a checklist of all the ordinary motives," Violet replied. "Money? The victims didn't have any. Not enough for anybody to care about, anyway. Maybe some kind of romantic deal—revenge or jealousy or whatever? No. Their consoles don't show any evidence of that kind of thing. And the interviews with their friends also came up empty. Family dispute? They all had loving families."

"We checked all of that, too. No family troubles. No police reports have ever been filed from their addresses," Kendall said. He started to rub his head again, but Violet grabbed his hand.

"You're making me nervous," she said. "Can't you get another bad habit?"

She was teasing him, but she wished she hadn't done it. Because she saw the effect of her touch on Kendall: Instead of shaking off her hand and uttering a wisecrack about how it sure beat smoking, he remained perfectly still. He looked down at her hand, where it lay atop his.

And Violet saw, with a pang in her heart, that he was blushing.

After a few more awkward seconds had passed, she gently slipped her hand out from under his.

"Okay," he said, his voice brusque and businesslike as if he'd just remembered that he was in the middle of a workplace, "so you've got to face the fact that these might be random."

"Fine. But if they are—what then?"

"Then we're screwed. Because random crimes are absolutely the hardest to solve," he said. "If there's no pattern, there's no way to solve them unless we get lucky. Really, really luck—"

A fierce clatter arose from a far corner of the room. Kendall and Violet flinched in unison, their heads jerking in the direction of the noise. An unruly suspect had kicked and thrashed his way loose from a cop's grasp; his writhing lurch knocked six computer monitors from a shelf. They hit the ground in heavy succession, like six separate clumps of thunder: *Ka-thunk, ka-thunk, ka-thunk, ka-thunk, ka-thunk, ka-thunk.* Before Violet and Kendall could jump up and offer help, two other officers arrived and pitched in, grabbing the suspect's arms and setting him firmly back down in his chair. A ReadyRob scuttled in and began cleaning up the mess.

"Geez," Violet said. "Hard to concentrate around here. Always a crisis. Always some bad guy acting up." She let a second pass. "Do you ever think—" She stopped.

"Think what?"

Well, why not? Why not talk about it? This was *Kendall*. He'd been through everything she'd been through two years ago.

And he knew as much as she did about feelings and the deep, scary hold they had over human beings.

"Do you ever think that maybe—just *maybe*—we were better off when we had the Intercept?" Violet said. "I mean, we didn't have to worry about things like that." She tilted her head toward the corner where the altercation had occurred. "People didn't get out of control. The Intercept stopped them before they *could* get out of control. All we had to do was send a feeling back into their brains and *boom*. Total safety."

It was, she knew, a tricky conversation to be having with Kendall, because he had invented the Intercept. Years ago, in his ramshackle lab back on Old Earth, he had discovered the precise neurobiological formula that turned feelings into Wi-Fi signals that could be picked up, stored, and then sent back into the source—the very brain that had generated the emotions. In one daring, brilliant stroke, his invention had changed civilization.

"No." He said it with quiet sadness. And Violet knew the origin of that sadness. With his words, he was turning his back on his own creation. "As much trouble as we have right now," he added, "we're better off this way, as messy as it makes things. We're better off with imperfect freedom instead of perfect security. We're better off without the Intercept. You and I both know it."

She didn't need to answer out loud. The expression on her face did all her talking.

If that's true, Kendall, then why didn't we destroy it completely? Why did we let a piece of it survive?

Redshift

In the moonlight, New Earth glowed with a ghostly blue-white shimmer.

Violet had just reached the bottom step of the entrance to her apartment building. It was a cool night. She wished she'd thrown on a jacket. *Doesn't matter,* she reminded herself, with a little shiver of happiness. *I'll be dancing in a few minutes, anyway. And that always makes me sweat. In a good way.*

She'd spent the evening reviewing, yet again, all the public information that was available about the lives of the four victims. Any similarities, any odd overlaps? If there were, she'd find them. Eventually. She was fighting Kendall's randomness theory as hard as she could.

Finally, a little after midnight, she had unstrapped her console and let it drop onto her kitchen table, where she had been working. She massaged her wrist.

She was tired of questions. She wanted to go out. And she deserved to, right?

So she'd pulled on a white lacey top and black jeans and

headed for the stairwell, reattaching her console as she raced down the stairs. She was too impatient to wait for the elevator.

Now she surveyed the silent, misty street in front of her.

Should she call for a Uni? The single-wheeled, driverless vehicles were the easiest means of transport around New Earth. They weren't expensive, but they still cost money. Taking a tram would be cheaper, but slower. And she was eager to get there.

Violet tapped the Uni app on her console. Less than a minute later, the round yellow plastic vehicle with the big wheel in the center rounded the corner and bobbed to a stop. Violet climbed in, causing the globe to quiver and lean precariously in her direction, but it never tipped over. Violet punched in the coordinates of her destination on the bright red dashboard and clicked the seat harness into place across her shoulders. To her relief, this was an older model of Uni; it did not feature the annoyingly perky audio track that started out with *Good evening! How are you?* This Uni was blessedly silent.

The silence ended when Violet reached Redshift. Cars were stacked three and four deep at the curb, and the gap between the curb and the golden double doors was packed with people. Each time someone activated those doors—and someone was *always* activating them, going in or coming out—the pounding racket from the band inside sprang forth like a million jack-in-the-boxes flying open all at once, an explosion of bass beats and ear-mashing guitar riffs. Strobe lights pulsed and wheeled from the roof of the club, draping the street in crisscrossing stripes of red and blue and purple and green, a perpetually melting rainbow of shrieking colors.

Violet had known perfectly well that Redshift would be cataclysmically crowded tonight because it was cataclysmically crowded *every* night. In fact, she had counted on it. Craved it, even.

Violet slid out of the tilting Uni. It righted itself the moment she stood up on the sidewalk and, with a mincing chirp, wobbled off in response to a summons from somebody else's console.

She approached the doors. The bouncer, his arms crossed tightly in front of his massive chest, held up a meaty palm to stop her progress. He gave her a long, squinty-eyed appraisal, interspersed with a series of slow insinuating blinks. Then he waved her over next to him so that three women trying to exit the club could get past.

The bouncer was a short, mean-looking man about Violet's age with a shaved head and sharp blue eyes that shifted around constantly, watching everything. There was an Old Earth feel about him; it simmered in his shabby black tunic and ragged-hemmed trousers and in his surly, defensive stance. A small silver hoop glinted from his right earlobe. Both arms bristled with tattoos.

"Hey, Violet," he said. His face broke open into a smile, and the nastiness vanished. "Didn't think you were coming by tonight." He flicked his head at two couples who had approached the door behind Violet, signaling them that it was okay to enter.

"Last-minute decision," she replied.

"Sometimes those are the best kind."

Violet gave him a playful punch on his bicep. It felt like she'd struck a wrought iron railing.

"Hey," he went on, "my mom said she got roped into attending your trial. Did she seriously call the judge an idiot?"

"Of course she did. Hey, I gotta get in there. See you around, Tin Man."

That was the nickname he'd had on Old Earth, the one his little sister, Molly, had given him.

"You be careful," he called out to her back. "And don't stay too late, girl." He grinned to make it seem as if he was kidding, but Violet knew that he really wasn't. He was as bad as Delia when it came to the whole controlling thing. Why couldn't they just leave her alone? She was young. She was single. The Intercept was gone. Nobody was keeping track of her except *her*. She could do whatever the hell she wanted to. Feel what she wanted to feel. Be where she wanted to be.

And where she wanted to be right now was right *here*.

A kaleidoscope of wild colors and riotous, full-throttle music swept her up as she entered the club. It was like being smashed in the face—in a good way—by two tornadoes, one right after the other, and then scooped up by a hurricane and dumped in a vat of sweat-sticky ecstasy.

Tightly packed bodies jumped and writhed on the dance floor. People weren't really paired off; instead they broke in and out of vague, ever-shifting orbits of other people, creating one hot, mashed-up creature with arms and legs everywhere and thousands of faces. Violet slipped easily in between two people she was pretty sure she'd danced with before, a man and a woman. She closed her eyes and joined the massive surge that pulsed in time with the music. Up on the stage, a band she liked—she couldn't remember the name—rocked hard. The lead singer was dressed in a long, red velvet coat trimmed in frilly lace and a high black stovepipe hat; she spat out long bristling strings of indecipherable lyrics. Her body mic turned the words into pure snarling bliss.

And Violet loved every bit of it. She loved the rampaging

lights. She loved the amplified growls and the gyrating bodies She loved the livid mix of people and flying hair and pure sensation.

The best part was this: For the next few hours, she didn't have to think. She didn't have to think about *anything*. She didn't have to think about her failing business, or about her father, whom she hadn't visited in weeks, or about Kendall and about how she felt—or didn't feel—about him, or about Charlotte Bainbridge's grief and pain. Or about how she didn't know if the other three people had killed themselves or been murdered. And if they *had* been murdered, why and by whom?

Wait. *Dammit.* Suddenly she was thinking again. She tried to dance harder, hoping the questions would go away, but no luck.

She needed a drink.

Violet turned sideways and slipped between two couples. The bar was a high copper counter that kinked and twisted its way, snakelike, across the entire length of the back wall. Behind it, a dozen tuxedoed bartenders, female and male, flipped bottles and glasses into the air in a perpetual frenzy of dazzling balance and gasp-inducing dexterity; the end of every performance was a magnificent and faintly ironic bow—and the presentation of a fantastically complicated drink.

"Hey, Violet." The bartender with the short purple dreads and two nose rings grinned and pointed at her. "Looking good."

"Casey. Hey. How's it going?"

"It's going." They both laughed. "One Neptunia Node," the bartender added. "Coming up."

Violet grabbed a stool, ready for the show.

Casey flipped two bottles in the air. In the midst of the third pair of alternating somersaults, a tall glass whose inner rim had been rubbed with salt somehow was whisked into place at the exact spot it needed to be in order to receive the arcing crystalline waterfall of a Neptunia Node. Not a single drop spilled.

Violet picked up the bright blue drink and polished it off in one quick, nifty swallow. She felt a spike of glorious, thought-killing dizziness. She gave the stool a twirl, specifically to keep the dizziness going. Her gaze swiveled around the room. Hey—was somebody waving at her from the dance floor?

Yeah. She knew that guy. Didn't she? Maybe. Maybe not.

Didn't matter. The band's beat was getting faster and louder, faster and louder. Deliciously hypnotic. She wasn't sure what time it was, but she knew one thing for sure: It was *way* too soon to go home.

14

Pattern Recognition

So I thought about this all night, Vi, and I think I've figured it out."

Jonetta stood in front of Violet's desk, practically levitating with excitement.

"I *mean*," she added, "it's just a *theory* and all, but I really . . . well, anyway, tell me how this sounds to you. Everybody who's died has been relatively young, right? And we're going on the assumption that they didn't do this to themselves, right? Because it doesn't make sense that so many people in a row would take their own lives, right? And *so*," Jonetta said, leaning across the desk with a dramatic flourish, "maybe that's the key."

Violet stared at her. Her eyeballs felt like somebody had tried to polish them with sandpaper. The Headache had returned, only right now it was THE HEADACHE.

She felt utterly and completely dreadful.

"*What's* the key?" Violet said, her voice low and slow.

She had stumbled back home from Redshift just before

dawn. It didn't seem worth it to untangle her sheets and fall back into bed; she would only have nabbed an hour or so of sleep before her alarm went off. So she'd poured herself a glass of orange juice and waited for the sun to rise.

It turned out that she couldn't drink the juice, after all. Just lifting the glass and *thinking* about swallowing it caused a massive wave of nausea to burble and thrash in her stomach. She gave up, took a shower, got dressed.

Now she was here. If she was going to suffer, she might as well suffer while doing paperwork.

"The key is my *theory*," Jonetta said. She was still leaning, but the close-up look at Violet's bloated face caused her to back off and stand up straight again. "Okay, so because the victims have all been young, maybe it means that somebody *old* is doing this—killing people and making it look like suicide. Somebody who thinks young people are ruining New Earth."

"What would make somebody think that?"

"Don't know." She pondered. "Because we're too noisy?"

"Right. And we talk funny. And we don't keep our rooms clean. Come *on*." Violet rolled her eyes. That was a mistake: She felt another steep black wave of nausea. She would have been more than happy to blame Jonetta for it, but she knew the truth: The sloshing in her belly had nothing to do with her annoying assistant and everything to do with too many Neptunia Nodes. She swallowed hard, trying to push the sick feeling back down.

"We can speculate all day long, Jonetta," Violet added, "but we need proof. As in *facts*. As in something beyond wild theories." *And I need a big glass of water and some aspirin.*

"I've been collecting all the information I can," Jonetta said, ignoring Violet's disdainful tone and rattling right on. "I made a lot of calls about the Wilton twins. Their dad and mom both work at the metallurgy lab." She checked the notes on her wrist console. "Amy Wilton was in the engineering department. Charles Wilton had been a sailor on Old Earth, but up here he got the only job he could find. So he was head of maintenance there."

"That lab's had a ton of layoffs."

"Right. So the metallurgy division has a lot fewer employees than it used to. The Wiltons were lucky to hang on to their jobs."

Violet nodded. Occupations that were once crucial for constructing a new world had become less important as New Earth matured. People now switched out their jobs two or three—sometimes four or five—times a year.

Like somebody who starts out in a comfortable position at Protocol Hall monitoring Intercept feeds and then becomes a broke detective with an endless hangover. Violet often missed the stability of her old job. And she was only eighteen. For families, the shifts and dislocations must be even harder.

"Anything more on Wendell Prokop?"

Jonetta checked her console again. "He was the only person who still worked at the transport origination point. There used to be thousands."

"Is he related to Arianna Prokop?"

"*Oh*, yeah." Jonetta rolled her eyes. "That's his mom. She's the reason he kept his job. Threw her weight around so he didn't get fired, even though he was pretty much a loser. I talked to some of his friends and got the lowdown."

"Some friends."

"They weren't being mean. I got the sense they'd been hoping he would pull himself together one day. Get motivated." Jonetta shrugged. "People talk, Violet. And as detectives, we oughta be glad they do."

The *we* wasn't lost on Violet, but she was too tired to react. By now she'd downed three glasses of water in a row. She stood by the window, listening intently as Jonetta continued.

"Anyway, I know Arianna Prokop's a pretty big deal. Do you know her?"

"Not really. When I was a kid, I met her once or twice in my dad's office. That was it," Violet replied. "But my dad talked about her a lot. He admired her. Depended on her. She was part of the team that built New Earth's platform. She's a geological physicist. In fact, she's the one who figured out how to suspend the weight of New Earth over Old Earth." Violet realized that she'd become so involved in her conversation with Jonetta that she'd forgotten all about THE HEADACHE. As a consequence, she could now officially downgrade it to merely the Headache. With any luck, it would soon shrink back to just a regular old headache again. "She never mentioned having a son."

"From what I heard, Wendell wasn't the kind of kid you bragged about," Jonetta said.

The elongated beeping sound startled both of them. It came from the communication console on Jonetta's desk in the outer office.

"I'll get it," Jonetta said.

Violet started to reply with something along the lines of "How nice of you *to do your job*" but she stopped herself. Jonetta *had* been doing her job. And Violet's job, too, while she was at it.

"Hey, Vi—it's Rez."

Violet touched her console. A bright orange dot ascended, displaying Rez's serious, scowling face. The image wasn't cluttered with wavy lines. It must be a rare clear day down on Old Earth, she surmised, when the toxic clouds were momentarily pried apart by a determined wind, and the signal was managing to slip through without interference.

She noticed the gray ridge of rock that rose in the distance behind Rez's head. And above that, a darker gray sky shot through with short broken threads of reddish-brown clouds, spreading over the mountaintop. It was a dingy, uninspiring scene. Old Earth looked different, Violet thought, when you were viewing it through the haze of a hangover. Even one that was now on the run.

On the screen, Rez squinted at her. "You look terrible. Are you sick or something?"

"I'm fine."

"Okay, good," Rez said, moving on. "Anyway, I wanted to tell you that I got the word this morning. Official permission to fire up the quantum computers. Kendall got it done."

"So you're calling to thank me."

"Um, sure. Sure, yeah." The idea of thanking her had never occurred to him, Violet knew. She was teasing him. But he did have something on his mind. He looked down and then back up at the console again. "But the thing is—"

"What's going on, Rez?"

"Look, I can design the rides myself. Really cool ones. Fast, stomach-dropping, spiraling ones. And I can build them; I know where to scavenge the materials, and I've been building things my whole life. And I can do the energy schematics and the topographical charts and the logistical calculations. But I'm having trouble with the . . . the *human* part."

"The human part," Violet said. "You lost me."

"Yeah. Like knowing what sorts of rides will appeal to people. Figuring out what they like to do with their free time. How do they decide that? What sort of algorithm do they use?"

"It's not about *algorithms*, Rez."

"It's not?"

"No, it's not."

"Then what's it about?"

"Joy."

"Huh?"

"People make decisions based on what brings them joy. You know—happiness, pleasure, euphoria. The works." Violet saw by his face—he was squinting, and the frown bit deep—that he still wasn't with her. "Okay. Let's try this. You need to discover what makes people feel the way *you* feel when . . . let's see. How about when you're first sitting down at your computer? When you've got a really hard problem to solve?"

He nodded. The light of comprehension slowly came into his eyes, relaxing his features. "That's it. You get what I'm talking about."

"Lucky for you, I speak Rez." He had been a challenge for her from the first day they'd sat down next to each other in their shared cubicle. Little by little, she'd learned how to deal with him, which meant learning how not to be frustrated by his personality. *Or by what passes for a personality*, she thought.

"Whatever," Rez said. "So will you help me? With that part, I mean?"

"Which part?"

"The part about why people want to ride rides. Have fun."

"Sure."

She wouldn't mind a diversion. Because unless she figured out the reason behind the rash of deaths, she'd definitely be needing something to take her mind off the spectacle of watching Crowley & Associates dwindle. And falter. And fade. And tumble. And then go totally out of business.

The particulars came slamming at her all over again: The Bainbridge case was her last chance. She didn't know why she felt that way, but she did. If only she could solve it—*big if*—and if solving that one solved the other three as well, she'd finally make a name for herself. She wouldn't just be getting by on her father's name.

And if she couldn't . . .

"So I'll send you sketches of the rides I have in mind," Rez said, interrupting her familiar worry over worst-case scenarios.

If she didn't know better, Violet would've said that he sounded almost happy. "And," he went on, "you can tell me if they'll work. If they'll bring people . . ." His voice trailed off. He took a deep breath.

"Joy," she said.

"Yeah. That."

"Say it, Rez."

Another deep breath. "Come on, Violet. I've got work to do, okay? Gotta go."

"You can't even say the word?"

"Sure I can. I just . . . No. This is stupid." He shrugged.

Violet felt a spike of intense guilt. She knew one of the reasons Rez didn't like to talk about his emotions. And it had nothing to do with the Intercept. Or with his personality, warped as it was.

It had to do with her.

Two years ago, while they were working together at Protocol Hall, Rez had developed a very large and very inconvenient, unreciprocated crush on her. It was obvious to everybody. And instead of having a frank conversation with him and letting him down easy, Violet had used his affection for her own purposes. It was a lousy thing to do, even if it was for a good cause. *Which it definitely was*, she reminded herself defensively. *It was.*

Later, in the midst of the greatest crisis New Earth had ever known, when an underground group that opposed the Intercept kidnapped Violet and her father, Rez had done a favor for the Rebels. Just one small thing. He did it, he later explained, in a momentary gust of anger against Violet. She didn't love him. She would never love him. Motivated by hurt and disappointment, and maybe a touch of embarrassment, too, he had lashed out. Later he confessed, apologized, and was sent to prison.

But she and Rez had worked it out. They were friends again. She trusted him now. And he trusted her.

The trouble was, Rez still didn't trust emotions. And he might never do so again, Violet thought.

"Keep an eye on your console," he said. "I'll send you the drawings I've already done. See what you think."

"Deal." The second Violet clicked off, the Headache returned. And she had a ton of reports to read and interviews to undertake. It was her own fault. This was a workday, and she had known that a workday awaited her even as she'd ordered her fourth Neptunia Node. Or had it been her fifth?

Violet rubbed the back of her neck. *Sometimes I'm not a very good friend to myself.*

Jonetta, of course, had gotten a great night's sleep. Which was nice for her, but also irritating, especially if you were her boss and you were supposed to be setting the agenda—and yet here you were, with a clanging brain and a bad bellyache and an even worse kind of ache, too: the ache of knowing you weren't really doing your best these days.

From the outer office, Violet heard the steady *click-clickety-click-click* of Jonetta's fingernails striking the keyboard. Her secretary was always working.

"Hey," Violet called out. "Did you get a chance to make some—"

Before she was able to say the word *coffee*, an explosion blasted Violet clean out of her seat.

Trigger-Trap

eathers.

She opened her eyes and saw instantly that she was surrounded by feathers. Down they drifted, hundreds of them, soft and silky and mesmerizing. They danced past Violet's bleary gaze.

Endless feathers.

The feathers were familiar. Violet had seen something similar before, hadn't she? A soft and strange snowfall of feathers?

Yes. She had. Two years ago, when Protocol Hall was destroyed in a blinding blast of hot fury. There were feathers then, too, a sifting-down of bits and dabs and threads and fragments and soft, floating flecks.

But these things—the things streaming past her eyes right now—weren't really feathers, she was slowly, *slowly* realizing. They only seemed like feathers in their elegant fall and quiet accumulation.

She forgot about feathers. Her body felt . . . *weird*. Were her arms and legs still attached? Yes. Okay—good.

But they seemed to be twisted into funny positions.

"Violet?"

She was lying on her side. That much, she could tell; she felt a dull pain in her left ear and realized the whole side of her face was smushed hard against the floor. She was sore everywhere, and raw, and confused.

And somebody somewhere was saying her name.

"Violet? Hey, are you okay?"

She blinked. She tried to move. Moving hurt. She groaned, and then she tried again.

"Go slow," the voice said. "I think you're just shaken up. Nothing looks broken. But you've got some cuts and bruises. Maybe a concussion. So take it easy."

Someone was touching her arm. She realized it was Kendall, and she started to speak to him, but her mouth was too dry.

"I . . . I can't . . ." It came out sounding like *canth*.

"Relax. Just relax for a minute."

She needed to sit up. She let Kendall help her do that. He was kneeling beside her, keeping a hand on her back so she wouldn't fall over.

"How's Jonetta?" Violet said, suddenly remembering her assistant. "Is she—"

"She's fine."

Violet felt a surge of relief so intense that it increased her dizziness. She looked around. Everything was covered in a fine gray-white mist. It was as if an overcast day had suddenly split wide open, revealing the tiny gray particles inside its foggy little heart.

What she'd thought were feathers were actually tiny pieces of paper. The tiny pieces of paper were actually the unpaid bills—the ones she'd stacked in the corner. The blast had shredded them, lifting them high in the air, and when they fell, they stalled in lazy drifts and slovenly heaps that continued to rustle and simmer.

All that paper—the same unpaid bills that were driving her crazy—had cushioned her fall.

Ironic, Violet thought, and that was her first clue that she was okay. If she could think of the word *ironic*, then her brain was actually functioning.

Her desk was still in one piece, but it had a large slashing crack down the front of it. The walls of her office were missing chunks here and there and were dented in a few places, but they were basically okay. The ceiling was minus a few tiles, but it, too, had held firm.

She looked up at Kendall. "How did you—"

"I've got an alert on my console. If an alarm goes off here or at your apartment, it lets me know."

She wasn't sure she liked the sound of that—it had a vaguely stalker vibe in there somewhere—but she was too woozy to argue.

"Once I knew you were safe," Kendall went on, "I called for the ReadyRobs." He nodded toward six small silver rectangles lined up along one wall. ReadyRobs—robots dispatched by the police and fire departments for heavy-duty jobs—would handle the cleanup. Violet had seen their handiwork two years ago, in the aftermath of Ogden Crowley's kidnapping; with a discreet series of *whirrrrr*s and a swift dazzle of *shush*es and a busy weave of synchronized mechanical arms, the ReadyRobs had restored the apartment that she and her father shared back then to its original state. In minutes.

Kendall helped her rise. She was shaky, but she could manage. Now she saw how many people were jammed into her office. It looked like a tram stop at rush hour. There were five officers near the front door, tapping out notes on consoles.

Another three were examining debris with green-gloved hands. And two more were on either side of Jonetta in the outer office. They had just gotten her to her feet as well.

"Hey, Vi," Jonetta said. "How're you doing?"

Some things never change, Violet thought. If she wasn't feeling like hell right at the moment, she would've given Jonetta a stern lecture—the 857th time, give or take, that she'd delivered said lecture—about the whole nickname business. But anger took too much effort. Maybe later.

Violet gave her an *I'm-okay* wave. Then she turned back to Kendall. "So it had to be a pretty mild explosion. Otherwise, Jonetta and I would be floating in pieces with the dust particles."

"Yeah," he said. "We're still trying to figure out what happened."

"I already know." Jonetta's voice was as perky as ever, despite what they'd been through.

"You do?" Violet said.

"Absolutely. It had to be a keyboard trigger-trap. It's a low-level explosive device embedded in a computer. They're programmed to go off when you reach a certain number of keystrokes—two thousand, say, or three or four. Eliminates the need for a remote detonator."

"I know what a trigger-trap is," Kendall said. "But what makes you suspect one in this case?"

"A second before the explosion, the computer screen went black," Jonetta answered. "And then there was a red dot, right in the center. Classic signature of a trigger-trap. My brother, Rodney, is a computer guy. Taught me all he knows—and he knows a *lot*. Trigger-traps are mostly used for practical jokes. They're not intended to really hurt anybody. Just to get a laugh." She looked around at the smoking mess of what had formerly been the ready-for-business offices of Crowley & Associates. "But in this case, maybe somebody miscalculated and set the intensity too high."

"You think?" Violet said. She couldn't resist sarcasm. Jonetta's calm explanation had begun to annoy her. "No. This was a warning," she added darkly.

"About what?" Kendall asked. "Which of your cases do you think this is related to?"

Um, well, actually . . . there's only the one. The one you already know about.

But Violet didn't want to say that out loud, because if she did, she might as well have *LOSER* tattooed on her forehead. No one thought this detective business was going to work out, and she wanted to prove everyone wrong. If Kendall knew the extent of her troubles, he'd try to help. And she didn't want his help.

Actually, she didn't want *anybody's* help. With anything. She could do it all by herself.

She looked at Jonetta. *Not a word about our embarrassing lack of clients, okay?*

Violet was relieved. Jonetta's face told her that she understood.

"The Bainbridge case," Violet declared.

"Why would somebody not want you to look into Amelia Bainbridge's death?" Kendall asked.

Violet shrugged. "I don't know. Maybe because we're getting too close to something."

"Like what?"

"If I knew *that*, I'd already have the case solved." Her back was starting to ache. The Headache had flown back with a vengeance, and this time it had nothing to do with how late she'd been out last night. It was related to the fact that she'd been thrown to the floor in a blast from a trigger-trap.

Jonetta picked up a chair. She set it right-side up again, and then she started on her desk, sweeping off the dust with both hands. She turned her lamp on and off, on and off, to make sure it still worked. "Kendall," she said, "can you ask somebody from Tech Division to come over and check my computer? Make sure there aren't any more nasty surprises in there? I'd ask my brother to do it, but he just started a new job today. Can't get here for hours."

"Sure," he replied. He looked at Violet. "And there's something else I'm going to do, too."

"What?"

"I'm going to post a couple of cops at the door for a few days. At least until we get a clue about who did this."

"No way. Absolutely *not*." Violet crossed her arms. She was still fuming silently about the fact that Kendall had rigged up his console to keep tabs on her. She'd discuss it with him later—and by "discuss," she meant that she'd tell him to cut it out. But this? This was *way* over the line. It couldn't wait for a nice, calm conversation later on. "I run a detective agency," Violet declared. "How many clients do you think we'd get if people saw cops hanging around?"

We'd fail even faster than we're failing now, she thought.

"I hear you, but you need some protection," Kendall said. "It's not safe with just you and Jonetta here."

"Having cops hanging around won't protect us. Whoever did this could just set another trigger-trap remotely. They don't have to actually touch the computer."

Jonetta joined the argument—but on the wrong side. "Yep, they do. Trigger-traps can't be set remotely. They're about as low-tech as you can get. They *detonate* remotely after the set number of keystrokes, but to plant the trigger, you've got to be on the premises."

Frustrated, Violet frowned and thought for a moment.

"What if there were more people here? People other than cops, I mean. What if I promised to hire somebody else?"

As soon as the last sentence was out, Violet caught the expression that flickered across Jonetta's face: *Hire somebody else? And pay them with* what*?* Her assistant kept quiet, however.

"Like who?" Kendall sounded skeptical.

"Tin Man." She wasn't sure how his name had come to her, but there it was. And it made sense; Tin Man was devoted to her. And the size of his biceps ended a lot of arguments with rowdy people before those arguments even got started.

"So you think he'd be willing to do that? Quit his job as a bouncer at Redshift?" Kendall asked.

"Maybe," Violet said. "He might not have to quit. He might be looking for a day job. And besides, everybody's changing jobs all the time, anyway. They have to. Until we figure out who set the trigger-trap, he's the best protection I could ask for."

Kendall considered her idea. *The tables are* so *turned*, Violet reflected as she watched him. *She* used to worry constantly about *him*.

"Okay," he finally said. "But you've got to take this seriously, Violet. It was just a trigger-trap today. Tomorrow, it could be something a lot worse. So you'll keep your friends close, right?"

A cop across the room had fired up the ReadyRobs, and now the *whir-shush*, *whir-shush*, *whir-shush* sounds made by the little machines filled the office. Violet had to raise her voice to be heard.

"Yeah."

He wasn't finished. *Of course he's not finished*, Violet thought wearily.

"And you promise," he said, "that you'll get yourself checked out by a doctor. To make sure you don't have any internal injuries."

"Yeah. I'll call Shura." There were definite perks to having a best friend who was a physician.

"And you'll take a moment and think about who might have done this."

"Yeah."

"And why."

"Yeah."

"And you'll let me know who has access to the office."

"Yeah."

"And you'll try to remember if anything else suspicious has gone on lately."

"Yeah."

"And you'll take it easy for the rest of the day."

"Nope."

Kendall sighed.

"What's so important that it can't wait, Violet?"

"My case."

Violet had decided that maybe she'd dismissed Jonetta's idea too quickly. Maybe her secretary was onto something. The victims were young. So maybe the perpetrator *was* somebody old and bitter. Maybe it really *was* some kind of age-related rage.

She knew the perfect place to start checking out the theory—a place that was positively full of potential suspects.

Starbridge

Violet hesitated. She stood in the doorway of her father's apartment. He was sitting in his reading chair, oblivious to the world, totally focused on the battered hardcover from Old Earth that lay open on his lap. She didn't want to startle him.

"Hi, Dad," she said quietly.

He looked up. His facial expression instantly shifted from annoyed to joyous. "Violet! So nice to see you, sweetheart. You said you were coming by, but I didn't know it would be so soon."

"I figured you'd be worried when you heard about the explosion."

"It's all over the news. And yes, I *was* concerned."

"I'm fine, Dad. Absolutely fine."

Ogden Crowley closed his book and set it aside. He tried to stand up. It was always a terrible struggle for him. He was the strongest man Violet had ever known, but he couldn't lift himself out of his chair without help. His strength was in his mind, not his body.

She didn't rush over to give him a hand. He would rather fail on his own than succeed with somebody else's help. And so she waited, watching. To save his pride, she looked around the apartment.

The living room was spacious and elegant, presided over by a crystal chandelier whose wilderness of tiny facets caught the sunlight and sliced it into tiny shivering rainbows that shimmied around the room. The walls were snowy white. The carpet was a lush dark green. The heavy drapes were a deep scarlet. Those drapes were gathered on either side of an immensely tall window that ran the length of an entire wall. From here, Ogden could look out across the splendid vistas and glistening towers of the world he had created, dream by dream.

Each time Violet visited Starbridge, New Earth's retirement community, with its vast replicating hive of specially equipped apartments, she felt the same thing: a sort of hybrid emotion composed of happiness and anguish. She loved her father and was glad to see him, but it was hard to watch someone you cared about grow older. More feeble, more helpless. Even if she didn't visit for long periods of time, she knew what was happening here. Life was a one-way journey toward the dark.

Day by day, the sadness seemed to spread a little further in Violet's heart, like a crack in a vase.

Her father took a deep breath. He steeled himself and gripped the arms of the chair tightly with his withered hands. Pushing down with a fury that was reflected on his face—his eyes widened, and two shiny pearls of sweat rolled from his temple to his chin—he tried again to rise. And again.

Finally, he let out a deep, frustrated sigh. He relaxed his hands. He sat back against the thickly padded chair, panting.

"These old bones," he said lightly, casually, once he'd caught his breath, "are giving me fits today. Just not getting the job done." He smiled as if it were a rare thing, as if, had she only come tomorrow, things would be different.

But things would never be different for Ogden Crowley. As a small boy, he'd been grievously injured during the Mineral Wars on Old Earth; his right leg was useless now, gouged with scary-looking scars. Age and overwork had run roughshod over the rest of him.

Violet walked toward his chair. With a simple supple motion, she sat down on the floor next to it, close enough for him to be able to reach out and touch the top of her head. When she was a little girl, this had been their nightly ritual. She would sit cross-legged on the floor, and they would talk, talk, talk, weaving a spell of words around themselves like a soft cocoon that only had room for two.

"You're sure you're okay?" he asked.

"Yeah. I'm fine, Dad."

"Any leads?"

"Not yet. Kendall and his team are working on it, but trigger-traps are hard to trace."

"So that's what it was."

"Best guess."

He nodded.

"Back when I was president," he said, "I would have speculated that they were trying to get to *me* through you. But now? Hardly. I'm just another old man. Put out to pasture." He frowned and waved a gnarled hand in the air as if he wanted to bat away the noxious fumes of self-pity. "Are you working on anything controversial? Anything that would make somebody mad enough to attack you? You should have Jonetta go through the list. How many cases do you have going right now?"

Violet paused. She didn't want him to know how bleak her business prospects really were. It would only worry him.

Um, there's just the one case, Dad. And even that came after a long, long dry spell.

He'd figure out in a flash that one case wouldn't pay the bills. And offer to help. The notion of needing help made her cringe inwardly. She was entirely her father's daughter, a thought that made her proud.

"Um, total number of cases?" she murmured. "I'm not really sure." Quickly, she added, "But there *is* one that's a little different. You read about the suicides, right? Four of them, one right after another?"

His face clouded over. "Terribly sad news. Tragic at any age, but they were all so young. With so much to live for. So much to look forward to. If it had happened on Old Earth, I could understand it. That's such a hopeless, depressing place. But here? Here on New Earth?" He turned his head sideways and down so that he could look at Violet. Perplexity filled his rheumy eyes. "It doesn't make any sense."

"Maybe it *does* make sense."

"What do you mean?"

"What if they weren't suicides?"

Ogden's expression reflected his surprise.

"The first victim's mother," Violet continued, "hired me to investigate. She doesn't believe her daughter killed herself. She says that's impossible."

His features relaxed again. "To be sure, Violet, it's a very hard thing to accept about your own flesh and blood—that your child was in such pain she would rather die than endure life another second."

"But what if she's right? What if it was murder? And what if the murderer was able to make it *look* like suicide just to throw off suspicion?"

He considered her words.

"Well," he said, musing aloud. "I'm wondering how some-body would pull it off in the first place. Making a murder look like suicide is not a simple task. Captain Mayhew runs a top-flight forensics team. He's not going to be easily fooled. And why would somebody want to kill that particular girl, anyway? Or those twins? What's the motive? Wendell wasn't adding much to society, but he was a harmless kid. How would his death help anybody? I remember when Arianna would bring him around sometimes, trying to motivate him, showing him how hard she worked." He shook his head. "Out of the entire population of New Earth, why go after those young people?"

"You said it yourself, Dad. They're all young."

"What?"

"Meaning," Violet said, her voice growing more emphatic the longer she talked, "that maybe somebody is deliberately tar-geting young people. It was Jonetta's idea, and I think it's a good one. There's always been tension on New Earth between the young and the founding generation, right? Especially since you lifted immigration restrictions from Old Earth. Thousands of young people have come up here in the past two years. The young outnumber the old by a lot now, right?"

"Yes."

"So maybe somebody's jealous. Maybe they think the influx of younger people somehow endangers New Earth. I don't know." Violet shrugged. "It's just a theory."

"They might be right."

"What?"

"Well, every civilization has to constantly renew itself," her father said thoughtfully. "But it's a balance. Because while the young have more energy, the old have more wisdom. We cre-ated New Earth with a careful balance of young and old. That's why I restricted entrance from Old Earth. To keep that balance.

I maintained a very careful watch on age levels. But then we opened the gates to New Earth and let everyone come up. Only the prisoners were left behind on Old Earth. And a few hundred people who wanted to end their days there.

"And so now, here on New Earth, no one adjusts the population for optimal age equilibrium anymore. And we're definitely skewing young."

"So you think New Earth is out of balance?"

"I do."

Violet contemplated this. She was thinking about potential suspects. "So does anybody else at Starbridge feel that way, too?"

Her father smiled a rueful smile. "Sweetheart, *everybody* at Starbridge feels that way."

So the suspect pool had just increased by several thousand. Violet let out a small groan of discouragement.

"Well," she said, "I'm going to do my best to find out the truth. I made a promise to Mrs. Bainbridge."

"That's my girl."

The warm tone of her father's voice had a definite effect on Violet. She wanted him to think well of her. She was his reflection in the world now. Since his retirement, he was rarely seen on the streets of New Earth; he was too old and too weak and often too sick to go out for any length of time. In many ways, his legacy—and the legacy of her mother as well—was in Violet's hands.

She couldn't think about that too often or she got sort of frozen with the responsibility of it all.

"So maybe," Violet said, getting back to business before emotion overtook her, "the killer can sense I'm getting close to the answer. So they want to shut me down. Send me a warning. Get me to back off."

"That would explain the trigger-trap."

"Yeah. It was a close call. Jonetta's been pretty cool about it—actually almost *too* cool about it—but still—" Violet broke off her sentence and shivered.

"She's a brave girl," Ogden said. "Her father told me she was, and she's proved it. Lucien Loring is an old and dear friend, and I'm glad you could find a spot for Jonetta. Have you met Rodney yet? Her older brother?"

"No. Just missed him. A few times he came to take her to lunch, but I was out on a case."

"He's a bright young man. Rather reminds me of your friend Steven Reznik." Ogden changed his position in the chair, in search of a comfort that would never come. "Reznik sent me a note, you know. From prison. Apologizing. Did I ever tell you that?"

"No. You didn't."

"It was thoughtful. And sincere. It was about how emotions can get hold of us and make us do things we never believed we could do. He wasn't making excuses. He just wanted me to know how sorry he was. He'd learned the astonishing power of emotions. Before—just working his shift with you in Protocol Hall, monitoring the Intercept—he hadn't thought of feelings that way. He *should* have, of course; he saw it every day during the interventions. He saw people brought to their knees by love or anger or jealousy or fear. But he never put it all together. He was too mesmerized by the technology itself, he told me, to think of emotions as powerful in their own right. As guideposts for a life, in both good and bad ways.

"Anyway," her father went on, "I appreciated his note. Very much. And it convinced me once again that I made the right decision when I shut down the Intercept." He paused. "I've always identified with those leaders back on Old Earth, the ones who ruled in the twentieth and twenty-first centuries. They knew how destructive an atomic bomb could be. First they wanted it built, because it was for a good cause. And then they saw where it might lead, so they tried to keep a lid on the technology. They did their best to keep it out of the hands of those who were power-mad or greedy or just plain evil."

"But they didn't succeed, Dad," Violet said. "Bad people *did* get hold of atomic weapons. And used them. That's part of what destroyed Old Earth."

"Eventually, yes. But the leaders tried. And sometimes that's all we can do. We can try." He glanced down at one of his gnarled hands. He drew it into a fist and then let his hand relax again, like a problem considered and solved. "I had to take a long, hard look at the Intercept, and that's when I told myself, 'It's magnificent—but it's much too dangerous.' So all in all, I think we're better off without it. Absolutely."

An uneasy feeling fluttered in Violet's stomach. This time, she couldn't blame a Neptunia Node.

Whenever her father talked so ardently, so passionately, about the fundamental rightness of destroying the Intercept, Violet always had the impression that there was really only one person he was trying to convince.

Himself.

17

Delia

What's this?"

Delia held the small gift-wrapped package that Violet had just handed her. The wrapping was an elegant silver foil made up of myriad light-catching crinkles.

The two of them stood in the foyer of the small home where Delia lived with her son, Tin Man. Delia dressed proudly every day in her Old Earth clothes: baggy trousers with a rope belt; too-big tunic that slouched off one shoulder; stained boots that had been mended and re-mended so many times that they were basically layers of interlocking stitching separated by brief patches of stiff, dried-out leather. Because of that leather, she crackled when she walked.

Tin Man was somewhere in a back room, getting ready for work at Redshift.

Delia prodded the package with a tentative finger. She liked and trusted Violet, but she was a suspicious woman. Violet understood why. Until two years ago, Delia's entire life had been spent on Old Earth. There, in that dark and dangerous place, suspicion was your best friend. It kept you alert. And being alert kept you alive.

"I promise it won't explode," Violet said.

Delia cocked an eyebrow. "Not funny, my girl. Not funny at all. I heard about what happened at your office this morning. Everybody's talking about it. Thank goodness there weren't any injuries. You know what? I wish you'd be more careful. You young people, you think you're indestructible. Let me tell you something, Violet—you're not. Nobody is."

"Oh, come on. You can lecture me some other time." Violet grinned. "Don't you want to know what I brought you?"

Delia flicked a fingernail at the small rectangle. Then she lifted it to her ear and shook it, trying to figure out the contents from any answering rattle. "If this is some kind of trick, I swear I'm going to—"

"*Delia.* For God's sake, open the present!"

"All right, all right." Gingerly, she peeled back the wrapping, loosening one small flap and then another. Finally, she was able to draw out the wooden box. The top was stamped EARL GREY TEA in ancient lettering. Delia looked at Violet, and then she looked back down at the box. She tried to pry up the lid, but it wouldn't budge.

"Let me help," Violet said. She slid off the lid, moving it smoothly through the two parallel grooves cut along the top. Nestled in the crinkly tissue paper were six tea bags. Their strings and tags were wound in a dainty bundle.

For a long moment, Delia did not speak. Violet understood. Tea bags had a special resonance for Delia, and the intense emotions generated by this gift were surely tumbling inside her.

Back on Old Earth, where Delia had lived with Tin Man and her daughter, Molly, tea bags represented a fabulous degree of luxury. They were more than just scarce; they were a reminder of all that had been lost when the earth imploded, when it was decimated by rampaging human greed and jagged-edged ignorance. A reminder of long-vanished days of leisure and contemplation and quiet conversation, of afternoons when people might spend many hours sipping a hot beverage out of delicate china cups. And perched enticingly on the edge of the saucer would be a small round cookie or crumbly biscuit.

Once the Water Wars and the Mineral Wars had begun, little rituals like afternoon tea became more than just quaint relics of a permanently vanished era; they were poignant symbols of all that had been lost. The memories were hurtful.

But Delia, during her long, ragged, difficult years on Old Earth, had squirreled away a tea bag. A single tea bag. She stored it in a small sack in the bombed-out husk of a structure that she called home. She used the tea bag over and over again, until every last bit of flavor from the tea leaves had long been leached out, until the thin paper was in danger of shredding each time she added hot water. Still she kept making cups of tea, tea that wasn't really tea at all anymore, just water.

And when Violet came to Old Earth and Delia rescued her from a street gang intent on robbing her, out came the tea bag. Delia used it to make a hot beverage that might, she hoped, bring some comfort to the mysterious young woman from New Earth who had shown up out of the blue—or, this being Old Earth, out of the gray.

Things were very different now for Delia and Tin Man. They were safe. They lived in a nice New Earth home in the city of Higgsville. Delia worked as assistant manager of a store; Tin Man had his job at Redshift. But for Delia Tolliver, a tea bag could never be just a tea bag.

"Tea," Delia said.

"Yeah."

"Tea," Delia repeated. She swallowed hard.

Violet wondered if it was all coming back to her now: the terrible dangers of Old Earth, with its radiation-blurred sunsets and its putrid oceans and its foul, pestilential rivers. She wondered if Delia was picturing Molly, her little girl, who had died at five years old of Missip Fever.

Maybe the tea bags had been a mistake, after all.

I'm worse than the Intercept, Violet chastised herself. *Now* I'm *the instigator of painful emotions.*

"This," Delia suddenly declared, "is wonderful. I'm going to enjoy every sip." She lifted the box again. She squared her shoulders. She could do this.

Violet was relieved.

Her relief was immediately shoved aside by guilt. Her motives weren't pure. She had brought the gift because she wanted an excuse to visit today.

"Can I make you a cup?" Delia said.

"No, I'm good."

"Well, then, come on in. And like I said, Tin Man should be out in a second."

They settled in the small living room. Beige couch, two chairs, square coffee table—the furniture was simple and serviceable, as was most all of the furniture on New Earth, where everything had to be measured and weighed. The only unique element here was the striking painting that hung on the wall behind the couch. It was a large, lovely portrait of a smiling young girl, running headlong, arms and legs extended in a full beautiful stride that made it look as if she might go airborne in the very next second, her hair flying out behind her. Tucked away in the lower right-hand corner of the picture was the artist's signature:

SHURA LU
2294

The girl in the portrait was Molly.

"Must have been scary," Delia said as she settled down on the couch next to Violet. "The attack at your office, I mean. Any idea who did it?"

"We're still going through the clues. And yeah, it was a shock." Violet looked around. "You know what? You and Tin Man have really made this place a home."

"Home." Delia seemed to be tasting the word. "Yeah, I guess so. But you know what, Violet? Sometimes I miss Old Earth. I know it sounds crazy, but I do."

It didn't sound crazy. Violet had heard Kendall say the same thing—that as vicious and violent and shadow-shrouded as Old Earth was, if you were born there, a part of you always missed it. You couldn't help yourself. And sometimes, Violet knew, you missed it even if you *hadn't* been born there.

"I wish," Delia added, "that I could go back. Just for a visit. But it's hard." She didn't have to explain further. Trips were expensive. And they took a fearsome toll on the body, especially for older people like Delia.

"Yeah," Violet said. "I've had to rely on console feeds lately. I'm not supposed to go back for a while."

Delia's face split open with a devilish grin. "Do you ever think of just sneaking back? Like you did that time when I first met you?"

"Sure. The only thing that stops me is not wanting to end up in a HoverUp by the time I'm twenty-five," Violet said. Rubbing her forearm, she finished her thought. "Shura went with me for my last bone-density scan. The specialist was clear. No more trips to Old Earth for six to eight months. Shura's trying to come up with something that will counteract the calcium-leach from the rapid gravity fluctuations, but for the time being I'm stuck on New Earth."

"Stuck. Oh, *riiiiiight*," Delia said, the sarcasm stretching out her voice. She swept an arm around the room. "It's just so *awful* here. How do you *stand* it? All these blue skies and sunshine and pretty houses and good food. It's *killing* us, Violet. Swear."

"Okay, okay," Violet said. She laughed. "I get you."

Delia's mood shifted. "Truth is, though, I do hate to see Old Earth abandoned. Just left to rot. Sooner or later, I bet it's going to disintegrate entirely. It'll become this dead thing that New Earth hauls around for a while and finally lets go of."

Violet thought about Rez's plan to rejuvenate Old Earth. Maybe it wasn't as far-fetched as it seemed. Maybe it would answer a deep desire that simmered in a lot of souls—her own, certainly, and Delia's, too.

Violet's console chimed. She looked down at the ID and frowned: *Jonetta*. She didn't want to deal with her secretary's chipper cheerfulness right now.

She declined the call. Jonetta could leave a message.

"Hey, Violet."

Another voice in the room. She'd know it anywhere. Tin Man entered from the short hallway leading to the back of the house. He walked toward her with his brisk, confident stride, all swinging arms and broad shoulders and big grin. The silver hoop in his earlobe winked and glittered. Even though Violet had talked to him just the night before at Redshift, she was struck anew by his looks. He had changed so dramatically from the first time she had seen him two years ago.

She remembered the moment well, because it turned out to be the opening act for the most intense drama that New Earth had ever seen. Violet was monitoring a drone feed from Old

Earth. Tin Man was running away from a cop. Back then, Tin Man was bone-skinny and as pale as skim milk; his scrawny, undernourished body looked like a tent pole from which his raggedy clothes flapped and wheeled.

Not anymore. Now he was cut, on account of the intense workout regimen he'd undertaken in his new home. His skin had the warm, golden hue that came from the generous sun of New Earth. He was a new man.

Yet the original Tin Man—wary, with a warrior's heart—still lived inside him. Violet could see it in his eyes. And that wasn't a bad thing. In fact, it was a very *good* thing, given what she wanted him to do for her.

"Tin Man. Hey."

"How're you doing? Been *so* long since I've seen you, girl." He smirked. Violet let him have his little joke; he liked to tease her about how many nights in a row she visited Redshift. Sometimes it was more than teasing. She knew he was genuinely concerned about her—a fact that infuriated her. She didn't need a babysitter.

"Don't let me interrupt you guys," Tin Man added. "I'm leaving for work in a second, anyway."

"Actually, I need to talk to you, too," Violet said.

Curiosity put a light in his eyes. "What's up?"

"I want to hire you."

"Already got a job."

"This'll be better."

Intrigued, Tin Man sat down in one of the chairs. He barely fit, so broad was his heavily muscled torso.

"I need help," Violet said. "Somebody set a trigger-trap at my office today."

"So I heard."

"And you didn't ask if I was okay?"

He shrugged. "I can *see* you're okay." He grinned. "Fact is, Violet, it's going to take a lot more than a trigger-trap to stop you from whatever it is that somebody doesn't want you to do."

"It was still scary as hell. That's why I need somebody else around the office."

"You mean like a bodyguard?"

"No. I mean like another investigator. I can take care of myself. I just need help with a case."

He frowned. "I don't have any experience in detective work."

"Neither did I."

Delia spoke up. "I've never much liked your job at that club, Tommy. All the late hours in that place. All those strangers. I'd love for you to get away from there."

Tin Man gave Violet a meaningful glance. He wasn't going to let Delia know that Violet was at Redshift almost as often as he was. But he was letting Violet know: *I could if I wanted to.*

Violet was relieved at his silence. She didn't like the idea of Delia judging her. *It's my business what I do at night. Nobody else's.*

"We can discuss salary and all of that another time," Violet said. "But you'll think about it? Coming to work with me?"

"Yeah. I'll think about it." He stood up. "Gotta get going." He hesitated, arms at his sides, balancing himself evenly on his black-booted feet. He had one more thing to say.

He rolled up his shirtsleeve. In the crook of his left elbow was a thick scar, a raggedy-edged patch of red, corrugated skin. It marked the spot where a younger Tin Man had tried to gouge out the Intercept chip from under his skin. Back when the Intercept was running full-time, a lot of people on Old Earth had done the same thing: They attempted to get rid of their chips so that the Intercept couldn't access them. Some of the DIY chip removals ended in death when infection set in.

"See this?" Tin Man said. He ran a thumb across the bumpy, rutted surface of the twisted scar.

Violet didn't answer. He didn't need her to. He knew she was seeing it.

"I'm glad we're friends now," he said. "I really am. You've done a lot for my mom and me. We owe you our lives." Slowly, as he continued to speak, his tone grew more emphatic. "But I want you to know something. I don't ever forget. This scar doesn't *let* me forget. I know what can happen when the Intercept is operational. I know the power it has. The terrible, terrible power. So if anything ever changed—and if you were on the other side again, on the side of the Intercept—I'd fight you with every bit of strength I had. I wouldn't think twice about it. I'd destroy you. And I'd do what you did. I'd destroy the Intercept all over again."

Violet was a bit shocked. His declaration had come out of nowhere.

But had it? she asked herself. The truth was, she had no idea what it had felt like to live on Old Earth in the days of the Intercept. She could listen to their stories of what it had been like—the sudden and terrible interventions, when emotions were inserted back into the consciousness with a vivid, punitive fury—but she couldn't *know*.

Not like they knew.

She didn't carry the memory in her bones like they did.

From her seat on the couch, Delia cleared her throat to get their attention. She had pushed up the sleeve of her tunic. The crook of her left elbow showed the ghostly remnant of her own small scar, the aftermath of a botched attempt to remove her chip. It wasn't as ghastly as her son's scar, but it was still there. A permanent reminder of how they both had suffered. And how everyone they had known on Old Earth had suffered, too.

"If the Intercept ever returns," Delia said quietly, "we'll fight you with anything we have. Sticks and rocks. Whatever."

Violet loved these people, and she knew they loved her. But there was something inside them that ran even deeper and truer than love: their sense of justice. If they ever suspected that she hadn't completely destroyed the Intercept, what would they do?

She knew the answer. She just didn't want to think about it.

She shook her head. Forced a smile.

"Come on, guys. The Intercept is over. It's gone," Violet declared. Had she said it too quickly, too firmly? She worried, for the space of a single breath, that Delia and Tin Man might have picked up on her nervousness.

"Fine," Tin Man said. "Great. But I need to be clear with you before I come on board—if I *do* come on board, that is. If the Intercept ever shows up again, I'm with the Rebels." The Rebels of Light was the name of the group that had kidnapped Ogden Crowley two years ago. Some of them had died when New Earth's police force came after them. The survivors were locked up in Old Earth prisons.

"No problem." Violet smiled. "If the Intercept shows up, I'll be with the Rebels, too."

Tin Man looked satisfied with her answer. "And now I really do have to go," he said. "People will be lining up at the door. Once they get close enough to hear the music and feel the heat from the dance floor, they get pretty antsy." He leaned over and kissed Delia on the cheek. "Later, Mom."

Now he turned to Violet, and she saw that his smirk had returned. He was his mother's son—meaning that he couldn't resist teasing her one more time. He wouldn't openly snitch on her to Delia about how often she hung out at Redshift but he'd make her squirm.

"Oh, and Violet?" he said. "You should come check out Redshift sometime. I think you'd like it."

Secrets and Lies

It was time.

Violet knew it was time—okay, it was way *past* time—but she still didn't want to do it. She didn't want to tell Kendall about Rez's suspicion that someone might be trying to resurrect the Intercept.

She texted him:

U free?

He texted back:

Y

She replied:

Perey Park in ten

The park was her go-to place. It was the spot where she and Shura had spent so much of their free time when they were growing up. Located smack in the middle of Hawking, anchored by a round granite fountain in the middle, Perey Park was lovely in a simple, unfussy way. The grass was a soft green carpet. The trees that bordered the walking path were tall and chocolate-brown and friendly looking. And the whole place had a faintly magical quality, a kind of glow, like the memory of a birthday party from childhood.

"So," Kendall said. He sat down next to her on the bench. He'd driven them here in his official police vehicle. She hadn't said much during the ride. "Here we are in Violet and Shura's secret hangout."

"Huh?"

"That's how I used to think of this place. You guys came here all the time, right?"

"We had a lot to talk about back then."

"Like what?"

Like you. She had been desperately in love with Danny Mayhew—that is, the guy she *thought* was Danny Mayhew, but who was really Kendall, the same guy who was sitting next to her right now—and Shura had helped her deal.

"Like all kinds of stuff," she said.

"You don't talk about Shura so much anymore."

Violet stood up. She didn't feel like sitting. She also didn't feel like talking about Shura and the changes to their friendship. "Can we walk around?"

"Absolutely."

Their feet crunched along the gravel path. Their paces matched up well, without either one having to adjust speed.

"So there's something I need to tell you," Violet said.

"Shoot."

"When I talked to Rez the other day, he mentioned something."

"Okay."

"That something was the Intercept."

"It's not a dirty word, Violet. People still talk about it. They probably always will."

"I know that."

Kendall stopped. She stopped, too.

"There's something you don't want to tell me," he said.

"How did you figure that out?"

"Come on. We've been through too much. I can tell when you're holding back."

She took a deep breath.

"Rez thinks that somebody may be trying to get it up and running again." There. She'd said it. She was apprehensive; she didn't know what Kendall's reaction would be. His feelings about the Intercept had always been so intense. He'd created it. Overseen its installation on New Earth. And then he'd watched as the dark side of his great creation had emerged, like a scaly, red-eyed, triple-headed monster from the depths of a cave.

"Can't be," he declared flatly.

"But Rez says—"

"Rez is wrong. There's no way. The Intercept is way too complicated for anybody to build from scratch."

"What if they didn't have to build it from scratch?"

"Meaning?"

"You know what I mean. Maybe they found the notebook pages. The ones we grabbed from the floor of Protocol Hall before it exploded."

She watched Kendall's face.

Talking about what happened that day had been forbidden from the moment they'd made their decision to do it. They had both agreed to that, without either having to say so out loud. For two years now, they had kept that unspoken promise.

Violet had just broken the pact. In the middle of a walk in the park.

He looked around. She did, too. No one else was present, but they were still cautious. They would always be cautious when it came to the Intercept.

"Impossible," he said. He didn't sound like himself anymore. Gone was the confidence, the self-assurance that typically defined Kendall Mayhew. He sounded . . . *nervous*. "Totally impossible."

"Is it?"

"I've had those pages locked away for two years. In a special place. A place where nobody can get to them. And even if somebody *did* get to them, they wouldn't be able to do anything."

"Why not?"

"Because they're not *me*. And only a handful of people would have the technical skills to whip up a new Intercept with only a few pages of notes to go on. Maybe less than a handful."

"Think back," Violet said. "Back to when you and Danny were living on Old Earth and you were working on the Intercept. Way back then. Well, who knew about *you*? Who would've ever envisioned some totally anonymous genius in a scruffy lab?"

He didn't say anything, but she could sense he was listening. So she continued. "What if there's another *you* out there—some unknown kid in a basement lab? And somehow they got those notes? And they're re-upping the Intercept? Dusting off the code? And maybe Rez just happened to stumble across it."

"I told you. It's impossible." The word *impossible* came out of him with marginally less conviction than before. "Okay," Kendall finally said. "I'll look into it. I'll talk to Rez and ask him what he saw. And I'll do it without tipping him off." He paused. "I hope it doesn't turn out that—"

"I know," she said. "You hope you don't find out that it's Rez himself. Playing some kind of game. As revenge, maybe, for his prison time. Right?"

"Basically, yeah."

"Because he's one of the very few people with the skills to get the Intercept up and running again."

Kendall nodded.

Both were quiet for a long moment. By now, darkness had swallowed the park. Shapes were still discernible, but specifics were not. Objects were reduced to their blunt essence: fountain, tree, bench. The gentle, radiant magic that was present here in the daytime had vanished along with the sunshine.

They were standing side by side. Violet touched Kendall's arm. She was struck by the fact that no matter where they were standing in relation to each other—close or distant—they would be linked forever. Linked by their friendship and linked by what they'd done. It had seemed wrong to not be touching him at such a moment. She hoped he wouldn't misinterpret her gesture, and think that maybe—

"What happened to us, Violet?"

She was startled. They didn't talk about their relationship anymore. They. Just. Didn't. They had tried to, early on, in the days just after the Intercept's destruction. But it was difficult and painful, and so they had backed off into neutral corners, heeding an unstated but crucial rule: no conversation about the Relationship. They wanted the friendship to continue—and if that was going to happen, then they couldn't discuss the fate of the romance.

But here he was, bringing it up.

Maybe it was because she was touching him. Maybe it was because the trigger-trap had gone off at her office; she knew how much Kendall worried about her, which sort of made her mad and sort of didn't. Maybe it was the darkness. Or maybe it was the fact that they were standing fairly close, the way they had done two years ago, just before he'd kissed her for the very first time.

"What happened?" he repeated, in a soft voice. "Once I'd told you the truth about who I was, I thought we could be together. I mean—I'm the same person. The same person you fell in love with. When you thought I was Danny."

She didn't know how to respond. Everything he said was true; she *had* fallen in love with him. Hard. And he *was* the same guy she had known back then. Older, sure—but the same guy. The only thing that had changed was his name. And what's a name? A name is *nothing*, right? Nothing at all.

But she just didn't feel it anymore.

She wanted to, but she didn't. She wanted to love him the way she had loved him before, with that swirly feeling that started in her stomach and made her fingertips tingle and then made her sort of dizzy every time she saw him and every time she even *thought* about seeing him. Or thought about him, period.

The feeling that, back when the Intercept was up and running, probably left a burn mark in the digital archive. That's how hot it was.

But the feeling just wasn't there anymore. She knew she was breaking his heart, and she was doing it slowly, piece by piece, each time they got together and he searched her eyes for the light he used to see there, that golden one that was like no other. And each time, she could sense his disappointment. They still had a good time together, and they talked and they laughed and they hung out, and she really looked forward to seeing him— but it wasn't romantic love, at least on her side. She didn't know why. She only knew what she felt.

Or what she *didn't* feel.

She took a quick glimpse at the crook of her left elbow. Nothing. *Of course there's nothing. The Intercept's been gone for two years.* But it was more than that. More than just the absence of the Intercept. It was another kind of absence, too. She didn't know what to do about Kendall. How to relate to him, especially when she saw his yearning. And his pain.

And that was one of the reasons why she hung out at Redshift, night after night, and she danced and she laughed and she flirted and she tried to jump-start other feelings in herself, feelings that would equal in intensity what she'd once felt for this guy.

The guy standing in front of her right now, the guy whose face she couldn't see very well anymore because of the darkness. But she didn't need to see his features. She knew them so very, very well. She knew how he looked when he was sad, so she knew how he looked right then.

"I don't know what happened, Kendall," she said. "You're my friend, though, okay? Always."

It was not what he wanted to hear. But he wouldn't push her. She knew that.

"Okay," he said. His tone changed. It was brusque now. All business. "I've got to get back to the station. And get in touch with Rez."

"And I've got a case to work on." She had checked her messages during the drive to the park. There were a bunch of annoying ones from Jonetta, who had rattled on and on about dozens of different things, things that Violet just *had* to take care of *right away*—but the one on the top of the heap was this: Charlotte Bainbridge wanted Violet to stop by tonight. No matter how late it was.

That was where she was headed next.

19

The Peanut Butter Principle

eff Bainbridge never took his eyes off his plate. He didn't eat a single thing during Violet's visit, but he sat in his chair at the kitchen table and stared at the food. His mother had made his favorite nighttime snack—saltine crackers with lots of peanut butter—and he studied the square crackers and the tufted tan gobs as if the whole thing constituted a dense mathematical code he was solely responsible for cracking.

Peanut butter.

Stepping into the brightly lit Bainbridge kitchen right behind Charlotte, Violet paused when she saw Jeff's plate. She remembered the first time her mother had introduced her to peanut butter.

She was probably four years old. They sat on the balcony in red chairs, her mother's big chair and Violet's small one, and they watched the light along the horizon of New Earth. The slow withdrawal of the sun's radiance left behind a watery trail of pink and bronze. *This may be a fancy new world filled with wonders aplenty,* Lucretia Crowley had said, *but the most wonderful thing of all is still peanut butter. Here, sweetheart. Taste this.*

Lucretia smiled and handed her half a piece of toast on a small plate. Swirled atop the bread was some kind of brown stuff.

Violet touched the substance with her tongue. Let some of it hang around in her mouth. *Delicious.* Like a kind of salty ribbon of deep flavor. She eagerly licked the rest of it off and wadded the crunchy bread and popped it in her mouth. She handed the plate back to her mother. *More, please,* she said. Lucretia laughed.

Violet could still hear that gentle laugh echoing in the caverns of her mind. Her mother's love rose up and encircled her all over again.

If this were two years ago, Violet realized, the Intercept would have been whirling and churning at this point, registering the intense memory—the one with peanut butter and a mother's love. Then later, if Violet broke the law, the memory would quickly be sent back into her brain. Because this kind of moment—sweet and joyous and gone forever—could bring you to your knees.

But the Intercept was gone.

"Would you like something to eat?" Charlotte asked.

Violet shook her head. She'd finally managed to stop staring at Jeff's plate. No wonder her client had the wrong idea. "I'm good."

"Well, then," Charlotte said. "Let's sit down. I'm glad you could come by. I heard about the explosion. I'm so relieved you and your assistant weren't hurt." As soon as they had settled around the table, she pulled a note from her pocket. It had been crumpled at one point, as if someone had tried to throw it away and smoothed back out again.

"Naturally, the police searched Amelia's room," Charlotte said. "They didn't find anything. But this morning I was doing the laundry. I came across Amelia's jeans in the hamper. And in the pocket, I found . . . this."

Violet was aware of a sudden sinking feeling. If this was a suicide note, then the case was over. Charlotte would dismiss her. And to her surprise, Violet realized that her disappointment wasn't just about the loss of revenue. It was about Amelia herself; she didn't want to believe that the young woman had been responsible for her own death.

"I think Amelia intended to throw it away," Charlotte continued, "but she couldn't. She knew it might be important. But she also wanted it out of her sight." The woman took a deep breath. "It's a page from her journal. She had ripped it out. It's from last week." She handed it to Violet.

It's not my fault. I've tried and tried to explain that. But I just can't make any progress. It's not about me at all. I had nothing to do with it.

"And this is definitely Amelia's handwriting?" Violet asked.

"Oh, yes. She didn't want to keep a digital journal. She liked the old-fashioned kind. This page is from the one I bought for her right after her father died. She needed to write down her feelings. Losing her dad was very, very hard." Charlotte reached over and tucked a cloud of Jeff's frizzy hair behind his ear. He didn't react at all. "It was hard for all of us, of course. Right, Jeff?"

The boy nodded slowly. Eyes still on the peanut butter.

Violet said, "Any idea what she's talking about in this note?

When she says, 'It's not my fault'? And who is she trying to explain it to?"

"No clue." Charlotte was still watching Jeff. She nudged the plate closer to him. "Sweetie? Aren't you hungry? You hardly ate any dinner."

He shook his head.

"Clearly," Violet said, "someone was bothering your daughter. I wonder why she didn't want to share it. You two were close, right?"

"We talked all the time," Charlotte said. "Amelia knew she could tell me anything."

Jeff had made a small noise. Violet thought it was a hiccough, or a burp, but then he repeated it.

"What?" Charlotte said.

He murmured the word again: *Scared.*

His mother leaned closer to him. "Jeff, what are you saying? If you know something about what your sister was going through, I hope you will—"

He jumped up from his chair, knocking it over behind him. His voice was husky. "She was scared, okay? She was really, really scared." He was breathing hard and fast, and when Charlotte tried to reach out and pull him closer, he squirmed away. "She didn't want anybody to know. But I caught her crying one day. I asked her what was wrong. She said, 'You wouldn't understand.' I'd never seen her scared before. She was brave, okay? Really brave. Like Amelia Earhart."

Charlotte reached out and took Jeff's hand. She held it, and with her eyes she coaxed him to sit down again. Finally, he did.

"Yes," Charlotte said in a low, soothing voice. "She really was brave. Just like Amelia Earhart." She turned to Violet. "It was my husband's idea to name her *Amelia*. He wanted her to have a bond with all the strong women who had lived before her, back on Old Earth."

Jeff had settled down. Violet wanted to get more information from him and figured it was okay to do so.

"Any idea who she was scared of? Even a guess?"

He shook his head.

"Okay," Violet said. "Were there any changes in her behavior? In her daily routine?"

Another negative head shake.

Violet was running out of ideas. "Jonetta checked her console," she said, turning back to Charlotte. "The only calls Amelia made or received for the past few months were from the list you gave us—her friends and teachers. And you and Jeff. No unknown callers."

"So whoever was frightening her must have been someone she already knew and saw in person," Charlotte said. "But who?"

Restless, Charlotte abruptly rose from her chair. She paced back and forth. "New Earth wasn't supposed to be like this. It was supposed to be a safe place. But if something like *this* could happen..."

The unfinished sentence hung in the air, menacing and mournful.

Olde Earth World

Violet was astonished. Totally, utterly astonished.

She knew Rez was good with computers, but this was . . . this was *way* beyond talent. And way beyond computers.

This was *art*.

Rez had sent the sketches to her console very early the next morning, when it was still dark outside. Violet knew the exact moment when the message arrived, even though her console was on vibrate, because she was already awake.

An hour ago, she'd finally given up on sleep. All night long, she had thrashed and flailed, her dreams infused with the terrible image of children plunging into bottomless chasms, their screams bouncing against the sides. After one last appalling dream, Violet stopped chasing after sleep; she lay in bed, staring at a ceiling she couldn't see. Part of the sheet was wound around her torso, and another part was bunched behind her knees. A third part was looped around her right foot.

Maybe I'll never get out of bed again. Yeah, I'll just stay right

*here until I starve to death, and they'll find my rotting corpse
and the smell will be so gross that—*

Her console made no sound, but a muted orange jewel rose
an inch from the screen. She retrieved it from her bedside table.
An auxiliary jewel—it was a sort of azure—was attached to
the main one. She touched it.

And there it was.

Violet felt a tingling in her fingertips—the same tingling she
had felt, two long years ago, when she was first falling in love.
The same tingling she still felt when she looked at one of
Shura's paintings.

The tingling made her feel *life*—her own life, and the life
of the world around her, the earnest flow and the constant
turnings—lifting up inside her like a private sunrise.

For the moment, she didn't mind all the crap that was going
on. She didn't mind the weirdness with Kendall. She didn't
mind the fact that she couldn't figure out the meaning of the
page from Amelia Bainbridge's journal. She didn't mind the fact
that she still didn't know what linked the suicides. Or the fact
that she'd just spent two sleepless hours obsessing over who
might be trying to bring back the Intercept.

All she cared about was the sketch that shimmered just
above her console screen, a three-dimensional holographic
image so gorgeous that it gave her goose bumps.

It was a rendering of the roller coaster Rez dreamed of building. But it wasn't like any roller coaster Violet had ever seen
before. Even though it was not a video, the picture seemed to
move. The sides were made of crisscrossing steel beams that
made the track undulate like a dark sinuous eel, curving up to
a bucking crescendo and then suddenly breaking off, leaving
only a steep drop and a fierce sweep of pure mystery. The
coaster track dissolved into the horizon . . .

. . . and then—*whoosh!*—it abruptly split from that same horizon, diving and turning in an elegant tangle of angled steel and twisted iron, swimming in and out of the horizon's powdery smudge of light and diminishing landscape.

There were no cars on this coaster track. Those would come later. For now, it was a track, a pathway, a direction, an idea; it was a swooping staircase that steadily escalated toward the unfolding promise of tomorrow.

By now, she was sitting up in bed. She couldn't take her eyes off the screen.

Her console chirped. Rez was phoning. He had to know if she'd seen the coaster.

"I didn't wake you up, did I?" he said. The sketch whisked away, replaced by an image of his somber face and dark glittering eyes. He looked tired but happy. He'd clearly been working long and hard on his plans for Olde Earth World. "I set it to go into your Storage Jewel if you didn't acknowledge the signal. So you'd get it later."

"I'm awake."

"Good. So what do you think?"

"I think . . . I think it's *the best thing ever*," Violet said. Not very specific, but she couldn't come up with anything else. She had to let him know how much she loved the coaster, but the right words seemed just out of reach. "I guess I thought it would be more like a regular sketch. Just pencil lines. Without all the color and light and . . . and imagination." Her breathing was returning to normal. "It's absolutely *great*, Rez. How did you—"

"Hang on." The screen went gray for a second, and when the image resolved itself, Rez wasn't alone anymore. Shura stood beside him. "She helped," he said, pointing at Shura.

Violet was surprised, but this time, the surprise included a

crease of annoyance. Shura hadn't said a word about going to
Old Earth. They didn't send console messages back and forth
every hour or so like they used to do, but if her best friend was
working on a project with Rez, well, *naturally* she'd expect to
get a heads-up about it.

"Hey, girl," Shura said.

"Hey. So—you and Rez."

Truth was, Violet realized, she should have known Shura
was involved, from the moment she saw the picture. Those colors, the way they zipped and blended—that was pure Shura.
Choosing between art and medicine had been the most important decision of Shura's life. Violet understood why her friend
had decided to become a doctor, but she still mourned the loss
of the paintings that would never be. Shura was that good.

Shura shrugged. "Sort of. I had to be down here for a few
days, anyway, for my research on viruses. I ran into Rez. He told
me his idea. I think it's pretty cool. Oh, and I heard about the
trigger-trap. Glad you're okay."

"Yeah," Violet said. "I'm totally fine."

Some other feeling was pulling at her. She couldn't name it.
Well, maybe she could, but it didn't make any sense.

Was it possible that she was—and here Violet wanted to
scoff at the very thought—*jealous* of Shura? Because Shura was
spending time with Rez?

Oh, come on. Get a grip.

Rez leaned his head into the console picture again. "I've got
tons more sketches to show you, Violet. The Ferris wheel is
going to be amazing. And there's a hoverboard ride around the
melting ice caps and a ride that goes through areas made un-
inhabitable by radioactive wastes—I'm inventing a sealed-off
car, so it's perfectly safe—and there's a—"

"Okay, Rez. Okay."

"Just wanted you to understand the scope of this," he said. "Now that I can do quantum computing, it's all going to come together very fast."

"Speaking of fast," Shura said, "I have to get going. I left some experiments running in my lab."

"Okay," Violet said. "See you around." Neutral voice.

"Yeah. See you around." Shura's image vanished from Violet's console.

Rez had moved over so that his face would occupy more of the screen. "You really like it?" he asked.

Violet had never seen him so curious about anybody's reaction to what he created. Usually Rez didn't care what you thought. He did what he did.

"It looks fantastic," Violet said.

He beamed with pleasure. She'd never seen Rez beam before. Another change.

"As long as I have something to work on," he said, "I think I'll be able to stand it. My parole. At first, I wasn't sure. When I thought about how much time I had left, I got so upset that I—"

He didn't finish his sentence. Violet was sort of glad he didn't; it was hard to see her friend in emotional distress.

"Anyway," Rez said, moving on, "it's easier now. I have Olde Earth World to design."

"One question."

"Okay."

"I know these rides are cool, Rez, but it's still Old Earth. I mean, it's still a pretty gross place, right? Depressing? And violent? Are people really going to enjoy rides that take them through polluted oceans and across melting ice caps? Won't they be too freaked out to have fun?"

He didn't look upset by the question, as Violet feared he

might. He nodded tboughtfully. He even gave her a hint of a smile—again, a very un-Rez-like thing to do.

"I worried about that, too," he said. "And then I found this quotation from an Old Earth writer. His name was Oscar Wilde. He said, 'It was like feasting with panthers; the danger was half the excitement.' That's what I think about Olde Earth World—the danger is half the excitement."

It made sense in a funny, twisted, Rez-like way. "Maybe it'll work," she said. "And no matter what, that coaster's going to be gorgeous."

She had another question for him. If he hadn't called her today, she was going to call him; she had to know the answer. Kendall hadn't asked him yet about the Intercept; if he had, Rez would have already told her about it.

"Hey," she said, using her best fake-casual voice. "Remember when you told me it looked like somebody might be trying to get the Intercept up and running again?"

"Yeah."

"Any more signs of that?"

"Nope."

Relief. Violet started to sign off. Maybe she'd get a few hours of sleep after all.

"But," Rez added, "I haven't checked in a day or so. Now that I can do quantum computing, I don't have to use a back channel anymore. The old one where nobody goes unless they have to. It's like a dirt road. After somebody puts down a nice, shiny, new one, you don't use the crummy one."

So he hadn't kept tabs. It might still be happening. Violet's relief was replaced by anxiety. Or rather *re*-replaced.

"If somebody *was* trying to restore the Intercept," Violet said, "how technologically savvy would they have to be?"

"Very."

"Meaning . . . ?"

"Meaning that anybody below the genius level would be out of luck."

The relief came back again. Her dad once showed her a video of him playing a game called Ping-Pong. Her sudden mood swings felt like the little white ball, zinging back and forth over a net.

"Okay, great," she said.

"But."

"But?"

"But if somebody *was* trying to fire up the Intercept again, it would be hard to tell. Once they cracked the outer shell of the code, the rest of the operation wouldn't leave any traces. It was the initial breach that caught my attention."

Her mood slumped once again. Violet wasn't sure how much more emotional ping-ponging she could take.

"Okay," she said.

Time for truth. She had to ask him a serious, important question—the second-most serious, important question she had ever asked him. The first was two years ago, when she'd had to ask him if he had hacked her father's Intercept file. The answer was yes.

Now she had to do it again—ask a question that she really didn't want the answer to. But she had to do it. She needed to put all of her energy into investigating Amelia Bainbridge's death, and the deaths of the other three, and as long as this Intercept business was hanging out there, she was distracted. She couldn't do her job.

She had to know.

"Rez," she said.

"Yeah."

"Is it you?"

"Is it me what?"

"Are you the one who's trying to get the Intercept up and running again?"

His image on the screen changed. Now he was peering at her the way he might look at a peculiar insect that had survived Old Earth radiation but grown an extra head and four hundred new legs in the process. At first, he seemed incredulous, then half-amused, then upset. "Why would you think that—"

"Because you told me about it in the first place. Which would be a perfect way to deflect suspicion from yourself. And because you're a genius with computers. You'd be capable of doing this, unlike just about everybody else on New or Old Earth. And because—"

"Because why?"

Because you were in love with me once, and I didn't love you back, and so you did something sneaky and mean to retaliate— and maybe you're still in love with me. Maybe this is just another way to get back at me.

Bringing the Intercept back to life.

Another voice in her head pushed back.

So if Rez did it, then how did he get the pages? The ones that Kendall has been keeping under lock and key? The ones he'd need to get a new Intercept off the ground? How? Rez can't leave Old Earth. It's a condition of his parole.

All she said out loud was this: "I don't know. That's why I'm asking. And I'm hoping you'll be straight up with me. Because we're friends."

The face on Violet's console screen was deadly serious.

"The truth," Rez said in a slow, measured voice, as if he wanted to make damned sure she understood him, "is that I wouldn't bring it back even if I *did* know how to do it. But I don't. I swear, Violet. It's not me."

She believed him.

"Okay," she said. "Just so you know, though, Kendall's going to be asking you about it, too."

"Why? Wait—it's obvious." In a bitter voice, Rez went on. "He's trying to get me into trouble again, right? It's like he thinks there's only room for one genius at a time."

"That's not fair, Rez. He got you the approval to do quantum computing."

"Yeah, whatever." He signed off.

Violet jumped out of bed and started getting dressed. All at once, she was feeling pretty good. Better, at least, than she'd felt for days. Now that she knew who *wasn't* trying to revive the Intercept, she could start to figure out who *was*. Or maybe she wouldn't have to. Maybe the culprit had backed off. Gone back into hiding. And now she was free to focus on her case—the one she was actually being *paid* to work on. Jonetta was making some real headway. And Violet was thrilled that Rez's ideas for Old Earth were soaring. Olde Earth World was going to be a real thing. Not even the petty feud between the two men in her life could dent her good mood.

She was marginally hopeful again. Faintly optimistic.

Which was why, when the terrible thing happened the very next day, it hit Violet so hard. Hope had softened her up, encouraged her to lower her natural defenses. She had made herself utterly vulnerable.

And so her heartbreak was even greater.

A Last Glimpse

I t felt like a . . . well, it felt like a *twitch*.

The briefest flicker, located behind her right eyeball.

Twitch.

Just plain weird.

Delia opened her front door. Maybe some fresh air would help. She waved at a young woman walking by on the other side of the street. The woman didn't wave back, but the snub couldn't affect Delia's good mood. Because the morning felt freshly rinsed and clean, just as most mornings on New Earth did.

She missed sitting outside. She had done that frequently on Old Earth, even if it meant plopping down in the dirt. The air back there might smell foul and the horizon might be awash in smoke and flame, but Delia didn't care about any of that. She liked the outdoors. She liked the feel of the sun on her skin.

Here on New Earth, however, sitting in the dirt was not an option. For one thing, all she had was this tiny, sparkling-green lawn. No dirt in sight.

She closed the door.

Tin Man was still asleep. She had passed his room when she walked toward the kitchen, pulling his door shut so that he could get his rest. He never came home before three or four A.M. and often slept until just before dinnertime, when he would rise and start the ritual over again: leave for work in the evening, work until the wee hours, and then return home to sling his tired body into bed for a long, restorative slug of sleep.

Her son was eighteen now. A grown man. Living with his mom wasn't the ideal situation—Delia had no illusions about that—but for now, he had no choice. He didn't have enough money to live on his own. Frankly, she loved having her son around.

Twitch.

She frowned. She'd had a good night's sleep, so this weird squirmy thing in her head didn't make any sense. Maybe she needed more coffee. In the kitchen, she stood by the small window while she drank another cup. She loved looking at the distant hills from this window.

Twitch.

Molly had loved hills.

Delia's hand flew to her forehead. *Whoa*, she thought. *Where did* that *come from?*

It was true, though. Nobody loved running up and down hills more than her daughter, Molly. Hills were her favorite, but mostly she'd had to run through ugly alleys stacked with garbage and stewing with rats that were almost as big as she was. Hills were a special treat. And yet Molly loved to run, no matter where she was.

But why was Delia thinking about Molly now? She took great pains *not* to think about her, except under carefully controlled circumstances. Otherwise, she simply got too sad. Mind-numbingly sad. Darkly, deeply depressed. Sometimes, as a precaution, Delia temporarily took down Molly's portrait in the living room. There were days when the picture was too much. It made the loss too real. So she had to be careful. She had to ration the amount of Molly-memory she released into her thoughts.

Twitch.

Twitch.

With every twitch—and by now Delia believed that *twitch* was the perfect word for what she was feeling, for that funny crinkly thing that kept happening behind her eyes—the picture of Molly in her brain became clearer, more detailed, than even Shura's wonderful portrait. The colors popped: Molly's yellow hair, blue eyes, raspberry-pink cheeks.

Twitch.

Her little girl was gone. She'd never see her again. No matter what else happened in Delia's life, the one thing that would not happen, that *could* not happen, was seeing her daughter even one more time.

Not even once.

She wanted to . . . to *scream*. Yes. That was it. Delia wanted to throw back her head and let out a long animal howl, because she missed her little girl so much.

She wanted to let it out.

But she was *already* screaming. The screaming had started inside her head—inside the twitch, really—and by now it was a giant vortex of accelerating sound, rising, climbing, widening out.

Delia dropped her coffee cup. It shattered against the tile floor. She swayed back and forth, grabbing the edge of the counter to try to steady herself.

The scream was louder now.

Molly was gone, gone forever, and there was a hollowness

at the heart of the world, a great empty cave through which ancient winds rushed and sighed with nothing to get in their
way.

I'll never see her again. My Molly. My child.

Frantic, feeling her soul fill up with grief and pain, Delia
yanked open the drawer in which she kept the utensils. She
pawed madly through the contents: spatula, slotted spoon, ice
cream scoop—*there*. Yes. There it was.

The knife.

She pulled it out by its hard black handle. The screaming
was so loud now that it was drowning out everything, destroying it all—not only the thoughts in her head but the pictures,
too. The screaming was shattering the pictures, raking them
off the walls of her mind, ripping them apart. And that was *exactly* what Delia wanted, what Delia needed; those pictures
must be *eliminated*. Molly running, Molly laughing—she had
to cut those pictures out of her memory, out of her body itself.
Or else she would die from sadness.

And that was why Delia had to do it.

She had to get rid of the pictures. And if she got rid of the
pictures, she could get rid of the screaming.

*So much pain. Molly died in pain. I couldn't help her. She
looked at me—asking me with her eyes to relieve her pain—and
I couldn't.*

Delia was small, but she was strong. Old Earth had made her
strong.

*My little girl—suffering. Suffering like no one has ever suffered
before.*

Delia jammed the knife at the point on her left wrist where
the vessels seemed plump and ready, fat with blood, and then
she pulled the knife out again with a fierce jerk and she plunged

it right back in again. This time, she dragged it back all the way to her elbow.

The pain was vast and tremendous. She smiled.

The screaming subsided, and one word emerged, like the lone survivor of a shipwreck.

Molly.

Epiphany

Violet could not understand a word Tin Man was saying. She tried adjusting the clarity enhancer on her console—he had called her on an audio channel, with no video feed—but it didn't work. His agitation caused the words to come across as one long, anguished sentence in which sounds slid and bobbed and stretched and banged against each other, making no sense.

FoundherbloodydeadOhGodOhGodOh

"Slow down," she urged him. "Please. I can't—"

Someone else's voice took over. Tin Man must have handed off his console. The woman's voice was crisp.

"This is Captain Marlene Bowers of New Earth Security Service. Mr. Tolliver is being taken care of. He is experiencing considerable emotional distress. Would you be able to come over to the Tolliver home?"

"What's going on?" Violet said. She'd been having lunch at her desk while she reviewed the Bainbridge case, double-checking what she'd learned from Charlotte Bainbridge. She jumped to her feet. "What's happening? Where's Delia?"

"As I said, ma'am, Mr. Tolliver is—"

"*Ma'am?*" Violet shot back in an incredulous voice. No one called her *ma'am*. She was eighteen years old, for God's sake.

And then Violet realized that what some cop called her during a brief console call could be safely filed under Things That Don't Matter Right Now Because My Friend Is In Trouble.

"Sorry," Violet said. "Just tell him I'm on my way. I'll get there as fast as I can."

But it didn't matter.

It didn't matter how fast she traveled. As she was to discover, it wouldn't have mattered if she had gotten there in ten seconds or ten minutes or ten years. By the time Violet arrived at the little cottage, it had been over for some time.

Two ReadyRobs were carrying Delia's sheet-covered body out on a stretcher. Tin Man followed behind, stumbling and shaking, reaching out his hands, and sobbing so hard that his breathing had become a harsh rattle.

"Violet!" he cried out when he saw her. "Violet! I found her in the kitchen . . . she . . . she had . . . How could she . . ."

He staggered, nearly falling to the ground. Violet helped prop him up. Tin Man was much heavier than she was, but somehow she was able to keep him standing, staving off total collapse. Then she embraced him. Violet forgot about being a bad hugger and she held him, letting him weep, feeling his big body shudder.

The ReadyRobs finished loading the stretcher in the van. When they closed and latched the doors and signaled to the driver that it was time to pull away, Tin Man let out a howl so immense that Violet was afraid he was losing his mind. He let her lead him back inside the house. She guided him to a seat on the couch.

"What happened?" she asked quietly. She sat down beside him, keeping a hand on his arm. It was the only thing she could think of to do.

"I was *sleeping*. I can't believe I was . . . I was *sleeping*, Violet! My mother was in such emotional agony, and I was *asleep*. I'm so mad at myself. I'll never—" Tin Man pulled his wrist across his mouth to clear away the spit. "I'll never forgive myself. She'd used a knife to . . . to *cut* herself. Over and over again. Her wrist, her arm. By the time I found her, she was bleeding to death. *No*—she'd already bled to death. She was—" A storm of weeping forced Tin Man to stop his story.

"Was she upset about something?" Violet said. "Extra-upset, I mean?" She added the qualifier because Delia had once told her that anybody who hailed from Old Earth was always sad. Sadness was the baseline. Sadness was a given in that broken, harrowing place, and even coming to New Earth couldn't ever quite displace it. Delia had prided herself on keeping her own sadness at a manageable level, deflecting it with smart-ass jokes and a jaunty attitude. She didn't want her sadness to get out of hand. Part of that, she said, was sheer angry defiance; she never wanted to give the Intercept the satisfaction of an intense feeling.

"No," Tin Man replied, roaring the word. "No, no, no. She seemed . . . she was *fine*, Violet. She was looking forward to so much. She was happier than she'd been in a long time. She was just starting to enjoy life on New Earth." He put his face in his hands. Then he raised it again. "I *know* she was happy," he went on. "I know it for a fact. Because I called her just after midnight. From work. If I'd only known that it was the last time I would ever—" He shook his head. He had to go on. "I needed to tell her I was going to be late. There was a private party at Redshift and they wanted extra security. We only talked for a few minutes, but I told her something else, too.

"I told her I'd made up my mind. I was leaving the club. Coming to work for you. And she was *thrilled*, Violet. Totally thrilled." He uttered a low, puzzled moan. "So when did she decide she didn't want to live anymore? How would such an idea even occur to her?"

Violet listened. As she listened, a dark suspicion stirred in her mind.

She didn't want to think it. She was afraid to think it.

But it made sense. It was the only thing that *did* make sense.

She swallowed hard. She let a few seconds go by.

Was she sure? She shouldn't say it if she wasn't sure.

First, she needed to ask him a question. "Did Delia ever remove her Intercept chip?"

"What? No, she tried once—we all tried—but it didn't work. You saw the scar. The infection almost killed her."

Okay, then. *Yes*, Violet thought. *I'm sure.*

"The idea didn't just pop up in her mind," Violet said, choosing her words carefully. "The idea was *inserted* there. Deliberately." The same way a terrible idea had been slotted in the minds of Amelia Bainbridge and Wendell Prokop and the Wilton twins.

Violet had been working under the assumption that these were two separate investigations: the suicides that might not be suicides at all—and the possible revival of the Intercept.

But now she knew. They were linked. They *had* to be linked.

Someone had found the perfect way to make despondency blossom in someone's mind. To make death desirable. To make it seem like sweet relief.

Only one device ever created could force its way into

people's brains that way, jamming their synapses with vivid memories, lurid visions, devastating emotions.

Only one device could commandeer thoughts so that they would attack the thinker herself.

Only one device could turn your own feelings into a weapon and then use that weapon against you.

Only one.

It was terrifyingly clear.

The Intercept was back.

But how?

PART TWO

23

Gray Area

The color was astonishing. Each time Violet came down here, it was like she was seeing Old Earth for the first time. It was a gray beyond the outermost concept of gray; it was the gray of ash and dusk and dirt and old metal and abandonment. The gray of lost hope and disenchantment. Of regret and despair.

She stood at the edge of a great, ruined city.

Into the pilot drive of the self-service ferry from Thirlsome she had punched the coordinates that Rez had given her, and the craft had deposited her here, after a quick but scary ride across a sludge-crusted bay that glowered with a sullen radioactive orange.

Stepping out of the ferry, she reset her console to OET: Old Earth Time. Her console would do it automatically, of course, but Violet liked to do it manually. Somehow that small gesture helped her to reorient herself to this place, to adjust to the grim new reality. Things were still done by hand on Old Earth. The primitive ruled. Resetting her console lessened the sensory whiplash that came when she traveled from New Earth to Old Earth, from a world of golden promise to . . . what festered in front of her right now.

A world of endless gray.

This was how Violet had decided to handle her grief over Delia's death: By getting busy. By going down to Old Earth. By doing her job.

She had spent the previous day sitting in her office, staring at the wall. The damage done to that wall by the trigger-trap explosion had been repaired, and there was a funny shadow in one spot where the new plaster blended with the old. Violet's eyes stayed on that seam. Hour after hour.

She didn't eat. She didn't drink. She didn't answer her console. She had no recollection of getting up and going to the bathroom, although she must have.

She just stared.

She remembered Delia's saucy laugh. And Delia's red bandana. And Delia's frisky dark curls. And Delia's tea bag. She remembered the brave and funny and feisty and sometimes crude and rude and ornery—but when it came to Violet, always, *always* kind and loving—woman from Old Earth.

Delia Tolliver. Gone. Just . . . gone. Absent forever from the rest of Violet's life.

Delia's death was sparking the second-worst emotional pain Violet had ever endured. The first came when her mother died nine years ago. At the time, Violet believed that no pain henceforth could ever be so bad—so searing, so overwhelming. It was a pain that seemed to blot out the world. It made everything dark, like a permanent solar eclipse.

And she was right. Nothing else ever *would* be that bad. But now something was coming damned close: Delia's death. The anguish she was feeling was only marginally less horrible. Delia Tolliver had been a second mother to her.

So now she had lost two mothers.

The Long Stare had lasted the whole day. Jonetta didn't try to cheer her up, which Violet deeply appreciated. Somehow her assistant sensed that empty words—and they were all empty now, because they couldn't bring back Delia—would make things worse, not better, even if they were uttered with good intentions. Jonetta had kept her distance, only offering her coffee once, and when Violet shook her head to refuse it, she never offered again. Jonetta returned to her own desk, working quietly at the computer as the day slouched by.

Then evening had arrived. Violet suddenly jumped up from her chair. She needed to *work*. She needed to solve her case. She needed to be in motion. It was the only antidote to this sorrow.

She had turned and looked out the window at New Earth, at the beautiful dusk that the Color Corps concocted for that day. The sky was a deep violet shade. She remembered the moment when she was six years old and she'd asked her mother why they had named her Violet. Her mother said, "Because it's my favorite color. It's the color of the sky right before the sky goes to sleep, and it's already dreaming about the next day."

Dreaming about the next day: *Yes*. Rest was good, rest was necessary—but you should always be planning ahead.

That was the lesson Violet had taken from her mother's answer. Not when she was six, of course, but later, once she was grown up, once she'd been through all the pain and the heartache of losing her. Cry when you must, grieve as long as you need to, but then get to work. Violet is the color of dusk, but it's also the color of tomorrow.

She had to find out who had killed Delia and the others—and how that person had revived the Intercept in order to do it.

So that night, after the long hours of brooding and staring, brooding and staring, Violet had finally switched on the lights. She called Jonetta into her office. Her assistant stood in front of her desk.

"Okay," Violet said. "The suicides. How's the investigation coming along?"

Jonetta didn't say, "Are you okay?" or "What happened?" or anything of the sort. She nodded and then tapped the series of jewels that would bring up her console notes, as if it were the most natural thing in the world to be ignored for an entire day and then summoned to discuss a case as if nothing at all was amiss.

"Obviously, my theory was wrong," Jonetta said. "The killer's not just targeting young people. Delia's death breaks the pattern."

"Right. So what's next?"

Jonetta flipped to another section of her console notes.

"I sent you more information about Amelia's dad and the accident that killed him. Plus more information about the Wilton twins' parents. And Arianna Prokop. Just trying to find a link—*any* link—between the deaths. And—"

"Book me on a transport pod," Violet said, interrupting her. "I'm going to Old Earth."

"Why in the world do you need to go to—"

"I'm going to Old Earth."

Violet had made her decision in an instant. She'd solve the case in her own way. She would honor Delia's memory by following her instincts—a very Delia-like thing to do—no matter what anybody else thought about it.

And for Violet Crowley, all roads led to Old Earth.

Rez was waiting for her. Violet hadn't seen him right away, but when she turned to take in her surroundings, he appeared: Rez, her friend and former colleague, walking solemnly in her direction. He looked so . . . so totally Rez-like, by which she meant scruffy and preoccupied.

Behind him, the broken-off tops of bombed-out buildings regularly exhaled oily black gusts of smoke. The buildings had been smoldering for years, like tire fires. There was no one to put them out, once and for all. They had been burning ever since the Second Mineral War, when the bombs dropped from the sky in vicious multitudes, igniting the chain nuclear reactions that destroyed people and cities and landscapes and the last shreds of hope that civilization would come to its senses.

"Hey," Violet said.

"Hey."

He was glad to see her—at least that was the vibe she got, and with Rez, you had to go by the vibe. His greetings were never effusive.

"How was the ride in?" Rez asked.

He knew how the ride was because the ride was always the same. Rocky. Risky. Painful. Even misery-inducing. The few pods left in service were flimsy and shopworn, prone to a violent quaking as they dropped from New Earth's sweet manufactured atmosphere to the stale air of Old Earth. And the ferry from Thirlsome was ancient and even creakier than the pod. Kendall had once wisecracked that the ferry covered more distance rolling side to side than it did lurching forward. A lot of first-time riders ended up puking over the side—which didn't much matter, because the bay was already a stinking, soupy, goopy, polluted mess.

"It was fine," Violet said.

So if Rez knew how the ride was—and he did—why was he making small talk? Rez didn't do small talk. His typical behavior when he first approached her down here was to blurt out his latest technical dilemma as if he expected her to solve it. Like *that* was ever going to happen.

"Good," he said.

She had told him about Delia's death during the call to arrange this visit. Rez being Rez, he was, Violet knew, trying to figure out what to say to her. He hated clichés like "Sorry for your loss." But if you rejected clichés, you had to come up with something *else* to say. Something original. And for Rez, that was tough.

She waited another few seconds. When Rez didn't add to his "Good" remark, she said, "So can we head for the prison?"

She had to keep moving. If she slowed down, if she paused for any length of time for any reason, the grief would overwhelm her, like a steep gray wave closing over a clumsy swimmer.

And she would drown.

"Sure," Rez said. "Let's go."

Prisoner Number
57681299-17-WZN

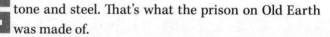tone and steel. That's what the prison on Old Earth was made of.

Wait. There was another ingredient, too, Violet realized.

Stone and steel and loneliness.

The loneliness seeped out of the thick gray walls. She could feel misery and despair, too, sliding off the rocks, but it was the loneliness that struck her. The walls had soaked up many, many years of the total and absolute loneliness of the prisoners they held in their grip. After a while, she surmised, the loneliness would be breathed out again on the other side of these walls, an endless, sorrowful exhalation. Hence they were streaked and slimed with a sticky moisture that was, Violet thought, the liquid equivalent of loneliness.

The mammoth prison had been carved into the belly of an Old Earth mountain. The small, dim cells were identically sized pockets scooped out of the rock, row by row. Prisoners never saw each other. But all through the long nights they surely could sense the vibrations as the mountain shifted and trembled in response to the human activity inside it, the low moans and the sad murmurings, the restless turnings, the nightmares.

This was where Tin Man Tolliver had served his time. And two years ago, this was where the Rebels of Light were taken after being found guilty of criminal conspiracy. The Rebels had opposed the Intercept from the beginning. They had managed to discover an antidote to it, a way of muting its power.

That was why Violet had come here. If anyone could figure out who might be accessing the Intercept again, she thought, it would be a Rebel. They had made a long, careful, and ultimately successful study of how to thwart its power.

She stood in the waiting room, mesmerized by the strange wet walls. The walls that seemed to weep with frustration and despair. The warden, Samantha Chivers, was on her way.

Rez had gone to check in with his parole officer. He had been an inmate here for a year and a half, serving his sentence for conspiracy and treason. He was still required to come to the prison twice a week, so that his parole officer would know where he was and what he was up to. Rez and Violet agreed to meet in the waiting room when they were finished with their respective tasks.

"Miss Crowley."

Chivers was an old woman. At least sixty, Violet guessed. She was petite, black-haired, dressed in a black tunic and black slacks. Her eyes fastened onto Violet's.

"Hey," Violet said.

"Good day," Chivers replied in a curt voice. It felt like a correction, not a greeting, as if Violet's *Hey* had somehow offended her.

I'm off to a great start, Violet thought dismally. *As usual.*

"I hope you will give my regards to your father," Chivers went on, her voice starched and formal. "He and I both endured the Second Mineral War here on Old Earth, back when we were kids. We stayed in touch, and I worked for New Earth Security Service. After I retired, Ogden asked me to do one last thing for him—come down here and whip the prison into shape." She looked around. "Quite the challenge, let me tell you."

"Right," Violet said. She was only as friendly as she had to be, to get what she wanted. She had never heard her father talk about the warden. This was clearly a job that nobody else had wanted.

"Please tell me again which inmate you would like to visit," Chivers said. Her finger was poised over her wrist console, ready to pull up the name and cell number.

"Paul Stark."

Chivers's face slowly rose. Once again, her eyes locked onto Violet's.

"Paul Stark," the warden repeated.

"Yeah."

"Leader of the Rebels of Light. The group that kidnapped your father two years ago."

"Yeah."

"Does President Crowley know that's who you want to see?"

"I didn't discuss it with him. Or ask his permission. I'm here on my own."

Chivers thought about that for a moment. Violet's honesty had apparently surprised her. Maybe she'd been expecting a lie, Violet thought—*Oh, yeah, my dad says it's all good*—which she could then have checked and disproven very easily. The truth was something new and different.

"I suppose I don't see the harm. The prisoner is in"—the warden's eyes dropped to her console again—"Section 3447-A. And in here, he's not 'Paul Stark.' He's Prisoner Number 57681299-17-WZN."

Violet let her inner smart-ass out for a spin. "Catchy," she said. "I'll bet he has a nickname by now. I bet almost nobody says, 'Hey, there, Prisoner Number 57681299-17-WZN! How you doin'?"

Delia would be so *proud of me.*

Chivers ignored her little joke. "I'll take you there myself."

With the warden leading the way, they walked through a twisting series of narrow corridors hacked out of the mountain's cold black heart. There was no conversation. With each turning, Violet felt as if the air were getting thinner, slowly but steadily. She knew this wasn't the case—the prison had an excellent air disbursement and filtration system—but it felt that way, anyway. The low-ceilinged hallway was lit by torches that hung on chains from the stone walls; the torches were placed every few feet, casting weird, gyrating shadows when anyone passed through.

The prison was a hellish maze. It was pierced by sudden tunnels that branched off unexpectedly and *whoops!-look-out* trapdoors and out-of-the-blue staircases chiseled into the walls, leading to unmarked locations.

Behind every iron door there was, Violet knew, a prisoner. And every prisoner had a face and a story. But you wouldn't know that human beings lurked behind those doors unless you were told, because no noise escaped from them. The thickness of the walls made the cells virtually soundproof. The prisoners might have been shouting or screaming or singing or calling for help, but no sound reached the hall. Violet could hear nothing beyond Chivers's breathing and the occasional echo of a guard's footsteps from far down the corridor.

At last they came to Section 3447-A. Two more turns

down two more corridors, and then a right and a left and another right, and there they were, standing in front of a cell. The iron door bore a nameplate inscribed PRISONER NUMBER 57681299-17-WZN.

"I'll send my assistant to take you back when you're ready," Chivers said. "Just text me."

"My console will work down here?"

An amused smile cracked Chivers's grim face. "No. It won't. You'll have to use this." She drew a square, clunky console from the pocket of her tunic and handed it to Violet. An antenna sprouted from the top. Clearly it was a purpose-built device for use within the thick-walled prison. Violet had a fleeting, disturbing notion: If she hadn't asked, would the warden have even told her that regular consoles had no signal capacity inside the mountain? Or would she have let Violet try and try and try to contact her office, to no avail, until finally—maybe a dozen years from now—Chivers sent somebody down to check on her, whereupon they'd find a rat-gnawed corpse? *Poor girl never called*, Chivers would say, explaining how Violet was left to perish under thousands of tons of stone and steel. *We just thought her interview was running long.*

"Okay, thanks," Violet said. No use picking a fight. She was close to her goal now.

Chivers pulled open the cell door.

"You've got a visitor," she called out into the blackness, and then she stepped to one side, letting Violet enter.

Violet felt the rush of chilly air as the cell door was slammed shut behind her. She heard the meaty, solid *ka-thwunk* sound as the bolt was pushed along the oiled groove and rammed home in the socket in the wall. She envisioned Chivers striding away from the cell, heading back down the corridor—but she couldn't hear her footsteps. Outside noises did not exist anymore.

There was no escape now.

She switched on the flashlight app on the console. From a small, exceptionally dark corner of this small, exceptionally dark cell, she saw a figure emerge. He moved slowly, haltingly. He was slightly stooped, and as he approached her, Violet heard the air currents growing louder and stronger, as if they were on a rheostat.

Paul used a HoverUp. He'd been injured many years ago, as a police officer working the streets of Old Earth, when a criminal's slab gun had melted his spinal cord.

"Violet," he said. His voice was weary and flat, but not unwelcoming.

"Hey, Paul."

Now his face was visible as he moved into the tiny circle of light provided by the console. She was shocked but had the good grace not to show it.

Two years had passed since Violet had seen Paul Stark. She knew prison would alter him—but *this* much?

His eyes had sunk so deep in his head that the pupils were only a rumor. He had always worn his graying hair cut very short—he'd been a cop, like Kendall, and every cop she knew favored the bullet-headed look—but now the decision was out of his hands; his hair was gone, leaving a pale, flaking scalp. The rest of his skin was yellowish-brown. His body was thin and frail.

"Nice to see you," he said. With a tease in his voice, he added, "Actually, it's nice to see *anybody*."

Violet smiled. Good to hear him make a joke.

She should have visited before now. She knew that. Paul had fought on behalf of his deepest convictions, and while there was no question he had to be removed from society—he had violated New Earth laws and put many lives in jeopardy, including Ogden Crowley's—his crimes were not motivated by greed or ambition or cruelty or vengeance. He and his fellow Rebels had believed the Intercept was a very bad thing, and they were determined to shut it down.

She and Paul had started out on different sides but ended up on the same side. She admired him. And she knew he admired her, too.

"I need your help," she said.

"Me? Help *you*?" He waved at the stone walls that rose all around him. "My ability to get things done is a little restricted these days. In case you haven't noticed. So if there's anybody around here who needs help—it's me. Not you. Not the proprietor of Crowley & Associates Detective Agency, the pride of New Earth." He smiled. The smile stripped off a bit of the sadness from his face.

"How'd you hear about that?"

"Information is a commodity in this place. Just like candy bars and cigarettes and burner consoles. We're let out of our cells once a month for exercise. That's when the bartering happens. You pay for what you need with whatever you have. And I pay for information. It's what keeps me going. Just some general details about New Earth."

Violet didn't ask how he paid for that information. Better not to know.

"Well, I think you *can* help me," she said. "Maybe a lot." There were no chairs in the cell. Paul stood, but Violet sat down on the cold stone floor. She didn't mind. She was too focused to be aware of any discomfort. "I'm working on a case right now that's got me stumped. Totally stumped. And it's an important one. It could affect the fate of New Earth."

He chuckled. "You never bother with the small stuff, do you, Violet? No runaway dogs or cheating boyfriends for *your* detective agency. No, sir. You skip right on up to the fate-of-New-Earth stuff."

"Call me an overachiever."

"I think I can just call you Ogden Crowley's daughter. Comes to the same thing." Now he, too, became serious, letting the smile die on his face. "Okay. I know you wouldn't have come all this way unless it was pretty damned important. Tell me what's going on. And what—if anything—I can do."

She told him about the suicides. And about how someone might be persuading the victims to take their own lives so that their deaths only *looked* like suicides.

"So how," he said, "do you force people to kill themselves?"

She paused. She knew the answer would hit him hard. "I'm guessing here, but what I *think* you do is put ideas in their heads. Visions. Memories. Bad ones. Ones they can't live with. Somehow the pictures are getting into their heads. And words. Words that sap all the life force from them. According to some written notes at the death scenes, it's like a . . . a screaming." She took a deep breath. "And we both know what kind of device would be able to implant a screaming in the mind."

His face changed. It had had very little color to begin with, and now even that scant bit drained away. "No." A choked whisper instead of a word.

"Yeah. Yeah, I think so."

"But the Intercept was *destroyed*. You destroyed it—you and Kendall Mayhew. Protocol Hall, the entire computer infrastructure—you blew it up. It's *gone*, Violet. It doesn't exist anymore."

"Wishful thinking, as it turns out."

He shook his head.

"Can it really be true?" he said. "The Intercept . . . is *back*?"

"The evidence sure points that way."

Now his incredulity turned into agitation. "But how could somebody just—*wait*. Hold on." He waved a bony hand in front of his eyes, like someone clearing a dirty windshield. "Never mind *how* it found its way back into operation. No time for that now. What can I do to help you fight it? Get rid of it again?"

"I can't totally dismiss the *how*. I've got to figure out who revived it. That may be the key to shutting it down for the second time. That's why I wanted to talk to you. When you were running the Rebels of Light, I know you tried everything you could think of to get rid of the Intercept. Violence didn't come into the picture until you had exhausted every other avenue."

"So you read the statement I made at my trial."

Violet frowned. "Of course I did, Paul. I followed the proceedings every day. The title of your manifesto is how it went from being known as *the Intercept* to *the Dark Intercept*. You renamed it. And you and your group almost cost my father his life."

"I never meant to—"

"Forget it," she said, cutting him off. "That's over and done with. And you're serving your time. I brought it up because in the early days, when you had just formed the Rebels, you told the court that you tried to find somebody who understood the Intercept well enough to fight it."

"That's right. A genius who'd be the equal of Kendall Mayhew—someone who could, in effect, undo what he'd done." He snapped his fingers. "I get it. You're thinking that if somebody could *un*ravel it, then maybe they could—well, *ravel* it. From scratch."

"Yeah. So who'd you find?"

He shook his head. "Nobody, Violet. I'm sorry, but the answer is *nobody*. We got lucky when we discovered the drug that would make people immune to it for short periods of time.

But that's what it was—luck." He moved restlessly around the small cell. Violet was tempted to call it *pacing*, but it really wasn't; it was a sort of slouchy lurch, the same style of movement that everyone in a HoverUp tended to use. "Now, the truth is," Paul added, "plenty of people might be able to build it from Kendall's notebook. If they had the formulas, the schematics, the computer coding—yeah, okay. Sure. That's paint-by-numbers stuff. But to rebuild the Intercept from the ground up? Without instructions? Nope. No way. Now, if your killer had Kendall's notes, he would have a chance. But that's impossible because you and Kendall destroyed every last particle of it. Right?"

Violet didn't answer. She was remembering the day two years ago when she and Kendall set the detonator, dumped Kendall's notes on the floor of Protocol Hall, and then raced down the steps of the immense glass-walled tower, searching for a safe place to ride out the blast, the one that would destroy the Intercept forever—and along with it, any possibility of ever rebuilding it.

And then, at the last minute, she had whirled around, run back inside, grabbed some pages scattered across the floor, and . . .

"Right, Violet?" Paul said.

"What? Oh, right. Absolutely."

"Okay, then. Nobody on New Earth—or Old Earth, for that matter—could re-create the Intercept without a template," Paul concluded. "Not your buddy Steve Reznik, as smart as he is. Not even Kendall Mayhew could reproduce all of his work, most likely, without the original diagrams to go by. The Intercept is a once-in-a-lifetime creation." He frowned. "So how *is* somebody doing it? The schematics were destroyed. And just as puzzling—*why* is somebody doing it? Why harm those particular people?"

"That's what I've got to find out."

"You're looking for a deranged killer who also has the technical ability to rig up a new Intercept. With nothing to go on."

She nodded, but that wasn't quite accurate. The killer might very well have something to go on.

The thought dug at Violet's conscience.

"Hey," Paul said. "Can I change the subject for a minute?"

"Sure."

He looked around, embarrassed. "I don't know how to ask this, but . . . do you ever hear anything about Michelle? I've never even seen her. Not once. I've sent her messages over the years, whenever the warden lets me, but Michelle . . . won't answer."

Michelle Callahan was his wife. She had also been the police chief on New Earth, back when the Rebels were trying to take down the Intercept. In the midst of an epic battle, she, too, had disobeyed the authorities of New Earth. She was serving her sentence in this very same prison.

"No," Violet said. "I'm sorry. I don't know anything about her."

He didn't speak for a time. The jets of his HoverUp made a *whish-whoosh, whish-whoosh* sound.

"I miss her," he said. "In spite of everything she did to me, I miss her. I always will."

Violet nodded as if she were thinking about Paul and Michelle, but she really wasn't. She was thinking about secrets. Right now, the weight of her worst secret—the one she shared with Kendall—was pressing down on her with a force that rivaled all the stones in this mountain prison combined.

Rez stood in the waiting room. He was reading a long article on his console about the harvesting and repurposing of neutrinos. Violet knew the topic because he launched into the technical details the moment she appeared—and he didn't take a breath until she held up her hand like a stop sign.

"How'd it go with your parole officer?" she asked.

"He's pretty bored by Olde Earth World. But I don't care. I'm just supposed to keep him in the loop. And that's done. Now we can go look at the progress I've made on the Riptide Ride."

"The what?"

He grinned. Violet couldn't ever recall seeing Reznik grin before. Smile, yes; smirk, absolutely. But grin? A grin was a sign of an easygoing joy. There was nothing easygoing about Steve Reznik.

"The Riptide Ride," he repeated. He didn't repeat it in an irritated, *why-didn't-you-listen-in-the-first-place* way. He repeated it with a little sprig of delight in his voice, as if he couldn't say it enough times. "That's the tentative name. I may change my mind later. But for now, that's it. The coaster's going to dip in and out of the ocean. It'll be under the surface at least 60 percent of the time."

"Um . . . won't the riders get a little wet?"

"The cars'll be covered. Bubble-tops," he replied patiently. "The coaster will go from land to water to land and then back to water again. A lot of swooping. A lot of climbing and diving. It's going to go on for hundreds of miles. I've already put in the first sections of track—well, the scaffolding for the track sections, at least. Now that I can crank out the specs on the quantum computer, the progress has been *amazing*."

Violet started to ask him more about it, but then she realized that, right at the moment, she didn't care about the Rip-Roaring Whatever-the-Hell-It-Was. She didn't care about any of the other rides, either, that Rez was so eager to tell her about. She just didn't.

She was tired. She was discouraged. She was right back where she'd started from. Paul Stark hadn't offered any useful information. And her grief for Delia had suddenly emerged again with a fresh fierceness. She'd managed to put it aside long enough to conduct the interview, but now it was back.

"Hey, Rez. Can I take a rain check on the . . . um . . . the . . ." She was blanking on the name again.

"The Riptide Ride."

"Yeah. That."

He shrugged. "Sure."

She could see how disappointed he was, but so be it. She'd look at the sites for his rides later.

She had to hurry back to New Earth. And go to work.

Dance Fever

But she didn't go to work.

By the time she alighted on New Earth, it was already dark. Violet found herself heading instinctively toward Redshift. She was still in a sort of mild shock over Delia's death and over her certainty that somebody had revived the Intercept. She still hadn't found any answers for Charlotte and Jeff Bainbridge. She didn't know what linked the victims. But instead of going back to the office and devising a strategy, she went out to do the only thing she seemed to do well these days: dance.

Another bouncer guarded the entrance to Redshift. She was a lithe, muscular woman with black skin, peroxide-blond dreads, a bright purple tank top, and crinkly black yoga pants.

"Name?" The bouncer kept a protective hand on the golden double doors in case she didn't like the answer.

"Violet Crowley."

The woman's eyes widened. She dropped her hand and stepped to the side.

"Go on."

Violet usually hated that—hated the automatic deference that came from being the daughter of New Earth's first president. Tonight, it was kind of nice. Saved her from a few seconds of arguing.

The moment she pushed opened the double doors, she was engulfed by colors and sounds and the complicated smell of overheated bodies and a hundred different perfumes. And once those doors closed behind her, she was captured by the music and the flashing lights and the thick crush of people. She felt her troubles dissolve in the heat and the noise, just melting away. She didn't have a specific dance partner; she didn't need one. It was the kind of night when being young and being on New Earth—and being in motion—were the only things that mattered.

And that feeling, in turn, reminded her of a line from a poem her father had read to her once. Ogden Crowley loved to take a big book down from the long shelf in his library and move slowly to his reading chair and then share a favorite poem with her. It was always a poem from long ago:

Bliss was it in that dawn to be alive, but to be young was very heaven!

"Violet! Hey, Violet! Over here!"

Without stopping the wild, made-up dance she was doing, she looked around for the source of the greeting. The bearded face was semi-familiar. Some guy she'd gone to school with. And his name was . . . Don? Doug? Dante? Dominic? Dimitri? She vaguely remembered that he'd asked her out a few times. She had turned him down, but in a nice way. Now he was next to her, dancing even faster than she was, his long blondish-white hair flying out behind him.

"Hey!" she shouted even though she knew he'd never be able to hear her over the music.

"Wanna dance?" he said. Or at least that's what she assumed he said. It reminded her of communicating with somebody on Old Earth. You had to do a lot of guesswork. And filling in the blanks.

She nodded. He nodded. Before she knew it, they were together, jumping and crashing happily against other people, people who laughed and pushed them back toward each other. Violet spun around until she felt terrifically dizzy. She almost lost her balance a few times, but there was always somebody to grab her before she hit the floor.

And that was how she spent the next several hours, shaking off the worries that had been following her around for days. She drank more than she should have—Don or Doug or whatever the hell he called himself kept bringing her fresh Neptunia Nodes before she'd finished with the one she already had—and she danced and she danced. If an emotion started to rise in her, she countered it with another drink, another mad flurry of dancing. She fought back against the feeling, so that it couldn't bother her anymore.

I finally know what to do about emotions, she thought. *Never stand still long enough to let them catch up to you.*

Oliver's Final Ride

liver Crosby sat in his car.

The darkness was absolute. It felt like the last word in an argument. Oliver didn't mind that; he found it rather comforting to be held in the night's tight grip. He couldn't move. He couldn't drive away. He couldn't drive away even if he wanted to, which he didn't, but the decision was now officially out of his hands.

The lot was empty now except for his car and one other, in the far corner. He knew this lot *so* well. He'd parked here every weekday for a year and a half. The New Earth authorities— busybodies, know-it-alls—were always harping at you to take a tram to work, to save wear and tear on the roads, to be mindful of the crucial ecological balance. But Oliver liked to drive. In fact, he loved it. What nineteen-year-old didn't? And so he'd said to hell with them. He'd drive whenever he damned well pleased.

Inside the block-long, four-story brick box next to the lot, its windows lightless because the workday was long over, was his former office. He could still see the inside of that office in his mind's eye, just the way he had arranged it, just the way it looked on his last day at work: desk, chair, computer.

He had designed guidance systems for self-propelled transport pods. He was very good at his job. And proud of what he produced. Pods were a challenge; you had to factor in the tremendous heat created by a controlled plummet down to Old Earth and, on the return trip, the equally ferocious heat generated by the propulsion system that lifted the pod from the gritty surface of that dying relic of a planet.

Yet as orders for pods had begun to drop dramatically, the company shifted to making decorative keyboard covers for desktop consoles. Pretty flowers and dancing unicorns and happy dolphins. In assorted colors.

Oliver Crosby was laid off, along with about four-fifths of his department. After a long search, he'd found a job with a company that made guidance systems for self-propelled vacuum cleaners.

It wasn't great, but it would do. At least he wouldn't have to move back in with his parents. Or download dolphin images all day long. He was fairly happy. Moderately satisfied.

Until.

Until today, when he'd felt a funny twitch in his head, just after lunchtime. It wasn't a big deal.

Then it intensified.

Twitch. Twitch. Twitch.

He shook his head. Shook it again. The twitches had started coming faster. He didn't see how it could get any worse.

And then it did.

At that point, Oliver did what he always did when he was nervous, jittery, or unsettled for any reason: He drove. He walked out of his new office in the new building and he got in his car and he drove the streets of New Earth, moving from Franklinton to L'Engletown to Farraday to Mendeleev Crossing and back to Franklinton. Then he drove that route all over again.

The afternoon slanted into dusky twilight. The twilight collapsed into night.

By now, the twitches had taken over his brain, and it was all he could do to keep hanging on to the steering wheel. He was like a man clutching a bobbing buoy in the midst of a frantic, roiling, deadly ocean.

A picture moved into his line of sight. It wasn't real; it was happening in his brain, which somehow made it *more* real than the images right in front of him, images of roads and trees and other cars—and it clung to his thoughts like the wrapper on a piece of candy.

He was back in his office, in the job he loved. Designing guidance systems. Busy and fulfilled.

You'll never be that happy again. Ever.

The words hit hard. A deep sadness moved unstoppably through his body.

That was the peak. And you're only nineteen. So think of all the years you have left—all those long, empty years, working at a job you don't really like. A job anybody could do.

He had stopped at a drugstore along the way. He thought the PharmRob who waited on him might ask if he was okay— by now Oliver was flinching with every twitch, wasn't he?—but it didn't, which made him realize his body wasn't jerking or flailing or flinching or *anything*. It was all happening inside his head.

He pulled into this parking lot. The one he knew so well. The lot made him remember everything.

Never.

Never, never, never.

Never again will you be as happy as you were back then. Your joy is all behind you now.

Oliver felt a rush of oncoming bleakness. He had a vision of trudging through the days ahead, counting the hours, counting the *minutes*, until he would be old and gray, and death would rescue him.

You don't have to wait. You can do it yourself. And avoid all of the pain between now and then.

Oliver opened the bottle of sleeping pills.

Something inside him, a last vestige of the carefree guy he'd been, the one who loved the open road and who had friends and plans and a future, put up a brief, brave fight. But the screaming in his head won.

Your joy is all behind you now.

There's nothing left. Just long days of emptiness and pain.

You know what to do.

He flung his head back, dumping the entire contents of the bottle into his mouth. He choked and gagged but somehow managed to swallow the pills, washing them down with a desperate gulp from the bottle of water he kept in his cup holder.

It was a cool night. The heat of the engine had caused condensation to form on the inside of his windshield. With a trembling fingertip, Oliver wrote the word in the moisture, a word that began to dissolve as the water evaporated. The streaming droplets made it look as if the word itself was weeping:

SCREAM

Hangover City

"m . . . Vi? Vi? I hate to wake you up, but you're sort of . . . well, drooling on the files—"

Jonetta was taking pains to keep her voice soft and low. But it still sounded to Violet like the roar of ten thousand transport pods with leaky manifolds.

She tried to lift her head.

Damn. Jonetta was right. She was stuck.

She tried again. This time she was able to free her cheek from the desk, but the effort came with an unseemly smooching sound. It left an icky-looking spot on the documents she'd been using as a pillow.

How long had she been asleep in her desk chair, with the side of her face spit-glued to the paperwork? And how had she even *gotten* here in the first place?

She had no memory of leaving Redshift.

No memory of making the trip from the club to her office in the middle of the night.

It was totally embarrassing. Jonetta was the only witness to her degradation, but it was still totally embarrassing.

"What time is—"

"It's just after eight," Jonetta said perkily. "Can I get you some coffee, Vi?"

Violet didn't even have the oomph right now to get mad about the very latest *Vi* violation. The Headache was back. Her mouth felt like somebody had stored their dirty socks in there. Her stomach was swishing back and forth. Plus, she needed to pee.

Violet tried to stand.

Whoa.

Before she'd taken half a step, she fell back into her chair. It was the infernal dizziness, caused by drinking too much in too short a period of time. Her knees felt wobbly. She remained sitting.

"How did I—"

"Don't know. You were like that when I got here." Jonetta handed her a mug of coffee. Violet wasn't crazy about coffee, but right now she needed it. Whether or not she liked it was irrelevant. She polished off half the mug in one swallow.

"Thanks." Her mouth began to register the heat of the beverage she'd just consumed. Violet didn't care. A seared tongue was nothing compared to a troubled mind.

"Sure," Jonetta said. "Ready to run down today's agenda?"

No. She most assuredly was *not* ready to run down today's agenda. What she was ready to do was to sit here and drink coffee for the next several hours—or the next several days—and figure out, as soon as her head cleared, the possibly humiliating specifics of what she had done last night at Redshift. And why.

The *why* was the key. Why was she behaving this way? What

was her problem? Ever since the Intercept had gone away, Violet had watched herself grow more and more reckless. Having fun was one thing; incapacitating herself was another thing altogether. It was almost as if the Intercept was a parent, and that parent had gone on vacation with the parting words "I trust you to behave."

Bad decision, Violet thought ruefully.

She assumed she was seconds away from being fired by Charlotte Bainbridge. And after that, she'd lose her office and her business. And after that—

"Call on line two," Jonetta said. She had been waiting for Violet's reply to her question about the day's agenda when the office phone rang. Two long steps had taken Jonetta back to her own desk, where she answered it and then made her announcement to Violet.

This is it, Violet thought. *It's going to be Charlotte Bainbridge, demanding a full refund, telling me I'm off the case, and telling me that, furthermore, I've made no progress on her case because I'm a lazy jerk who wastes valuable time while her daughter's killer is still out there somewhere, ready to—*

"It's somebody named Dave," Jonetta added.

Dave? She didn't know a Dave, did she?

"Um . . . hello?" Violet said. She squinted at her console. It was some guy with a beard. His face didn't ring any bells. Wait, did this guy ask her out in high school?

"Hey," he said. He looked embarrassed, his glance shifting right and left and then returning to the center of the console screen. "Listen. I need to tell you that I've thought about it, and while I'm really flattered, I just can't see how it would work, and so I think at this point we ought to just—"

"How *what* would work?"

"You don't remember?"

"Remember *what*?" Now she was concerned. What had she done last night?

"You said . . . you said we ought to get married. And I was like, hell yeah. I mean, we danced great together. But I really don't think that—"

"Whoa. Whoa. WHOA." Violet sprang up from her chair, a gesture that caused the Headache to intensify into a violent thumping. For a brief, horrified second, she thought she might throw up. Was he going to say that they'd actually gone somewhere—like that quickie wedding chapel in Franklinton—and gotten *married*?

Her voice became a strangled squawk. "What are you talking about?"

"It seemed like a great idea last night, but now that I've given it some thought," he said, "I realize that dancing with somebody one time—when you've both had too much to drink—probably isn't the basis for a lasting marriage."

"Agreed," Violet said. Her horror continued to mount. Was this stranger actually her *husband* now?

"So we're good? We can call off the engagement?"

The fact that he had used the word *engagement* and not *marriage* instantly caused such a tsunami of relief to flood through her body that she thought she might keel over. "Yeah," she muttered. "Let's call it off." *Because I don't even know you, Dave.*

"See you around," he said. "Maybe tonight at Redshift?"

Apparently, her almost-husband didn't learn from his mistakes. It really wasn't going to work.

"Um . . . maybe." She clicked off her console. She took a series of deep, restorative breaths.

But her relief was short-lived. The grubby fact dawned on her that she'd come very close to marrying some guy she barely knew.

Okay, some guy that *she did not know at all*.

What was she thinking? Shura would be horrified at how Violet was messing up her life. Kendall would be horrified, too. And her father—she couldn't stand to think of how disappointed *he* would be. The thought of his reaction made her cringe.

Violet executed a quick but solemn vow to herself: She was going to change. She *had* to change. Next time she needed to drown her sorrows, she'd stick to tea. She could toast Delia's memory when she did so.

"So am I invited to the wedding?"

She knew that voice. It was Tin Man. He leaned against one side of the threshold. His arms were crossed. He had a slight smile on his face, a smile that was right on the cusp of being a smirk.

"How did you—" Violet stopped. All kinds of conspiracy theories roosted in her head—Tin Man had tapped her console or Jonetta was eavesdropping and told him or he could actually read minds—before the truth struck her.

"It was a trick," Violet said. "And you did it."

"Yeah." Tin Man pushed himself away from the doorframe and came into her office. "Dave's an old buddy of mine. I needed to scare some sense into you."

Now that he was closer, she could see that he still wasn't himself. The skin around his eyes was smudged with fatigue. She knew the signs because she knew the feeling herself all too well: He was missing his mom.

It didn't matter how many practical jokes he played. He was grieving.

"And so," Violet said, "you told Dave to call me this morning and pretend . . ."

"You got it." Tin Man sat down. "Had you going there, right? You're still shaking."

"Nasty trick."

"But necessary. My mom was always worried about you, too, Violet. Did you know that? In one of the last conversations I had with her before she—"

He couldn't say the word. He gulped and went in another direction.

"Anyway, she said you were out of control. Taking too many wild chances. And that something bad was bound to happen. Believe me, my mom knew all about taking chances and paying the price for it. She wanted something better for you." Tin Man crossed one leg over the other knee. He fiddled with the sole of his boot. Whatever he was going to say next was as hard for him to say as the word *died*. That's why he was stalling. She knew him well enough to recognize the tactic. "A lot of people care about you, Violet, and they're all saying the same thing. You're being reckless, and you need to start taking care of yourself."

"You've got a hell of a nerve. Telling me what to do."

"So you disagree? You think you're just fine?"

No. She absolutely did *not* think she was just fine. The fact that she'd fallen for his little trick and thought that she actually might have married some guy and didn't even remember it proved to her that she wasn't fine. She was about ten thousand miles from "fine."

But it was *her* life. Nobody else's. She didn't want to live this way anymore, true, but that was *her* decision. She had come to it on her own, not because Tin Man or anybody else told her she had to change. Not even if Delia had told her to change.

Not even then.

"Listen," she said heatedly. She wanted him to understand. "Back when we had the Intercept, I had to watch everything I felt. I had to keep tabs on my emotions all the time. If I liked a guy—" She paused here, because the only guy she'd ever really liked that way was Danny, and she still couldn't talk about it because it had been so intense, and that's why she went with the generic "guy," as if she fell in love every three minutes or so. Which definitely was *not* the case.

"If I liked a guy," Violet repeated, starting again, "I'd try to disguise it. To myself, I mean. I tried to *not* feel it, because I hated the idea of the Intercept spying on me. Recording my feelings. You know?"

"I know," he said. Tin Man was listening intently. He really did seem to understand.

"So when the Intercept was destroyed," she continued, "it was like . . . like I was a cork that had been held underwater for years and years. And then the pressure was released." She flipped her hand toward the ceiling. "It's like—*whoosh!*—I went shooting off into the air. Really fast. Because I'd been holding everything down for so long. I just let it all go. That's when I started hanging out at Redshift. Admittedly way too much. And when people like Shura tried to point out to me that I was on the wrong path, I really resented it. I think I even told her to go to hell one night. My very best friend." She flung herself back in her chair.

"Not cool."

"Oh my God. I'm such an idiot."

Tin Man shook his head. "No. Not an idiot. You just don't know how to handle life without the Intercept. Nobody does, really. We're still learning. The lesson's harder for some than for others."

Violet absorbed what he'd said. "*You* seem to be doing okay. How did you—"

"You have to be your own Intercept."

She frowned. "What does *that* mean?"

He lifted his gaze. Sunlight was trundling in through the window behind Violet's desk. Another beautiful day on New Earth.

"It means," he said, "that you watch your emotions *yourself.* You remember them on your own. And when you need to, you use the memory of an emotion to adjust your behavior. Just like what the Intercept did—but without the pain. Without the anguish." He touched the scar in the crook of his left elbow. "I'm glad they left the chips in," he said. "It's a good way to remember how powerful feelings can be. How they can get the best of you if you let them. Rip you up. Twist you around and torment you."

When Tin Man spoke again, there was a slight hitch in his voice. Violet guessed that he was holding back tears. "I'll remember forever how it felt when I came into that kitchen," he said, "and found my mother's body. I was a mess. I was totally wrecked. I was . . . *undone.* I didn't see how I was going to go on with my life. Which is exactly how I felt when Molly died. But you know what, Violet? It's different this time. It's different because there's no Intercept.

"Now *I'm* in control. *I* get to decide which memories get recycled. Which ones I allow to come back and affect my life. Not the Intercept." He smiled. "You know my old job at Redshift? It's like that. I get to be the bouncer of my own emotions. If I don't want to let a feeling in, it doesn't get in. But if I *do* want to let it in, I open the door. And in it comes."

"Be your own Intercept," Violet said softly and slowly, exploring the concept even as she pronounced the words.

"Yeah. And believe me, it works. If *I* can do it, *you* can do it."

She started to ask another question when Jonetta showed up in the doorway. Her face looked stricken, and when she talked, she had trouble finding enough breath.

"Check your consoles—it happened again," Jonetta said, her voice trembling. "Another suicide. Some guy named Oliver Crosby."

Before Violet had a chance to react, her console chimed. Incoming call.

It was Kendall.

"I need to talk to you, Violet," he said. "Right away. I went by your apartment last night, but you weren't there."

He waited for an explanation. She didn't offer one.

My business, Kendall. Not yours.

"I was busy," she said. "And I'm sort of in the middle of something now, too. Can it wait?"

"No."

"Come on. What's so urgent that it can't—"

"It's about the Intercept."

"On my way."

The Key to Everything

Kendall's apartment was on the eleventh floor of a complex on Curie Street. A lot of cops lived in the same building—a beige box with a flat red roof and stucco sides and small slits for windows—because it was relatively cheap and close to the center of Hawking, handy for people whose lives were defined by responding to emergencies.

The person who opened the door after Violet's fierce and prolonged knocking was not Kendall but Sara Verity. She held a gray dusting rag in one hand. Her red curls were corralled back into a ponytail.

"Hey," Violet said.

"Come on in. I'm just finishing up. Kendall's in his study." Sara stepped to one side as Violet swept past her. The apartment smelled mildly fruity. Violet chalked that up to the furniture polish Sara had been using. Violet saw the can on Kendall's coffee table. The table gleamed. And you could actually see the surface. The table, in fact, looked better than it ever had before—which wasn't an especially high bar, Violet reminded herself, because in the past it had been not only dusty but also stacked up with a bewildering assortment of scribbled-on notebooks and chewed-at sprockets and grimy filters and greasy snippets of wires and tiny flywheels and portable electron microscopes and an untold number of mysterious gizmos, along with not-so-mysterious things like candy wrappers and half-empty coffee cups.

The apartment was much too small to have an actual study. That was just the name Kendall had given to the single bedroom, which he had turned into a combination laboratory and library about ten seconds after he'd first moved in. He had gotten rid of the bed and the dresser and jammed in a workbench and bookshelves and towering stacks of computers. He slept, Violet knew, on the couch in the living room—when he slept at all, that is, because Kendall considered sleep to be a self-indulgent luxury.

"Hey," he said. "Take a look."

He was sitting on a stool at the end of his workbench. The screen of a small laptop glowed in front of him.

"What's going on?" she asked. "What's that?"

"My own version of a trigger-trap. And it worked." He didn't say it triumphantly.

"Meaning . . . ?"

"Meaning I wasn't sure if somebody was really accessing the Intercept again. It just seemed so unlikely. Especially after I talked to Rez. He didn't have any real evidence. Just a few scraps from a bunch of old algorithms. Somebody would need a hell of a lot more than *that* to get the Intercept up and running again. The technical threshold would be daunting, not to mention the—"

"Got it, Kendall. So what did you *do*?"

He nodded toward the laptop. "I set a trap. I put in the old

Intercept coordinates. If somebody tried to fire it up—even just as a test—these numbers would climb until they reached a certain point. A level that I designated. At that moment, it would trip a silent alarm. Late last night, it happened." He pointed at the screen. "See this red spike? That's the Intercept. Rising from the dead."

Violet felt the bottom drop out of her world. "So somebody used it again."

"Yeah." His face was grim. "Briefly, but . . . yeah."

"Oh my God."

"And then I checked the news feed on my console. Another suicide." Kendall grimaced. "Do you know what I think? I think somebody is using the Intercept to cram terrible ideas into people's minds—ideas about how horrible life is, how futile. Based on their memories. And so the people kill themselves."

Violet could only look at him. For the moment, she was too stricken to speak. She was still reeling from the confirmation that the Intercept was alive again.

Kendall filled the gap. "The question is, how could somebody do it? How could they re-create the Intercept? Even *I* wouldn't be able to revive it without the original specs. And maybe not even then. Not that fast, anyway. It took me nearly a dozen years on Old Earth to invent the thing in the first place, and that was when I was working day and night, year after year, with no distractions."

"I know," Violet said. "I know." She shook her head. Squared her shoulders. She couldn't be stunned forever. There was work to be done. "I checked with Paul Stark down on Old Earth. I thought maybe he'd remember somebody who would be capable of this. Somebody who helped the Rebels two years ago."

"And?"

"No dice. He confirmed just what you said. Nobody's smart enough to create a whole new Intercept."

Kendall's eyes shifted in her direction. She could almost see his mind working faster now; she could almost feel the heat of the sparks generated by the runaway speed of its calculations. "Hold on. Not 'a whole new Intercept.' Just a part of it. And a relatively small part, all told. This isn't the entire system. This is just a little piece. A sort of mini-Intercept. Not one big enough or sophisticated enough to run an entire civilization like New Earth and Old Earth—but one that could control a few dozen people, tops."

"And maybe," Violet said, her voice growing graver as the terrible certainty dawned, "somebody could do that without having a full set of specs—just a few pages."

"Like the pages we rescued."

They were quiet for a few seconds. This was the biggest secret of their lives—and maybe the biggest regret, too.

"But you hid them in a safe place," Violet said. "Right?"

From the next room came the sound of the front door opening. Sara's voice called out, "All done! See you next week!"

"Thanks, Sara!" Kendall called back. The front door closed. "Of course I did. They're in a safe place."

"No office is completely burglar-proof, Kendall. Not even an office in a police station."

"I don't keep them at the station."

She stared at him. "You don't mean that you keep the pages *here*? In your *apartment*?"

He shrugged. "Wall safe in the hall closet. Behind Shura's portrait of Danny. I check every day to make sure they're still there. And it's a digital locking system with a tamper-proof, time-based algorithm plus nine additional layers of—"

"Doesn't matter," Violet said, interrupting him, impatience in her voice. "It's not secure. If somebody figured out how to break into the safe, they could make copies of the pages and then return them. You'd never know."

"I'd know."

"*How* would you know? If they circumvented the algorithm and sidestepped those nine layers of yours, they could cover their tracks. Let's face it, Kendall—you're a lot better at coming up with world-changing technologies than you are at keeping your stuff safe. You're focused on the big picture, right? Not low-level crap like burglar alarms. Using your brain for something like that is like building a rocket to cross a room. It's overkill."

"So you think . . ."

"Yeah. I do. I think somebody could've broken into the safe and grabbed those pages."

He frowned. "But they'd have to get *in* the apartment first. And there'd be traces if somebody did that."

"Sara Verity has a key, right? In case she comes by to clean when you're not home? And the building superintendent. I bet she's got a key, too, right? And me. I've got one. That's three people. Any one of us could have stolen the pages and used them."

Kendall shook his head stubbornly. "Sara doesn't have the technical expertise. She's never had any formal training with computers and wouldn't have the faintest clue what to do with those pages. The building superintendent? Ditto. And you? I'm assuming you don't consider yourself a suspect, Violet. Is that right?"

"Come on, Kendall. You know why I'm freaking out. The idea of the Intercept back in business, run by somebody who wants to *murder* people—it's a little on the scary side."

"Yeah. I get that." Deep sigh. "Okay, let's be detectives here. It's what you do, right?"

She started to give him a smart-ass response but held back. This was too important. Being pissed at him could wait.

"Yeah," she said. "It's what I do."

"So how many people would realistically be able to create a new version of the Intercept? Me, Rez, and maybe three or four other computer experts. Some we may not even know about. Now, of those particular people, how many theoretically have access to the pages we saved?"

"Only you."

"Right. Only me. And I'm giving myself the same break as I gave you; I'm not the bad guy. So where does that leave us?"

She nodded. "You're right. Rez has the knowledge, but he doesn't have the access to the pages. The only two people with knowledge *and* access are you and me." She sighed. "That's it, Kendall. We'll just arrest ourselves. Problem solved."

He laughed. She did, too. Violet was standing close to Kendall, and there was a part of her that wanted to reach out and touch him, just as she'd done in the park. Just as she'd longed to do back when she was still in love with him, two years ago.

Moments of tension did that to her sometimes. They sent her rocketing back into the past, when the problems seemed simpler, the issues less complex, the stakes lower. That wasn't the reality, of course; the world had been just as much of a mess back then as it was now. But nostalgia was like frost on a windshield. It distorted the view.

A flash of memory: the first time she and Kendall kissed. It was two years ago, just after she'd found out he wasn't Danny. Here in this very apartment. She wished she could feel that again, the special magic of a first kiss . . .

She shook her head.

No. The desire wasn't there anymore. She couldn't pretend that it was.

And besides, there was a crisis at hand. Her personal life was about 287th on the list of Things That Need Attention ASAP.

"Going forward," Violet said hastily, "make sure you keep an eye on your trigger-trap in case our killer tries to access it again. I'll check in with Jonetta. See if she's found any common thread linking the victims. That's all we can do. That—and hope that nobody else commits suicide in the meantime."

She had to go. She needed to get out of there quickly because she had work to do—and for another reason, too. She was afraid that Kendall was remembering that kiss right along with her, and maybe—in the heat of the crisis—he was hoping that she'd start to feel the same thing she had felt for him in the past, and that it could all be rekindled somehow, all that love brought back to life, just as the Intercept had been brought back to life.

Just like that.

But it couldn't. And not because Violet didn't have feelings. She had *those*, all right. Too many of them. In fact, as she bolted from Kendall's study and moved quickly through the fruity-smelling living room toward the front door, she was hit with a realization that surprised her.

She actually *was* feeling it all over again: the tingling anticipation of a kiss, the deep and fevered longing for a certain person's touch. But this time, the person she found herself thinking of, the person who—to her complete astonishment—inspired all of that internal chaos wasn't Kendall.

It was Rez.

Rodney to the Rescue

Did she have the wrong office?

Violet stopped dead in her tracks. A man she had never seen before was sitting at the front desk of what she'd assumed was Crowley & Associates Detective Agency, fiddling with Jonetta's computer—or, if this *wasn't* the office of Crowley & Associates Detective Agency, fiddling with a remarkably similar-looking computer kept in the same spot where Jonetta kept hers.

The man paid no attention to her. He was exceptionally thin and wore his hair in a shaggy blue-black Afro. He had the biggest hands and the skinniest fingers that Violet had ever seen. He poked at the keys on the keyboard one by one by one, alternating index fingers. He looked like a mad musician, some kind of deranged composer who hoped that if he just picked random keys and pressed them diligently he might, after a millennium or so, end up with a symphony.

Violet took a quick peek over her shoulder at the office door, which she had left open when she barreled in. On the frosted glass, she could see the letters painted on the front:

YCNEGA EVITCETED SETAICOSSA & YELWORC

Okay, she was in the right office. So who was this stranger? "Vi!"

Jonetta called her name as she came rushing out of Violet's office, waving a clipboard. "I was just checking the Wi-Fi in there to see if Rodney got everything put back right. It's working fine." She took note of Violet's stupefied stare. "Oh, you two haven't met yet. Rodney, this is my boss, Violet Crowley. Vi, this is my brother, Rodney. He's making sure that there are no more trigger-traps. I got worried after the latest suicide. Something weird is *definitely* going on."

Rodney looked up. His eyes widened when he saw Violet. He seemed too embarrassed to speak, and so in lieu of words, he swallowed hard several times and coughed.

"Glad you're here, Rodney," Violet said. "It was pretty scary the other day when that trigger-trap detonated. Good to be in the clear."

"You're not," he said.

"We're not?"

"Not yet," he clarified. "I've still got some protocols to run through." Down went his head again as he resumed poking at the keyboard. "Want to make sure it's totally clean."

"Okay, well, good," Violet said.

Jonetta waved the clipboard once more. "While he's finishing up, I've got some stuff to go over with you. Information about the case."

They withdrew into Violet's office. Violet sat down while

Jonetta fluttered around the room, half pacing, half hopping, as she talked. It made Violet dizzy just watching her.

"So I think—I *think*—I found it," Jonetta declared. "I mean, it's still pretty sketchy, and I don't have all the blank spaces filled in, and there's still a *ton* of questions and it might all turn out to be wrong and stupid and—"

"Jonetta." Violet willed her assistant to remain still for a tenth of a second. "Found *what*?"

"A link between the victims—Amelia Bainbridge and all the rest."

Violet sat up straighter in her chair. Could it be?

"Tell me," she said eagerly.

Jonetta grimaced ever so slightly as if she feared she'd over-sold her breakthrough. "Well, it's a link, yeah, but I still can't account for Delia Tolliver. Like we talked about, she breaks the pattern. But it works for all the others."

"We'll get to that. First tell me about the common element."

Abruptly, Jonetta stopped moving. She leaned across Violet's desk and uttered the word in a low, conspiratorial way. "Transportation," she said.

"Pardon?"

"Transportation. That's it. All the suicide victims except for Delia were involved with transportation. Or they *had* been involved with transportation. Nowadays, that sector has been almost totally wiped out by cuts to the pod program to Old Earth. Everything's changing so fast lately, right? People change jobs five times before breakfast, or so it seems."

Violet thought about it. "Amelia was still a student. She didn't have a job. How was she involved with transportation?"

By now, Jonetta had gone back to her march. It seemed to keep her brain going. "Her father was the one in transportation.

Frank Bainbridge. He was an engineer. He made the decision to shut down the transport site."

Violet nodded. "And the Wilton twins?"

"Their mom and dad had been laid off from the metallurgy lab. Lost their jobs when the transport division cut back but found other jobs."

"And Wendell Prokop's mom invented the entire transport system," Violet said, nodding. "Okay, so how about Oliver Crosby?"

"He used to work for a company that made guidance systems for pods."

"Used to?"

"Lost his position. A lot of companies went out of business when the immigration program changed and fewer pods were needed. But he found something else to do. So did the others. They landed on their feet—even though they had to sort of reinvent themselves to do it. All of them had worked with transport."

"Except for Delia."

"Right. Except for Delia."

Jonetta's information was interesting, but Violet didn't yet know what to do with it. How would it help them unmask the perpetrator—the person who had somehow reanimated the Intercept and was using it to kill?

She was quiet for a moment as she reflected on the newly unearthed facts.

Jonetta misinterpreted Violet's silence as a reproach.

"I know, I know," Jonetta said, "I have to keep digging. Right now, it's only a theory."

"So's gravity. But it seems to work pretty well." Violet smiled. She wasn't trying to be a smart-ass. It was just that her father had taught her to disdain the notion that theories were rickety, tentative things with no lasting value. Theories were *everything*, he believed, and he had transferred that belief to Violet with no lessening of intensity. A theory was the prime catalyst behind New Earth.

A rustle in the doorway instantly drew both of their gazes. Rodney stood there with a sheepish smile on his face. The moment he realized that his sister and her boss were looking back at him, he froze, and then he seemed to recoil in a spasm of embarrassment, ducking his head and coughing. He simply could not bear being looked at.

"Um . . . I'm sorta finished for now," he said. His eyes jumped all over room, anywhere except toward Violet and Jonetta. "No more trigger-traps. And I set a deflection code so nobody'll be able to reinstall one. Or if they do, I'll know about it. Right away."

"Thanks, Rodney," Violet said.

A vein in his forehead began to throb. Violet was half-afraid he would self-immolate from the sheer agony of being, even momentarily, the center of attention.

"Um . . . I . . . well," he said, swallowing between each word. "It's really no big deal. I utilized the Grafton-Boulan Coefficient Analytics and then spliced it with the Simpson-Sosa Sine Curve and—"

"Rodney," Jonetta said, interrupting him. "She doesn't care about any of that. Take the compliment and go home."

He dropped his head even lower. Then he backed out of the doorway, twirled, and fled.

Violet listened to his footsteps, a panicked-sounding patter that finally tailed off into a silence that meant he'd cleared the floor. "Your brother's a little on the shy side, huh?"

Jonetta rolled her eyes. "If somebody says hello to him he almost passes out. He used to be even *worse*, if you can believe it."

"Really."

"A few months ago, he was barely able to leave the house. He's better now. More confident."

"What changed?"

Another eye-roll. "He got a girlfriend. *That* was a first."

"A girlfriend."

"Yeah." Jonetta snickered. "She had to practically hit him over the head to get his attention, but once she did—wow. He's *really* into her now. Guess what they do on their wild and crazy dates? She asks him a bunch of heavy-duty questions about computers. And he takes his time answering her while she smiles and tells him how *brilliant* he is. Boring, right? I heard her do it one day when she dropped by here to pick him up. I'd asked him to work on my computer. You hadn't come in yet that morning. Late night at Redshift, I guess." If it was anybody but Jonetta, Violet would've suspected a dig. But not from her assistant. Jonetta didn't do digs.

"I guess," Violet said.

Jonetta snapped her fingers. "Hey. I think you know her. I just remembered—that day she came by the office, she told me that you guys are friends."

"What's her name?"

"Sara. Sara Verity."

Violet felt a funny prickling sensation on the back of her neck. Her palms started to sweat. So Sara had a means of getting advanced training in computers. Rodney Loring sounded like an excellent instructor.

What if Sara had broken into Kendall's safe and found the pages? The Intercept specs were sketchy, but to a person with

the proper expertise, they would be enough. Enough to jump-
start a junior version of the Intercept. Enough to create a device that could scoop up a person's worst memories and then
reinsert them at will, causing suicidal despair.

Rodney might very well be innocent. He might not know
what he'd done in those tutoring sessions. He might not realize how he had helped his girlfriend with her deadly plan.

If it was really her.

If Sara was the one who had hijacked the Intercept.

Wait. Maybe I'm making a big mistake here, Violet thought,
cautioning herself. *I have to give Sara a chance to defend herself before I go any further with this.*

Fine. She'd do just that.

Violet tapped her console. A yellow jewel rose with a fussy
shimmer. Sara answered before the end of the first chirp.

"Hey, Sara," Violet said. She forced herself to keep her voice
normal. Friendly, low-key. She smiled at the screen. "We said
we'd get together soon, right? I sure could use a quick break.
How about a walk in Perey Park?"

Peril in the Park

Sara stood at the edge of a small circle of yellow light beneath one of the streetlights. She looked left. She looked right. She clenched and unclenched her hands.

Violet had not noticed before just how much her friend had changed over the past year. Her hair had lost a lot of its springy bounce. It spread out, frizzy and listless, across hunched shoulders.

Why hadn't Violet observed that when she spotted Sara at TAP? Or later when she saw her at Kendall's apartment?

Because both times I was wrapped up in my own problems. And because I'm not really a very good friend.

Maybe if I'd been nicer to her, maybe if I'd looked closer and seen her suffering and tried to help . . . she wouldn't have resorted to this.

To doing what I think she's done.

"Hey, Sara."

Sara flinched. Her head flicked toward the sound. She hadn't seen Violet approaching. The park was growing darker by the minute; the shadows of the trees made sharply pointed stripes that lay across the wide expanse of grass. Wind hissed through the hedges lining the gravel path. The air smelled chilly, with the faint tang of cinnamon that air on New Earth always carried, thanks to the Scent Corps, a team of engineers who custom-crafted the atmosphere.

"Hey," Sara replied. Her tone was defensive, wary.

She stepped out of the light. Violet could no longer make out the details of her face.

"How's the job hunt coming?" Violet asked. She kept her voice blandly cordial. It was hard to do that because her heart was pounding.

Sara shrugged. "Can we walk? You said you wanted to take a walk."

"Sure."

The park was almost deserted. A young woman jogged past them; she was cooling down after a run, Violet surmised, because her husky breathing did not match the relative ease of her pace. Another woman went by in the opposite direction, wrangling a small leashed dog who had a yen to lunge and paw at the grass on the margins of the path.

Sara plunged her hands deep in the pockets of her jacket. Her head bobbed forward as she walked.

"I used to be so jealous of you and Shura," she muttered. "I'd watch you guys go around this park for hours and hours and *hours*. Talking and talking. Or just walking side by side." She sniffed. "I've never had a friend like that. Never."

So you were spying *on us? That's incredibly creepy. Disturbing and creepy.* Violet didn't say it out loud because she didn't want to rile her. Eventually, if Violet's hunch was correct, some riling would have to occur, but for now, she had a lot more information she needed to get from her.

"We don't hang out that much these days," Violet said. "Not since she graduated from medical school and opened her lab. And I opened my business."

Sara made a little snorting sound. "Right. Your business."

Violet fought to keep her face neutral. "Yeah."

"Why'd you want to have a detective agency, anyway? I mean, I hear it's not going so well." Sara snickered. "I mean, you've got a *lot* of bills. The stack's about a mile high."

The only way Sara would know that was if she'd snooped around the office when Violet wasn't there. And if Sara *had* snooped around the office, she could very well have set the trigger-trap on Jonetta's keyboard.

"How would you know?" Violet asked mildly.

Sara shrugged. "Lucky guess."

Violet still didn't react. There was more she needed to know.

"Business will pick up," Violet said. " And as for why I started it—well, it's kind of cool to help people."

Sara didn't answer.

They came to the end of the row and made a right turn, continuing up the other side of the park.

"You used to think so, too," Violet said softly.

"What are you talking about?"

"You used to like helping people, same as me. When you first started working in transport logistics. Remember? Two years ago? I needed to get to Old Earth. I didn't have official permission. And you came through. You helped me get there. Which helped me save my father's life."

For several minutes, the only sound was the light, rhythmic splashing of the fountain in the center of the park, where six jets of water—nearly invisible now in the semidarkness—leaped high in the air and then fell in the pool in a simple symphony of delicate splashes.

"I loved my job," Sara said. Her voice was wistful.

"I bet you miss it. Cleaning apartments—that's not exactly the same thing."

"No, it's not."

"And that makes you mad."

"Yeah. It does."

Violet could sense the anger rising again in Sara. She hoped to use that anger, to exploit it.

"I mean," Violet said, "it's not really fair, is it? You worked hard, and you did a good job. Everybody said so. And then— *boom*—you're out. Unemployed. Just because things changed. Just because my dad opened the border and let in the people from Old Earth. There weren't so many trips back and forth to Old Earth anymore. So they shut down the transport sites and stopped making pods. It wasn't fair. And you weren't the only one, right? Other people were in the same situation. A job they'd trained for, a job they loved with all their heart—gone. Over."

"Oh, the others did just *fine*," Sara shot back. "They used their connections. Or they were just lucky. They got other jobs. But not me. *Not me.*" She made a fist and stared at it. "I started thinking about all of this when Frank Bainbridge died last year. It was an accident; a pod exploded when he was standing too close to it. He was the one who'd started decommissioning the pods, one by one. I guess I was supposed to be sad that he died, but all I could think about was, *Yeah, take that, old man.* It backfired on him. His plan to shut down the transport system—it ended up killing him. *Ha.* It felt good to me, seeing his family suffer." She shuddered. She didn't seem to care anymore how that sounded. She stared at Violet. "I *loved* my job. I was good at it. Then they took it all away from me. They destroyed my life."

"And you deserved better."

"Yeah. You bet your ass I did." Anger invaded Sara's tone, like soldiers swarming over a hill. "*It wasn't supposed to be like this. New Earth was supposed to be* different. *It was supposed to be* fair. How did this happen? All the things our parents were told about this great new world. Well, when it came right down to it, New Earth turned out to be no better than the old. Maybe worse."

"Worse?"

"Yeah. Because nobody had any hope for Old Earth. That's what my parents told me. It was rotten and horrible, and everybody *knew* that. But New Earth—New Earth made *promises.* And then it broke them. New Earth gave us hope. And then it took it away. That's the worst thing of all."

She had increased her pace to match her mounting rage. Violet almost had to run to keep up with her.

"I don't know, Sara. Nobody ever said things would stay the same on New Earth. Things *can't* stay the same. Life is always changing. It has to. Sometimes changes are good and sometimes they're bad, but change has to happen. I know you get that."

A flamethrower would have generated less propulsive heat than Sara's response. "You have *no idea* what you're talking about." She shook her head. Something was rising in her, something dark and final. "I don't have to listen to any more bullshit from you, Violet. It was that father of yours who made this lousy world in the first place. And who brought in the Intercept." She uttered an evil-sounding laugh. "You may think it's gone, but it's—" She cut herself off.

"Sara." Violet reached out and clutched the sleeve of Sara's jacket. "Wait."

Sara jerked her arm out of Violet's grasp. Her breathing was shallow and ragged. "What do you *want* from me?"

"You have to stop, Sara. And you have to stop now."

"Stop what?"

"Don't play dumb. I know what you've done, Sara. I know all about it. You got Rodney Loring to help you rebuild the Intercept protocol. You reactivated it. You've been infiltrating the minds of people you hate—people who kept their jobs in transportation or who got other jobs when you couldn't. And you put terrible thoughts in their heads. Unbearable thoughts. It was your way of getting revenge on everyone you're jealous of—including *me*. That's why you went after Delia Tolliver, isn't it? To hurt me." Violet paused to catch her breath. The memory of Delia's face made it hard for her to go on. But she had to. "It's not right, Sara. You *know* it's not right. So you have to stop. Now."

"I don't know what you're talking about."

"Sara, this is *murder*."

"Go to hell."

Sara turned and ran, jumping off the path and heaving herself toward the interior of the park. Violet was quicker, though, and caught up in a flash. A thought skittered across her mind as she grabbed Sara's arm: *I need to call Kendall and get some backup.*

She'd needed to have brief physical contact with Sara to set the rest of her plan into motion, but once that was done . . .

Well, she didn't know *what* would happen next. She hadn't thought things out that far in advance.

Sara whirled around. It was too dark for Violet to see the expression on her face, or to note—as she would learn in a flurry of seconds—that Sara had raised a fist. The fist went crashing into the side of Violet's jaw.

Violet flew backward. Her head bounced against the ground. She moaned once.

And then lay motionless.

Confession

She was floating in a strange green sea.

No: She was flying across a vivid orange sky.

No: She was sleeping on a fluffy bed of pink cotton candy, and the bedposts were made of black licorice, and it was sweet and cool and—

"Vi. Vi? Vi!"

Pain shot through her head as she fought her way up to consciousness again. When she opened her eyes, Jonetta's face was positioned entirely too close.

"Okay," Violet muttered. "Okay, I'm awake."

"She's conscious!" Jonetta yelled, apparently calling out to others in the vicinity, but she failed to turn her head away, so Violet received the full blast.

The next thing she knew, she was being helped to her feet by Kendall. Behind him hovered a concerned-looking Shura, and behind Shura loomed an equally concerned-looking Tin Man. Violet recognized the surroundings; she was in her office.

Shura edged forward. "How's your balance?" she said.

"What happened?"

"Tin Man found you in the park and carried you back here."

Violet blinked. Her thoughts were still fuzzy and disorganized. Kendall continued to hold her up, and if he'd let go of her, she would have flopped right back down on the floor.

Her thought was a simple one:

I'm too old for this crap.

Shura was shining some kind of light in her right eye and then her left eye. Violet jerked and tried to recoil, but Shura held her chin firmly.

"I don't think it's a concussion," Shura said. She lowered the penlight and snapped it off. "But I'll need to do tests at my office to be sure. Tin Man, will you and Kendall help me get her into a chair so I can—"

"*Wait,*" Violet said. "Where's Sara?"

Kendall's answer was exactly what she didn't want to hear. "We don't know. When you didn't respond to Tin Man's console call, he checked with Jonetta. She said you'd gone to the park to meet Sara. He found you there. Out cold. No sign of Sara. He carried you back here."

Shura was talking again now, in a tone so accusatory that Violet would've preferred the penlight. "What were you *thinking*? Why did you go to the park alone? Sara's dangerous."

"Well, I know that *now,*" Violet replied, a trifle defensively. "I didn't know it *then*. She pretty much confessed." She gave them a brief rundown of the conversation she'd had with Sara. Then she turned to Kendall. "I don't know if she took the housecleaning job in order to get access to your safe or if it was just a lucky accident for her, but that's how she was able to get the Intercept. At least a portion of it. Enough to hack into the minds of our victims."

"How did she know what I kept in the safe?" Kendall asked.

"She probably didn't. Not at first, anyway," Violet replied. "Think of how many times we've hinted about it on our console calls over the past two years. We never mentioned it outright—but we didn't need to. Sara only had to overhear your side of the conversation once or twice to catch on. She might not be a computer genius—but she's not stupid."

"You're right," Kendall said. "I usually forgot she was even there. She sort of fades into the woodwork. She's quiet. And I guess I'm not surprised that she figured it out."

"Hold on," Shura said. "Figured out *what*? What was in that safe? And how does it relate to the Intercept? You guys destroyed it two years ago. Wasn't that the whole point of demolishing Protocol Hall?"

Violet and Kendall exchanged guilty glances. *Are you going to handle this one, or should I?*

Violet knew what she had to do. It had been mostly her decision, after all. She was the one who had run back into Protocol Hall at the last second and snatched up the pages.

She faced the others—Shura, Tin Man, and Jonetta—and, after taking a deep breath, she told them the truth. "We didn't destroy all of the specifications."

"What?" Shura asked. "*Why?*"

Violet gave her the only answer she could.

"I don't know." She struggled to put into words something she had only felt, not understood in a conscious way; it was a passionate conviction that lived far below the level of language. "I mean, I guess it just didn't seem right to completely destroy the Intercept. The technology was so beautiful. And the idea behind it—a perfect world, a *safe* world—was beautiful, too. So I did what I did. Just in case."

"In case *what*?" Shura said.

"In case," Violet answered, "we ever want to reinstall it. If people are ready for it. If the world seems like it can handle it."

A suddenly irritated Shura was ready with her response. "I can't *believe* you never told me this. I'm supposed to be your best friend." The way she'd said "supposed to be" made Violet feel a little bit lonely and a lot guilty.

Tin Man stepped between them. "If anybody has the right to be mad just now, it's me, okay? I *hate* the Intercept. I've hated it from the day I was born." He pointed to Kendall and then Violet. "And I'm not sure I can ever forgive you guys for keeping it alive. But that's not really the point just now, okay? There's a serial killer out there. And I know two things for sure—one, you have to take her down. Two, my mom would want me to help you do it."

"To accomplish that," Kendall said grimly, "we've got to find her first."

Violet shrugged. "No worries."

Tin Man's jaw shifted. He appeared to be holding back a great deal of skepticism. "What does *that* mean?"

"It means," Violet said, "that I know exactly where she is. Jonetta, how about giving me a hand over here so I can show them?"

The picture wavered, disappeared, and then reappeared again. For a moment it acquired the visual characteristics of pea soup, complete with the lumps of sickly green goo. Then that, too, vanished, and in its place was a very clear image of a shelf of red-hued rock.

They were clustered around Violet's console: Shura, Kendall, Jonetta, and Tin Man.

"Give me the location coordinates," Violet said.

Jonetta rattled off the longitude and latitude in a firm, clear voice. "And you know what that means," she added.

"Old Earth." Violet pronounced the words carefully. "Sara has gone down to Old Earth."

Tin Man still wasn't buying it. "How can you possibly know that?" he said. "Where's that picture coming from?"

Violet quickly explained the principle of the chip-jack. "Rez invented it back in our days at Protocol Hall. It's a transmitter that can hijack an Intercept signal. If the chip-jack comes into contact with somebody's Intercept chip, even for a second or so, it picks up the coordinates and so later it lets you—well, eavesdrop. That's the best way to describe it. You see what they're seeing. Hear what they're hearing. It's like you're right there with them, but it's only temporary. After a while, it stops working.

"I swiped it across Sara's chip when we were in the park," Violet added. "I grabbed her jacket. Right before she punched me."

"Hold on. Just hold on," Tin Man interjected. "I know that our Intercept chips were never removed, but they're not activated anymore. They're not connected to anything."

Kendall spoke up. He was in the outer office, using Jonetta's computer to complete his understanding of what Sara had done and how she had done it.

"That's what Sara figured out, with her boyfriend's unwitting help," he said. "She knows how to activate individual chips, one at a time. The Intercept archive as a whole isn't online anymore, but it doesn't have to be. Sara is pulling bad memories directly out of a victim's brain—and then she reinserts them at triple the intensity. That's where the despondency comes from. Whatever idea a person is most vulnerable to, whatever thought or memory makes them feel weak or filled with anguish—that's what Sara jams back into the brain through the Intercept chip. Over and over again, until they don't want to live anymore."

Tin Man nodded solemnly. "So that's what happened to my mother."

They were all silent for a moment. Jonetta put a hand on his shoulder.

Shura broke the spell. She pointed to the picture on Violet's console. "Sara's on the move."

"She won't get away," Violet said calmly. "We'll track her with the chip-jack. It'll work."

"You'd better hope so." Kendall waved a hand over the keyboard at which he had just been feverishly working. "I just hacked into Sara's file. That's how I know how she operates. She's got big plans—big, terrible plans."

"So Sara just left her plans in a file that anybody could find?" Violet said.

"Not anybody," Kendall replied. "Me."

"Oh. Right." Violet nodded. Sometimes she forgot just how brilliant he was.

She headed over to Jonetta's desk so that she could stand beside him. Peering down at the computer screen, she saw gyrating orange numbers that meant nothing to her, but she knew they meant a great deal to Kendall.

"Okay," Violet said. "What's this master plan of hers?"

"Right now, she's able to control a few people at a time. Here and there. But each time she succeeded, her ambition increased."

"Her ambition to do *what*?"

"To kill us all. Or, to be more specific, to have us kill ourselves."

"But how—" Violet's throat was bone dry. She had to take a

few quick swallows before she could go on. "Okay, so I know *how*. She's got the Intercept. But why go to Old Earth?"

"Best place to hide while she's refining her skills," Kendall answered. "The longer she's down there, the better she's going to get. She'll go from controlling one or two people at a time— to taking over New Earth. Even with just a tiny portion of the Intercept, she can do it. She's learned enough from Rodney to pull this off."

"Hold on," Shura said. "Sara's just a loser with a grudge. She can't possibly do something this . . . this *massive*."

"Don't underestimate her," Violet said. "And don't underestimate the corrosive power of disappointment. It's eaten away at Sara until there's nothing left that any of us would recognize. The woman you knew—the woman I knew—is gone. She's *gone*, okay? What's left is somebody with endless pain and a monumental hate—and access to a device that can get inside the mind of any of us, whenever she wants. If she learns how to do it on a mass scale—like Kendall says, we're in big trouble."

Violet looked into each friend's face, one by one, as she spoke her next words. She needed to be sure that everyone understood the full import of her proclamation: Kendall, Shura, Tin Man, Jonetta.

"I need every person in this room," she declared, "to join me and go down to Old Earth to stop her. It's going to be difficult. It's going to be dangerous. Some of us may not come back at all. Is that okay with everybody?"

No one answered out loud, but Violet read the answer in their eyes. They were with her all the way.

Jonetta had already begun raiding the supply cabinet, loading necessities in a red canvas tote: laptops, yellow rain slickers, bottles of water, spare consoles. Tin Man helped her. Shura checked the contents of her medical bag.

"So everybody's sure about this?" Kendall asked. "You all know what we're in for?"

Four grunts of agreement followed his question. The time for making speeches was over.

They moved toward the door.

"I'll be right there," Violet said. "Give me a minute. I left something back on my desk."

"We'll meet you out front," Kendall said. "But don't take too long."

Violet activated her console. A shimmering white dot arose. She touched it, and the ancient, sunken face of Ogden Crowley materialized on the screen. At the sight of him—she loved every wrinkle and groove in that face, she loved the set of that jaw and the banked fire in those watery eyes—Violet coughed, trying to get rid of the lump that had suddenly formed in her throat.

"Dad," she said once she'd heard his shaky *Hello*. "I'm sorry to wake you, but I need to say—" She faltered.

"What is it, sweetheart?"

"I just wanted to tell you how much I love you."

That wasn't their way. Violet and her father did not pepper their interactions with "I love you" the way some people did, as if every conversation was a stew that needed the same seasoning, over and over again. Ogden Crowley was too reserved and too practical to have any patience for that ritual, and he had raised Violet to be the same way. Violet had witnessed Shura and her parents ending each encounter with "I love you," but she'd never understood it. Why repeat something that the other person already knew?

Tonight, she finally understood. She was compelled to say it to her father. Out loud. In case she didn't make it back.

How could she ever have suspected—even for an instant—that he might be involved in resurrecting the Intercept? Ogden Crowley didn't operate that way. He was open and straightforward. He could be stubborn, and he always believed he knew best, but he wasn't sneaky.

She, on the other hand, *was* sneaky—but it was for a good cause. She couldn't tell her father where she was going and what she needed to do and the danger that waited for her down on Old Earth. He'd try to stop her. She was forced to lie to him.

"Violet?" he said. "Is everything okay?"

"Everything's fine, Dad."

By the time Violet joined her friends out on the street, she noticed something odd. She did a quick head count. It was true: Now she had five companions, not four.

Standing next to Jonetta was a little girl in a dark suit with a pissed-off expression on her face.

"Rachel?" Violet said. "What are *you* doing here?"

Rez's little sister held up her wrist. A black jewel bounced above the face of her console. "I came right over because the check you sent to settle your legal bill didn't go through. I just took a look at my account. I thought you might be working late and we could talk about it. I *also* thought you'd be alone. Sorry to embarrass you in front of your friends, but—"

"It's okay." Violet laughed a short, bitter laugh. "You know what, Rachel? Least of my worries right now."

Rachel seemed to realize, all at once, how strange it was for people to have gathered on the sidewalk in front of Violet's office at this time of night. "What's going on?" she said. She knew the faces that surrounded her, except for that of the large man with the tattoos and the ear piercings, because she'd sometimes tagged along when her big brother got together with his friends. "Jonetta? Kendall? Shura? What's the deal?"

Violet let Jonetta fill her in while she checked the chip-jack signal. She had to make sure they'd be able to find Sara. She also sent a text to Rez. He needed to know their plans.

"We've got to go, Rachel," Violet said once Jonetta had finished. "I'd appreciate it if you kept an eye on my office. And I'm trusting you not to tell anybody about this until we get back, okay? We're handling this ourselves. I'm partially responsible for what Sara's doing, and I don't want anybody else hurt."

Rachel's face still wore its pissed-off expression.

"Oh, *please*," the little girl said.

"What?"

"You don't actually believe I'm going to let you guys go down to Old Earth without me, right?"

Kendall spoke before Violet could. "No way," he said. "You're eleven years old."

"And I have an IQ of 257."

"Oh, yeah?" Kendall said. "Well, mine's 314."

"Oh, yeah? Well, I created a new version of calculus with analytic geometry before I turned eight. And last year, I totally rewrote the New Earth Judicial Code."

"Oh, yeah? Well, I—"

Shura took a step forward, putting herself between them. "Both of you—shut up. As entertaining as it is to watch you fight over who's the most amazing genius in the history of the universe, we're wasting time here. Rachel, sorry, but you can't go with us. It's just not safe."

Rachel shook her head. "You can't stop me. My brother's down there. I have to make sure he's okay."

Shura hesitated. The kid had a point. She turned to Kendall. Kendall turned to Violet. Violet turned back to Rachel.

"Let me guess," Violet said. "If we don't let you go, you'll run right to the authorities and tell them where we've gone."

"Count on it." Rachel's voice was firm.

"Tin Man?" Violet said. He was in charge of security, so it was his call. "What do you think?"

Tin Man crossed his arms. He'd been looking intently at Rachel for the last few minutes, and now he looked even harder. She stared right back at him, her eyes blazing.

While the rest of them were fussing and arguing, Violet realized, Tin Man had been taking the measure of this girl, assessing her fitness to join them on this life-or-death mission that could very well determine the fate of New Earth.

"The more the merrier," he said.

PART THREE

32

Into the Storm

By the time they arrived at the Kampura Caves on Thirlsome, a terrible storm had started to rage across Old Earth. The sky was black. Rain slashed down with such devilish fervor that it didn't feel like liquid at all but like sheets of cold darkness crashing to the ground. When lightning exploded, it lit up the sky for a wretched second, as if a spear had been driven into the heart of the world, splitting it into a million brilliant shards. Then the darkness instantly closed over everything once more.

They climbed ashore clumsily, turning up the collars of their slickers against the pounding rain. Violet went first. After her came Kendall, then Shura, then Tin Man, then Jonetta, and finally Rachel. The adult-size slicker was much too big for the girl, and the bottom hem dragged along the ground.

All of their collective strength was needed to tie off the ferry at the edge of the dock; the wind tore at the craft and yanked the ropes from their hands. The wind was so cold that Violet felt as if the skin were being stripped from her fingers.

"South," Jonetta said, checking the chip-jack readout on her console. "The signal's weak, but it looks like Sara's heading in that direction." Because it was night, the chip-jack showed only darkness; that was all Sara was seeing, too. From this point onward, they would use the chip-jack essentially as a trace.

They switched on flashlights, yet the frail beams made little difference in this world of absolute blackness.

At first no one spoke as they trudged along, fighting the razor-wire wind and the stinging rain and the brutal cold. Old Earth was unpleasant enough in the daytime, but at night, in the midst of a ravaging storm, it became as brutal and dangerous as a sworn enemy. They put their heads down and drove themselves forward, pushing back against the shrieking wind.

They stumbled over rocks and tripped into ice-covered gullies, fishing each other out of the shallow troughs and waiting until the shivering subsided before marching on. They rested at times, very briefly. They did not falter. And they did not quit.

These are my friends, Violet thought, and it caused a thickness to rise in her throat. *These are the people I love. We are warriors. We fight together.*

If Rez had been here, the circle would be complete. She tried his console repeatedly, but the storm was interfering with the signal. She smacked her console and cursed, and then smacked it and cursed again, knowing the gesture was pointless but doing it anyway. The signal would poke through the nasty weather precisely when it wanted to—and not a second before.

Rachel let out a squeal. She'd tripped over the long coat again, sliding sideways and teetering over a muddy swamp. She ended up on her butt.

"I've got her," Jonetta said. "You guys keep going."

But Rachel didn't want any help. She flapped a yellow sleeve angrily at her would-be rescuer. "I'm okay. I got this. Go on. I'll catch up. Just *go on.*"

"No way," Jonetta said. She grabbed Rachel's arm and tried to free her from the incredibly stubborn mud, gasping with effort as she yanked. The black goo sucked and pulled at Rachel's boots, which were also about four sizes too big for her.

At last there was a loud *pop!* as Rachel finally broke free. It sounded like a soap bubble bursting.

"Thanks," Rachel said. "I owe you one."

"I'll remember that when I need a good lawyer."

And then they ran to catch up with the others, who had been slowed up by a source more unlikely than a tumultuous storm: The smell.

Whenever the wind died down for a few blessed seconds, the smell of Old Earth wafted up from the charred and rancid landscape. They staggered under the blow. It was the deep, fungal smell of failure and futility, of a world destroyed long before its time by greed and shortsightedness. It was the rotting stench of lost hope.

Disgusted and revolted by the odor, Violet wondered how she could ever have been curious about this place, could ever have imagined that she cared for it. Or that she could ever have asked Rez to send her pictures of it from his console.

But it's different now, she reminded herself. *I'm seeing it at night, in the midst of a storm, while searching for a killer.* There were many sides to any given world, she decided, just as there were many sides to a person.

And this was Old Earth at its worst.

"Now go east," Jonetta called out. "No, wait—make that east-northeast. Three degrees east-northeast." She was shivering badly, and her words were quickly torn to bits by the wind. Somehow they understood her, anyway. She consulted the chip-jack signal on her console every few feet. When she needed to, she adjusted their route.

The odd thing was, of course, that the chosen destination was the last place in the world they really wanted to be: closer to a ruthless murderer. They were walking into a trap that wasn't a trap at all, not really, because they knew full well what awaited them when they got there. They would face the vicious wrath of a woman who had lost touch with her sense of what was good or decent or honorable, and who dreamed of dominion.

They marched for an hour.

Two.

Three.

Four.

Jonetta continued to call out changes in the coordinates. Violet could sense—but could not see, because of the blinding rain and battering wind—that they were getting close to the mountain in which the prison was located. Which also meant they were getting close to the first rides Rez was constructing for Olde Earth World. All of that—Rez's enthusiasm, his plans for the future, the future itself—seemed very far away now. A trapdoor had opened in Violet's soul, and all of the good and simple and ordinary things had dropped away.

A vivid flash of lightning suddenly illuminated the landscape. In that moment of clarity, they could see bits and pieces of Rez's project: the massive steel support beams for a tram track, the rudimentary framing for an enormous castle, the iron scaffolding that constituted the initial stage of the roller coaster.

"What's that?" Tin Man said. He'd flipped off the hood of his slicker to give himself a better look. He didn't stop walking, but his steps slowed a bit so he could behold the enormous structures taking shape in this, the most unlikely of places for new development.

"Olde Earth World," Violet replied.

He couldn't hear her over the roar of the wind. "WHAT?" he said.

"OLDE EARTH WORLD!" She shouted it this time, but he still couldn't hear.

Tin Man started to ask another question, but the rain was coming down too hard and too fast for him to walk any longer without his hood, so he nodded as if her answer had made perfect sense and covered his head once more.

Each time the lightning flashed, they were treated to another glimpse of Rez's amusement park—or at least the glittering bones of it, the preliminary infrastructure. The rides looked imaginative and sleek and appealing. *In other words, pure Rez*, Violet thought. Even if Tin Man didn't know precisely what it was, he would know it was something special.

Then the lightning would die in the sky, and the world was cloaked once more in solid darkness. The half-completed rides returned to the dream-state from which they had come. Reality meant rain and wind and cold, not trams and castles and coasters.

"I just don't see," Shura muttered to Violet, shouldering her way against the relentless rain, "how somebody could get that upset over a *job*. I mean, a job's a job. How could losing a job make Sara go so totally off the rails?"

"So a job's a job, is it?"

"Yeah."

"Is that how you feel about your painting? Or your medical practice?" Violet asked. She leaned forward as she trudged, folding her arms across the front of her slicker to keep the wind from peeling the material back from her body.

"Not the same thing."

"Really? Why not?"

"Well, because medicine and art are . . . well, what I *mean* is, Sara was basically a clerk in the transport unit," Shura said. "It's not a passion profession."

Violet shook her head. "It doesn't matter what anybody else thinks of it. She loved what she did. She felt she'd found her destiny. And then it was taken away from her."

Fighting a sudden upsurge in the wind, Shura and Violet were forced to lean forward even more severely, until their backs were nearly parallel to the ground.

"You almost sound like you sympathize with her," Shura said.

"No. I'm just saying that I understand what it's like to lose something you love. It makes you . . . a little crazy. Or a lot crazy. It can strip away your equilibrium just like *that*."

The wind apparently had a sense of humor, because right then a big gust of it nearly knocked them both sideways, abruptly stopping their conversation.

At some point—they could not have said precisely when—the dark clouds that had been blocking the moon drifted away. They didn't know how long it would last. They only knew that they were able to make out the general outline of this world by the shimmering glints of moonlight. It was far from bright, but the silvery reflections here and there were better than abject darkness.

"We're close," Jonetta said. "The signal is stronger than it's ever been."

They kept moving at the same pace but drew closer together,

making a tighter unit. They had no idea what they would find when they topped the next hill.

"Even stronger now," Jonetta said ominously.

They crested the hill and started down the other side. They fought to stay upright on the steep grade. Tin Man lost his balance and fell, nearly knocking Rachel over; she was grabbed at the last minute by Kendall, who kept her from flipping up in the air when Tin Man came rolling at her feet like a runaway log.

"It's here," Jonetta said.

They had reached the bottom of the hill. "These are the chip-jack coordinates," she added in an even firmer voice. "Sara's got to be right around here. Very, *very* close."

Another massive hill loomed ahead of them. Violet motioned to Kendall. He understood: They would climb it and then report back to the others. The chip-jack signal was still strong, but as yet there had been no sign of Sara.

Where *was* she?

"Wait here, guys," Violet said. They were too tired to argue.

She and Kendall scrambled up the side of the hill, moving very fast at first but then slowing down as the grade became steeper and the footing less secure. Violet could feel her heart jumping madly in her chest. What would she say to Sara when they found her? How would she persuade her to give up? What leverage did she have?

The crest of the hill was only a few grueling steps away. Violet grunted and hauled herself up. Kendall was right behind her. They reached the summit and took a deep breath. They both looked down.

And there she was.

Sara's Revenge

Sara stood in the middle of the rain-wrecked valley.

A spasm of lightning lit up the valley floor, and for an instant Violet could see her face clearly. Too clearly. It was warped and twisted with hate. Sara punched her right arm high into the air, brandishing her wrist console the way an enemy in a conventional battle would display a slab gun. The console was how she controlled the Intercept signal.

We'd be better off if it were *just a slab gun*, Violet thought. Her stomach gave a sickening lurch. *What she's got is far more lethal than a slab gun.*

Each of them had a chip embedded in the crook of the left arm. That chip was like an unlocked door to a house filled with treasure. The treasure was their brains, their thoughts, and if Sara completed her mastery of the technology, she could enter at will. Millions at a time. They would no longer control their own minds. She could fill those minds with images of doom and despondency. They would all be helpless.

Empty of will. Hollow of soul.

Now Sara looked up the hill at Violet. The tables had turned. The hunters were about to become the hunted.

Kendall grabbed his head with two hands. His body began to shake.

"Kendall!" Violet cried. She tried to touch him, but he shook her off. "Kendall, what's hap—"

"She's doing it," he said, his voice a choked, desperate whisper. "She's putting thoughts in my head—dark thoughts. Terrible thoughts." He uttered a low, long howl that seemed to come from the core of his being, tearing through layer after layer to get to the surface. It was filled with more pain than Violet had ever known could exist in a single human body. "I killed my brother!" Kendall cried. He was on his knees now, rocking back and forth. "I killed him because I didn't protect him. Oh my God—it was *me*. I caused him to die. I let him—"

He stopped. He jumped to his feet again. He looked down into the valley. "Look," he said to Violet, pointing at the woman below, the one who stood there with a smile on her face and a console raised up like a sword. "Now she's switched it off again. She wanted to show us how powerful she is."

"We're too close," Violet said. She grabbed his arm. "We have to run. Back the way we came. We have to get out of the range of her signal. We don't have any weapons; we can't fight her on our own."

"We'll have to figure out how to get close enough to get that console without getting zapped by the signal," Kendall said.

They spun around and fled, slipping and tumbling down the other side of the muddy hill they had ascended just seconds ago, through torrents of rain and giant tridents of lightning.

Could they find reinforcements on Old Earth? A few hundred people had stayed behind here, Violet knew, even after her father opened New Earth's borders two years earlier. The holdouts didn't want to come to the new land. Some said it was because they were too old to start somewhere new. Others were recluses. Here, their only company—along with inmates in the mountain prison, whom they never saw—were parolees like Rez.

But she didn't know how to find those last, lingering residents of Old Earth. They hid in caves or in trees or in the bombed-out buildings of the ghost cities. And they might not want to help, anyway.

The only people I can really depend on, Violet told herself, *are my friends.*

Those friends were huddled at the top of the next hill over.

"We have to go!" Kendall yelled. He and Violet had just come up alongside their companions. "Sara's increased her powers. She's right behind us. Come on—*run!*"

Nobody asked any questions. Questions were for later. Kendall had told them to run, and they had never heard such panic in his voice before, and so they ran. Or at least they achieved a close approximation of running, given their weary and depleted state. Violet led. Jonetta and Shura were behind her, and then Kendall. Tin Man was close behind him. Rachel wasn't keeping up, and so Tin Man, without breaking his stride, finally just scooped her up under his right arm.

"*Put me down!*" Rachel yelled, squirming and kicking.

Tin Man ignored her. After a few minutes she climbed on his back, like a kid watching a parade with her dad, so that they could make better time.

Up and down the muddy hills and across the jagged landscape went Violet and her friends, the same hills they had traversed in the opposite direction. They ran single file, and then they bunched up, Shura next to Kendall and Jonetta, with Tin Man and Violet a few steps behind, and then they stretched out single file again.

When they looked back, their hearts sank.

Sara was still coming, still following them with a tireless, machinelike intensity.

"My God," Jonetta sputtered. Her face was covered in mud. She had to wipe away great black smears of it before she could continue speaking. "How is she doing that?"

"Doesn't matter," Shura said. They'd gotten a decent lead, and she wanted some answers. "The question is—why don't we stand and fight?"

"Because she's got the Intercept," Violet said. "And until we can figure out how to distract her and grab her console, she can control us with our own emotions."

"Oh, come on," Shura said. "I bet we can just use willpower. Shut out any thoughts she tries to put in our minds. How hard can it be?"

All at once Violet realized that she and Tin Man were the only ones in the group who knew what an Intercept intervention felt like. The horror was profound. If you didn't know, you didn't know. If you knew, you never forgot it.

"You're just going to have to trust me on this, Shura," Violet said. "You don't want to mess with the Intercept. Even with the baby version she's got. Right now, she can't sustain the signal over a long distance. She needs to be close to us to make it work. So we have to keep moving."

They stumbled and lurched down another long, steep, muddy hill.

"Which way?" Rachel asked. They had paused at the bottom. She was shivering so badly that she had trouble getting the words out.

"Over there," Kendall said, pointing. A long, flat expanse of land was visible in the distance. At least they would not be wearing themselves out on the hills. They made a sharp right turn.

And still Sara came.

Violet constantly checked back over her shoulder, marking the progress of their pursuer. At times Sara seemed lose her grip for a few seconds. She was trying to access each of their minds, Violet surmised, and so she was forced to alternate, going from one person to another, like a symphony conductor signaling each section of the orchestra when its big moment came. That diluted her power. It was all that was keeping their minds out of her clutches. It was all that was saving them.

"We've got to get that console of hers," Tin Man said. He was half running, half walking alongside Violet.

"Yeah!" she yelled back. She had to yell; the wind had picked up again and was shrieking in her ears, making conversation difficult.

A figure suddenly appeared in the distance, approaching quickly and purposefully from another direction. Shura saw it first. She grabbed Violet's arm and pointed. Then Kendall and Tin Man saw it, too, and finally Jonetta and Rachel.

"It's Rez," Violet said.

How did she know? She didn't *know* how she knew, but she did.

Somehow she had recognized him, as far away as he was, on this night when the only light came from fragile, shifting shards of moonlight—visible when the clouds momentarily cleared—and from the erratic bursts of lightning. It was as if she'd sensed his presence through her skin—skin that was soaked and chilled.

And she was right. It was Steve Reznik.

When he reached them, shaking the rain off the shoulders of his overcoat and stomping the mud from his boots, the first thing he did was pull out a small device from the pocket of that coat. He didn't bother with greetings or hugs. The situation was dire. No time for frills.

"I've got this area rigged with DIY drones," Rez said. "I've been monitoring you since you arrived."

"And it didn't *occur* to you," Kendall declared hotly, "that maybe it would've been a good idea to, oh, I don't know... maybe *help* us?"

Rez shrugged. "Took me a while to get over here. Hell of a night. And besides, I *am* helping you." He held up the device. By the feeble light of her flashlight, Violet could see that it was a small metal box studded with rows of small lights. A stubby antenna jutted from the top.

Rez said, "This is what I was working on. I didn't even have time to answer Violet's console call. I had to focus. It's ready now."

"Unless it c-c-c-can make some hot c-c-cocoa," Rachel interjected, her frozen lips causing her to stutter, "I don't c-c-care."

For the first time, Rez realized that his little sister was present. He'd been too absorbed in showing them his invention to notice. Now his eyes widened. He reached out to her, moving a soaking-wet strand of hair off her forehead. He lifted the shoulders of her way-too-big raincoat, trying to pull the garment tighter around her small body to keep her warmer.

"Hey," he said.

"Hey," Rachel said.

They exchanged a brief, knowing smile.

Violet waited for Rez to whirl in her direction and explode, demanding to know why she'd endangered his sister's life by bringing her along. She waited, that is, for the standard *What-the-hell-were-you*-thinking? lecture that she'd heard so many times before in her life.

But it didn't happen. Rez said nothing about Rachel.

Why not? Why *wasn't* Rez angry that his little sister was smack in the middle of a jury-rigged mission on a calamitously cold, dark-as-doom, storm-smashed night on Old Earth? Violet only had a second to speculate, and what she came up with was this: They understood each other, Rez and Rachel, the moody genius and his brilliant sister. They let each other be who they were. They'd been doing it their whole lives. If Rachel wanted to be here, fighting the good fight, fine.

Now Violet had to focus. Rez was addressing the group.

"We've got to stop Sara as quickly as possible," he declared. "The more times she uses the Intercept, the better she gets with it. The only thing that's saved us so far is the fact that it's a pretty steep learning curve. I figure we have about an hour before she's got the thing licked."

"And then?" Tin Man said.

"And then she'll be able to handle multitudes at a time," Rez said. "Not just us—everybody. New Earth and the few people left on Old Earth, too. There'll be mass suicides. Right away. No question about it."

He said it so calmly, so casually, that at first the meaning didn't sink in. But then it did. Violet felt a cold shiver of intense fear, a fear greater than the fear she'd been feeling so far. A fear beyond and above fear. Because there was no real defense against an enemy who had the key to your brain.

"Violet."

Rez was addressing her. She shook off her newfound terror—or at least she found a decent hiding place for it—and faced him.

"Yeah."

"I need you and Tin Man to help me pinpoint the coordinates of Sara's Intercept signal. Kendall, you and Jonetta and Rachel stay here and keep an eye on Sara. Okay?"

"Okay," Kendall said reluctantly.

Rachel wasn't any happier about his orders, but she didn't complain. She wrapped her small arms around her torso, hunching up against the cold. Jonetta grunted.

Rez, Tin Man, and Violet headed across the top of the ridge. Rez kept the box tight against his side.

"What does that thing do?" Tin Man asked as they marched.

"Theoretically, it should block the Intercept signal between Sara and anybody she's trying to control," Rez said.

"*Theoretically?*" Tin Man roared back at him. "You mean it might not work?"

"I had a few hours to do what ought to require *years* in the lab. This is strictly a beta version." He shrugged. "So sue me."

"And if you *do* sue him," Violet put in, trying to tamp down the tension, "just know that he'll have the best lawyer on New Earth on his side."

They found the spot Rez had been looking for. He adjusted the antenna. While Violet and Tin Man fed him the coordinates, he calibrated the sensors on the side of the device. It began to glow with a soft bluish-white radiance. Then it emitted a soft whine. The whine cut through the brazen bluster of the storm, drilling through the noisy chaos like a lighthouse beam through heavy fog.

"What's it doing?" Violet asked.

Rez answered her without taking his eyes off the gauge on the device. "You remember, right, how the Rebels of Light were able to thwart the Intercept three years ago? How they blocked its effects?"

"Yeah. They used deckle. Everybody thought it was addictive, but it was actually a harmless drug. No worse than an aspirin. But it made the user immune to the Intercept."

"Right. So think of this as virtual deckle. It mimics the molecular structure of deckle with a unique electromagnetic wavelength frequency variation signature. It should block the Intercept signal she's broadcasting."

"*Should*," Tin Man muttered. "*Should*. Our lives are at stake here, buddy."

"I'm well aware of the contingent nature of this enterprise," Rez replied, "but I believe there's a cliché that summarizes your options at this point."

"What's that?"

"Beggars can't be choosers."

Once Rez had activated and synched his device with the coordinates of Sara's location, it took only minutes to work.

Violet stood on the ridge next to Rez and Tin Man. She swept her flashlight back and forth across the valley below. Sara had stopped. She looked confused and upset. She smacked her console repeatedly.

"How long will your little magic box keep working?" Tin Man said. There was grudging admiration in his voice.

"No idea," Rez replied. "It's beta, remember?" He adjusted the dial. "But it might cut out at any second, so we'd better get out of here. If our signal starts to weaken and hers comes back, Sara can tap the Intercept again. She could be inside our heads in seconds."

Violet started to ask him another question when she heard a commotion off to their left. A cascade of rocks had been loosened by a figure scrambling along the ridge. She swung the flashlight in that direction.

"Hey, guys!" Violet said. "Look—it's Sara!"

In the short time Violet had not been watching her, Sara had made a run for it, and she was getting away. She had reached the far end of the shelf of rock and, after only a second's hesitation, she jumped off into the darkness below.

No.

The word surged up inside Violet in a great, sweeping crescendo of feeling.

No.

No.

Sara would not escape. That *could not happen.*

The chip-jack signal was already weakening. If Sara fled into the wilds of Old Earth, they'd probably never find her again. She still had her console. She could still enact her plan. New Earth would never be safe.

"I'm going after her," Violet said.

Tin Man gave her a startled look. "Is that a good idea?"

"Absolutely not," Violet said.

She leaped off the ledge.

Ride at Your Own Risk

She was in the fight of her life.

And she was losing.

Violet had chased Sara across two high hills and across a frozen plain. Violet was a very fast runner, and under normal circumstances, she would easily have caught up to her. But these were not normal circumstances.

Sara had a hat, a scarf, a waterproof coat, and—crucial to her success—boots. Violet had no hat, no scarf, a thin coat, and—crucial to her failure—sneakers. Each time Violet began to make progress, her shoes slipped and buckled and she lost traction on the swampy ground. She fell to her knees. By the time she struggled upright again, Sara had widened her lead.

But Violet didn't give up. She *couldn't* give up. It wasn't a conscious choice anymore. Not giving up was simply *who she was*, as much a part of her essential being as her DNA. She blundered forward. Somewhere along the way she had lost her flashlight, but it didn't matter anymore. The beam was useless on this darkest of all dark nights.

She ignored the drumming ache in her legs and the fact that her fingers were totally numb. She couldn't feel her ears anymore, either. Or her nose. Or her toes. Her thoughts weren't really thoughts anymore but just primitive directives that flashed rhythmically in her mind:

Lift foot.

Put foot down.

Lift other foot.

Now put that foot down.

Move forward.

She only lost track of Sara once, and that was just for a few minutes. Soon, she was aware of Sara's presence just ahead of her again. Violet put her head down and willed herself to go faster, faster.

And then, before Violet realized quite how far they had come, they were at the foot of Rez's coaster. What did he call it, what silly name had he affixed to his latest wild idea? Violet, sick with exhaustion, racked her frozen brain.

Oh, yeah. The Riptide Ride.

A bright zigzag of lightning. The structure suddenly was gorgeously illuminated as if singled out by a circus spotlight. In that half second of brilliant light, Violet's eyes traveled up and up and up, straight to the top of the iron scaffolding.

Sara.

For there Sara was, climbing toward the outermost edge of the unfinished track, the part that hung out over the wind-whipped, churning ocean.

And she wasn't alone.

"Rachel!" Violet called out.

She couldn't believe it. At first, she thought she must be

hallucinating. How could Rachel have ended up here? She was back with the others, wasn't she? Safely distant from Sara and her madness?

No. She was right here, being dragged up the track of a half-finished coaster.

"Rachel!"

Another spasm of lightning and Violet saw them again. Sara was bent over, grabbing at the rails of the track with one hand, climbing slowly but persistently. With the other hand, she pulled Rachel along behind her.

Where was Sara taking her? And why?

It didn't make sense. The track wasn't finished; after the summit, it suddenly stopped, cut off in midair. That was as far as Rez had gotten on his Riptide Ride. There was a long, terrifying drop from that apex into the ocean below. One gigantic upward swoop of those girders and then, after the top . . . nothing.

Air. Space. Oblivion.

The waves slammed the pillars that had been sunk in the sand, as if the ocean was trying to tear the thing down while it still could, before the other half was built. As Violet began her climb, trying to keep Sara and Rachel in sight, she felt the massive vibrations as wave upon wave upon wave smashed against the pillars. It was jarring and unsettling. Could the track withstand these constant blows? Would it hold?

Rez built this, Violet reminded herself. *It'll hold.*

She climbed. Head down, body tilted at the waist, she slowly pulled herself up the track, hand over hand. The rain intensified again. The track grew even slicker. And the wind continued its determined effort to knock her legs out from under her. If she *did* lose her grip—well, it was a long way down.

And now she had reached the peak.

Standing before her, just a few agonizing feet away, were Sara and Rachel. Sara had stopped at the very edge of the track. Their backs were against the vast, storm-torn sky. Below them, the black ocean boiled and seethed. Over their heads, visible each time the lightning allowed it, was the faint white outline of the distant underside of New Earth, hovering like a whispered promise above the screaming nightmare of Old Earth.

"Stay away from us!" Sara yelled. "Don't come any closer!"

She redoubled her grip on Rachel's arm. She held up her other arm, the one with the console strapped to her wrist, making sure Violet could see it—and understand her power.

"Let Rachel go!" Violet called out, inching forward. "We can talk about it on the ground, okay? It's freezing up here."

As to validate her claim, a punch of icy wind hit Violet in the face. She nearly toppled off the track.

"What?" Sara yelled. "I can't hear you! You'll have to come closer!"

"I told you to let her go!"

Sara shook her head. "Still can't hear what you're saying. Come closer!"

Violet knew what Sara was doing, but she had no choice. She had to get to Rachel.

"Okay, Sara," Violet said, moving a bit closer, "I'm here. Look, I know you're hurting. We can help you. I promise. But first you have to let her go."

"No," Sara said. "I can't." She whispered into her console.

And that was when Violet felt it:

The twitch.

Within seconds, the twitch intensified. Transforming itself into . . . a scream. The scream picked up speed and momentum. The scream became . . . a *louder* scream. A *bigger* scream. Louder and bigger than the storm. The scream expanded to fill

Violet's entire skull. Everywhere her thoughts turned—right, left, up, down, as if they were trying all the exits—they collided with the scream.

Violet tried to fight back—but fight back against *what*? Her own brain?

With a sickening surge of insight, she realized that Rez's blocking device must have died.

The screaming in her mind grew louder still. There was no way to shut it down, no way to lessen it or redirect it. It was excruciating.

She closed her eyes. She was fresh out of ideas. She was ready to give up.

No. She already *had* given up. Her mind was filling with dark, foul images, with smelly things, with slithery things that cooed slyly to her, curling around her mind like the flick of a scorpion's tail. *It doesn't matter, it doesn't matter, why not die here and now? My friends are dying all around me. Why would I want to be alive when all of my friends are dead?*

My mother—she's dead.

My father—he'll be dead very soon.

The voice was her voice, but it also wasn't her voice. It was saying things that were true but also not true, things that were only true when she was feeling discouraged and sad.

The voice continued to whisper, *I'll be left alone. I am* already *alone. The emptiness—it surrounds me like this storm, screaming and twisting, squeezing my soul until there is nothing left, just a hollow, echoing place where my soul used to be . . .*

I am alone. I have no one. I have nothing.

I am nothing.

Violet clamped her hands on either side of her head. If she could have, she would've pushed those sides together, tight enough to smash open her skull. That prospect seemed far more palatable than putting up with the screaming for another second.

Then, like a tiny light in the distance on this dark, cold, wet, terrible night, she remembered something:

I can be my own Intercept.

Tin Man's words. Tin Man's idea. Tin Man, her friend. The son of the woman who'd been a second mother to her. She could keep Delia's memory alive by staying alive herself—and by deciding which ideas and images should have access to her mind. And which ones shouldn't.

Be my own Intercept.

She could let feelings linger when she wanted them to, not because an entity outside herself put them there.

Be my own Intercept.

She gritted her teeth. She focused. She gave it everything she had.

She began repeating the words to herself over and over again. She remembered Tin Man saying them, and so it was as if they were saying them together, a desperate duet.

Be my own Intercept.

Be my own Intercept.

Her words pushed back fiercely against the other words, the ones Sara was trying to inject into Violet's brain. *Life is meaningless. Nothing matters. I want to die.*

This was a fight, and Violet Crowley had never backed away from a fight in her life. Back and forth they went, the two sides vying for control of her mind.

Be my own Intercept.
I want to die.
Be my own Intercept.
I want to die.

Be my own Intercept.

I want to die.

Be my own Intercept.

I want to . . . I want to live.

She slammed shut the big iron door in her mind and twisted the lock.

I want to live.

Breathing hard, each breath tearing in and out of her body with its own savage certainty, Violet stood on the track and faced Sara. Her fists hung at her sides. The icy rain was pouring off her shoulders, streaming down her face, leaking into her shoes. Every part of her was drenched.

Yet she didn't feel misery. She felt joy.

Sara, too, was completely undone by the freezing rain, rain that cascaded out of a midnight-black and wind-mauled sky. Her hair was plastered around her face. Her coat and her boots were sopping. She stabbed at the buttons on her console, pushing them harder and harder, in case the voice activation feature was on the fritz.

"You want to die!" Sara called out to her. "You want to jump, don't you?"

"No."

"You *do*! You *do* want to die! Hear the screaming? *Hear* it? Don't you want to make it stop?" Sara kept speaking to her console, prodding the Intercept.

"Sara, it's over," Violet called back. "Let Rachel go. We'll climb back down. We'll go back to the others."

"I won't give you the girl!" Sara yelled. "She's my shield! I need her! As long as I have her, I can escape!"

Rachel still had not said a word. Violet squinted at the small wet face. Now she could see the reason for her silence: Rachel was paralyzed with fright. She might be brilliant, but she was still a little girl.

"Rachel, look at me," Violet said. "It's going to be okay."

Rachel shook her head. She seemed to rise momentarily from her trance. "I followed you, Violet. When you went after Sara. I was . . . I was just trying to help. I thought I could talk to her, make her see reason. But she grabbed me."

Because you're eleven years old, Violet wanted to yell at her. *You may be smarter than Einstein and Franklin and Hawking put together, but you're still just a kid.* Instead she said, "Rachel, just do what she says. Don't take any chances." Back to Sara: "Come on. It's me you want, not her. Let her go. We'll go back together."

"I . . . I can't!" Sara was sobbing now. With each sob, she shook the little girl's arm as if she were a rag doll. Rachel didn't cry out. She let herself be yanked and pulled as Sara's hysteria grew. "Don't you understand, Violet? I *can't*. I *can't* go back. Everything I wanted is *gone*. The job I loved, the life I wanted . . . *gone*. Gone *forever*. And the things I've done . . . unforgivable." Once again, she tightened her grip on Rachel's arm. Violet saw Rachel wince with pain. "Frank Bainbridge fired me. I was going to start with him, use the Intercept and make him kill himself. Make him *pay*. But then he died in an accident, before I got the chance, so I had to go after his daughter. I sent Amelia notes. Terrible notes. And then I made her kill herself."

"Sara, we can talk about all this when we get down. When all three of us are safe."

Violet inched toward them while Sara talked. Creeping closer. The footing was treacherous; the coaster track vibrated wildly in the harrowing wind, its stability compromised by being half-finished. Violet was terrified that she might stumble forward and fall into Sara, tipping all three of them over the edge.

"Sara, let her go. Please."

"There's no hope!"

"There's *always* hope!" Violet yelled back. She had to scream it, because the wind had suddenly picked up again, and she had to fight to be heard over the shattering noise.

Violet reached out.

"Give Rachel to me, Sara!" she hollered. "Pass her here! And then give me your hand."

Sara lifted her free hand. The gesture encouraged Violet to move even closer, to take another step toward her—and to the drop-off that was just inches from Sara's back.

"Closer!" Sara called. She wiggled the fingers of her outstretched hand. With her other hand, she redoubled her grip on Rachel's tiny wrist.

Violet took another step. A violent gust of wind almost up-ended her; for a heart-stopping second, she swayed precariously back and forth, finally regaining her balance.

"Just a little bit closer, Violet!" Sara yelled over the chaos of the wind, leaning forward, stretching out her arm. The desperate strain showed on her face. She had pulled Rachel very close to her now, an arm slung diagonally across the little girl's chest.

Violet gingerly took one more step. The tips of her fingers were just grazing Sara's fingertips when she saw it: the hysterical gleam in Sara's eyes. There was a calculating, diabolical look in those eyes, a look that Violet interpreted in a flash.

She's going to jump, and she wants to pull me over the edge, too.

Just as the thought registered in Violet's brain, Sara lunged forward, a crazed grin on her face. Her curved hand settled on Violet's forearm with a talon-like grip.

"We'll die together!" Sara screamed. She gave a mighty yank on Violet's arm. Rachel let out a small cry.

But Violet was ready. She had half a second to prepare, and so she lurched back and sideways, trying to free herself from Sara's hold. For an instant, the struggle was like a life-and-death version of a seesaw—Violet pulling one way, Sara pulling the other—until finally Violet was able to jerk her arm out of Sara's grip.

The link was broken.

Sara teetered wildly on the lip of the track's ending point. Her face was contorted. She held Rachel even tighter, pressing the child's body against her own.

Violet tried one more time to save them. She braced herself and leaned the upper half of her body forward, extending her arm to Sara. "Grab it!" Violet screamed. "You can do it! You can—"

Sara flew backward off the edge of the track, tumbling through the air into the hell-black, storm-shredded ocean hundreds of meters below. She never let of go Rachel, and so the little girl tumbled right along with her.

35

Rachel's Star

Thee it is."

Violet stopped at the sound of Shura's voice. She had been walking alongside her friend in a sort of daze, not really noticing the world that surrounded them.

They were here to see the small memorial that Steve Reznik had placed for his sister in Perey Park.

A week had passed since the night when Rachel Reznik was dragged into an Old Earth ocean by Sara Verity. Sara's body still had not been recovered, but divers sent down the very next day from New Earth had located Rachel's body right away. Their intention had been to bring her back to New Earth. Rachel and Rez's father, however, agreed with Rez:

Rachel deserved something different. Something special.

And so she had been cremated that very afternoon on Old Earth. It was done quickly and privately; Rez had wanted to handle things himself. He had described the aftermath to Violet, telling her how he had gently nestled his sister's ashes in a tiny wooden box. He placed the box inside a slightly bigger capsule, a biodegradable one that would disintegrate within hours. Then he used a small booster rocket to send the capsule into space. By day's end, Rachel's ashes were mingling with stardust, drifting through the galaxy as pure light.

"The marker's beautiful," Violet said. She had dropped to her knees to get a closer look at the square brass plate that read:

RACHEL REZNIK

ASTRA CASTRA, NUMEN LUMEN

The words were Latin for "The stars my camp, God my light." The marker was affixed to the base of a massive oak, one of the largest trees in Perey Park. Looking up from the spot where she knelt, Violet saw how the spreading network of leaf-furred branches reached with crooked beauty across the very sky that was Rachel's new home.

"Yes," Shura said. She had remained standing. "It really is."

The day was a splendid one. Warm sun, mild breeze. It was a vivid and dramatic contrast to what they had endured on Old Earth: howling wind, freezing rain that felt like little knives repeatedly stabbing the skin, a black horizon split open again and again by angry lightning. Sometimes, even now, that night seemed to Violet as if it had all been a dream—but other times, it was the present moment that seemed like the dream. The terror of Old Earth was the true thing, whereas the calmness and beauty of New Earth seemed like something one might wish for, yearn for, but that would never be real.

"I wonder," Shura said.

"Wonder what?"

"I wonder what Rachel would have done with her life. She was so smart."

Violet smiled. "You couldn't exactly ask her what she was

going to be when she grew up. She was already a lawyer. And a good one."

"She'd have to be, if she kept *your* butt out of jail."

"Can't argue with you there."

Violet stood up. She wiped off the dirt from the knees of her jeans. She felt a bit better now. Only a best friend knew exactly when to joke about the dark stuff.

She would never forget Rachel. She would never forget Delia, either, of course. Nor would she ever forget Amelia Bainbridge, Rita and Rosalinda Wilton, Wendell Prokop, and Oliver Crosby. Sara's other victims.

How could you mourn people you'd never even met?

It didn't make sense, maybe, but she did.

"I still can't get warm," Jonetta said. "Not after that night. How about you, Vi?"

A half an hour later, Violet was settled behind her desk. Jonetta breezed in, dropped her rear end into the only other chair in the room, and then proceeded to toss off the hated nickname.

Violet had said goodbye to Shura at the edge of Perey Park. Both of them needed to get back to work: Shura to her improvements on the HoverUp and her research on vaccines and her paintings, and Violet to . . . well, *something*. Something to take her mind off . . . everything.

But the first thing Violet faced out of the gate was Jonetta and a repeat performance of the *Vi* abomination.

Violet didn't care how much she and Jonetta had gone through together on Old Earth. She didn't care how instrumental Jonetta had been in solving the Bainbridge case. She didn't care how loyal and reliable Jonetta was.

Don't care, don't care, don't care.

She was going to put a stop to the vile *Vi* business, once and for all.

"Before I answer that," Violet said, "I've got a question for you."

"Okay." Jonetta stopped sorting the piles of unpaid bills on Violet's desk. "Shoot."

"I've told you over and over again *not* to call me *Vi*. And you keep doing it. Why?"

"Oh, that's an easy one."

"Really."

"Yeah. I kept wondering when you'd get around to asking me." She grinned. "Your dad told me to."

Now Violet was totally confused. Her *father* had encouraged Jonetta to piss her off? To keep on calling her by a nickname that Violet loathed and despised—and had made *quite clear* that she loathed and despised from the get-go?

"What are you talking about?" Violet's tone was even testier.

"Well," Jonetta said, "it's like this. I really, really wanted to work here. My dad talked to your dad, and your dad said he'd get you to hire me, and—"

"Ancient history," Violet snapped. "Get to the point."

"Okay, okay." Jonetta settled back in her seat. "Well, your dad made it happen. Just like he said he would. And when I visited him at Starbridge to thank him, the day before I started working here, he told me that he had one piece of advice.

"He said, 'Violet doesn't like being pushed around. *You* know that you'll be a great assistant—and soon, a lot more—and *I* know that you'll be a great assistant. But *Violet* doesn't know it yet. And if she focuses on the fact that I insisted she hire you, she never *will* know it. She's a wonderful young woman, but she's also stubborn. Holds a grudge. So you've got to take her mind off the circumstances of your hiring, or she'll never see past it.' And I said, 'How in the world can I do *that*, President Crowley?' And he said, 'Make her mad. Make her mad about something else—something unimportant, but irritating. She'll be so busy resenting you for the *small* thing that she'll forget to resent you for the *big* one. Before you know it, you'll be indispensable. Then it won't matter anymore.'"

Violet felt her irritation melt away. She laughed. "Sounds like my dad." She thought about it. "So he really said I was stubborn?"

"Yeah."

"Well, I guess it all worked out. But can we stop the *Vi* business now?"

"Absolutely. I don't like it, either."

Violet moved on to more serious matters.

"So how's your brother doing?"

"Rodney still can't talk about Sara," Jonetta said. "I mean, her death hit him hard, sure. But when he found out the rest of it—how Sara used him to get the information she needed to reboot the Intercept—he was totally devastated. The idea that he was involved in all those deaths. Even accidentally. It was shocking."

"There's a lot of shock to go around."

"Yeah. He'll be okay, though. He's a good guy. And strong. Hey, one more thing."

"What?"

Jonetta looked a little sheepish.

"Um," she said.

"Um?"

"Um, do you happen to know if Tin Man is dating anybody?"

Of all the things Jonetta might have asked her, *that* question would not have been in the top 250.

"No clue," Violet said.

"Okay. Well."

Jonetta returned to sorting the bills, shaking her head and rolling her eyes each time she came across one that featured an unbelievably ginormous total. Violet watched her for a minute or so. Then her thoughts began to drift—away from Jonetta, away from unpaid bills, away from this office and all of her responsibilities, away from New Earth itself.

She was thinking about the crazy-cold, storm-stunned night on Old Earth and how she had felt when she saw Rez's face as she and her friends were huddled, shivering and hopeless, upon the dark ridge.

Could she be falling in love with *Steve Reznik*? The same guy she'd totally rejected two years ago? It seemed . . . well, *impossible.*

He was weird, for one thing. He was on parole for a serious crime, for another. He barely talked unless the subject was computers. He wasn't handsome—not the way that Kendall was handsome. He was . . . he was *Rez*. He was just himself.

Yet when she thought about him, she got that funny flipping feeling in her stomach.

She looked down at the crook of her left elbow, at the small blue mark. What a relief it was to see . . . nothing. No spark, no flash.

And that, of course, was because the Intercept was gone. But she could tell herself that it was for a different reason:

Because she didn't feel anything.

Right?

Well . . .

She shook her head. This was ridiculous. Rez lived on Old Earth. He wasn't even around here. Nothing could happen between them even if she *did* want it to . . . which she didn't. Of course not.

Her console chirped. The ringtone told her it was Rez, calling from Old Earth. Calling her personally, not through the office console as he usually did. And Violet was aware once again of that flipping sensation in the pit of her stomach. Was she getting the flu?

Yeah. Had to be it.

She touched the rising orange jewel. His face materialized on her screen, and the stomach-flipping thing intensified.

"Rez," she said. "How're you doing?"

"I'm okay," he said. "I wanted to tell you that they shaved a few months off my parole, so I'll be back up to New Earth sooner than I expected. But that's not the only reason I called."

She waited. Her belly had settled down, so it definitely wasn't the flu.

But maybe that was bad news, not good. As Shura had pointed out two years ago when Violet was crushed out on Danny, "The flu, I can maybe cure. Being in love? Um, not so much."

Love? *Where did* that *come from?*

"Here's the thing," Rez was saying. "I've been thinking. As long as the Intercept's back up again, why don't we maybe use it a little? Run it on a limited basis? The chips are already in place. Instead of collecting emotions from everybody, I can rig it to just pick up negative feelings. Feelings that lead to crimes. Greed, rage, hate, lust, whatever. Just a trial run. It'll really help the cops. They're swamped these days, and this could be the answer."

She knew she needed to pay attention to the rest of what he was saying, but Violet's mind was stuck on *lust*. She shook her head. *Okay, focus.*

"What are you taking about?" she said. "After what we've been through, I can't believe this."

"Hold on. I've given it a ton of thought." Rez's voice crackled with excitement. His eyes gleamed with hopefulness.

She understood why he was proposing it. This was a fresh hurdle for him, a chance to work on something that was beyond his current skill level—which was, she knew, what Rez loved best in all the world. An intellectual challenge. And it also might help him take his mind off the loss of his little sister.

"If it works," he went on, "we'll never have to deal with anybody like Sara again. We'll pick up on the feelings that lead to the crimes—before the crimes even happen. And if the crimes *do* happen, we'll have the emotions to take down the criminals. Just send 'em right back into the bad guy's brain. I'll coordinate with Kendall. It'll be official. We can make this happen. What do you say?"

"I say no."

He seemed a little taken aback. "Is that really your only response?"

"Wait. Let me rephrase. *Hell* no."

His face crinkled up as a consequence of a deep frown.

"I thought you'd have an open mind about it," he muttered.

"Come on, Rez. I'm still getting over the frostbite in my hands and feet," Violet said. "And I still have to sit down with Charlotte Bainbridge and explain all of this to her—in more than just bullet points. Do you *seriously* want to play around with the very device that basically killed her daughter?" *And your sister, too*, she wanted to add but didn't because it seemed like a cheap shot.

"We're missing a golden opportunity." He sounded sullen and discouraged. The brooding frown still owned his face. "The research possibilities are—"

"No, Rez. That's final. And if you've got any bright ideas about doing it anyway, you know that Kendall will be monitoring all the channels, all the frequencies, all the time. If somebody so much as gets a dab of peanut butter on a computer keyboard, Kendall will know about it and investigate it. Just warning you."

"Fine. See you around, Violet." He clicked off the console. He'd wanted to sound snippy, she knew, and he had succeeded.

Well, he would get over it. She was used to Rez being mad at her. They had clashed a lot in those days back at Protocol Hall when they'd monitored the Intercept together, and they always made up. Because Rez never stayed upset. Or discouraged. He was the kind of guy who pushed and pushed, and if he didn't find a way to get what he wanted right away, he'd try another way, and then another, and another. Usually it was some kind of computer breakthrough he was after. Some new horizon of technology.

Violet turned around in her chair to look out her office window. New Earth sparkled in the sunshine of a spectacular day.

The only thing that made it less than perfect was a small, nagging worry.

Rez never gave up. And he had his eye, once again, on the Intercept.

ACKnowledgments

Climbing a roller-coaster track on a stormy night—not in a car but on foot, all by yourself, bent over, grabbing at the rails—while the fate of the world hangs in the balance: That, we decided, is just about the most exciting thing ever.

It was during a car ride to Dairy Queen one summer day that Thomas King, 13; Catherine King, 9; Elizabeth Clare King, 7; and I first came up with the roller-coaster-at-midnight scenario. (You'll be glad to know that I was driving.) Thanks to my three friends for helping me envision what became a pivotal moment in this book.

I am also grateful to Ali Fisher, my deft, funny, and imaginative editor at Tor; and Lisa Gallagher, wise agent and dear friend.